THE INN KEEPER

EMERSON PASS CONTEMPORARIES
BOOK FIVE

TESS THOMPSON

PRAISE FOR TESS THOMPSON

"I frequently found myself getting lost in the characters and forgetting that I was reading a book." - *Camille Di Maio, Bestselling author of The Memory of Us.*

"Highly recommended." - *Christine Nolfi, Award winning author of The Sweet Lake Series.*

"I loved this book!" - *Karen McQuestion, Bestselling author of Hello Love and Good Man, Dalton.*

Traded: Brody and Kara:
"I loved the sweetness of Tess Thompson's writing - the camaraderie and long-lasting friendships make you want to move to Cliffside and become one of the gang! Rated Hallmark for romance!" - *Stephanie Little BookPage*

"This story was well written. You felt what the characters were going through. It's one of those "I got to know what happens next" books. So intriguing you won't want to put it down." - *Lena Loves Books*

"This story has so much going on, but it intertwines within itself. You get second chance, lost loves, and new love. I could not put this book down! I am excited to start this series and have love for this little Bayside town that I am now fond off!" - *Crystal's Book World*

"This is a small town romance story at its best and I look forward to the next book in the series." - *Gillek2, Vine Voice*

"This is one of those books that make you love to be a reader and fan of the author." -*Pamela Lunder, Vine Voice*

Blue Midnight:
"This is a beautiful book with an unexpected twist that takes the story from romance to mystery and back again. I've already started the 2nd book in the series!" - *Mama O*

"This beautiful book captured my attention and never let it go. I did not want it to end and so very much look forward to reading the next book." - *Pris Shartle*

"I enjoyed this new book cover to cover. I read it on my long flight home from Ireland and it helped the time fly by, I wish it had been longer so my whole flight could have been lost to this lovely novel about second chances and finding the truth. Written with wisdom and humor this novel shares the raw emotions a new divorce can leave behind." - *J. Sorenson*

"Tess Thompson is definitely one of my auto-buy authors! I love her writing style. Her characters are so real to life that you just can't put the book down once you start! Blue Midnight makes you believe in second chances. It makes you believe that everyone deserves an HEA. I loved the twists and turns in this book, the mystery and suspense, the family dynamics and the restoration of trust and security." - *Angela MacIntyre*

"Tess writes books with real characters in them, characters with flaws and baggage and gives them a second chance. (Real people, some remind me of myself and my girlfriends.) Then she cleverly and thoroughly develops those characters and makes you feel deeply for them. Characters are complex and multifaceted, and the plot seems to unfold naturally, and never feels contrived." - *K. Lescinsky*

Caramel and Magnolias:

"Nobody writes characters like Tess Thompson. It's like she looks into our lives and creates her characters based on our best friends, our lovers, and our neighbors. Caramel and Magnolias, and the authors debut novel Riversong, have some of the best characters I've ever had a chance to fall in love with. I don't like leaving spoilers in reviews so just trust me, Nicholas Sparks has nothing on Tess Thompson, her writing flows so smoothly you can't help but to want to read on!" - *T. M. Frazier*

"I love Tess Thompson's books because I love good writing. Her prose is clean and tight, which are increasingly rare qualities, and manages to evoke a full range of emotions with both subtlety and power. Her fiction goes well beyond art imitating life. Thompson's characters are alive and fully-realized, the action is believable, and the story unfolds with the right balance of tension and exuberance. CARAMEL AND MAGNOLIAS is a pleasure to read." - *Tsuruoka*

"The author has an incredible way of painting an image with her words. Her storytelling is beautiful, and leaves you wanting more! I love that the story is about friendship (2 best friends) and love. The characters are richly drawn and I found myself rooting for them from the very beginning. I think you will, too!"
- *Fogvision*

"I got swept off my feet, my heartstrings were pulled, I held my breath, and tightened my muscles in suspense. Tess paints stunning scenery with her words and draws you in to the lives of her characters."- *T. Bean*

Duet For Three Hands:

"Tears trickled down the side of my face when I reached the end of this road. Not because the story left me feeling sad or disappointed, no. Rather, because I already missed them. My friends. Though it isn't goodbye, but see you later. And so I will sit impatiently waiting, with desperate eagerness to hear where life has taken you, what burdens have you downtrodden, and what triumphs warm your heart. And in the meantime, I will go out and live, keeping your lessons and friendship and love close, the light to guide me through any darkness. And to the author I say thank you. My heart, my soul -all of me - needed these words, these friends, this love. I am forever changed by the beauty of your talent." - *Lisa M.Gott*

"I am a great fan of Tess Thompson's books and this new one definitely shows her branching out with an engaging enjoyable historical drama/love story. She is a true pro in the way she weaves her storyline, develops true to life characters that you love! The background and setting is so picturesque and visible just from her words. Each book shows her expanding, growing and excelling in her art. Yet another one not to miss. Buy it you won't be disappointed. The ONLY disappointment is when it ends!!!" - *Sparky's Last*

"There are some definite villains in this book. Ohhhh, how I loved to hate them. But I have to give Thompson credit because they never came off as caricatures or one dimensional. They all felt authentic to me and (sadly) I could easily picture them. I loved to love some and loved to hate others." - *The Baking Bookworm*

"I stayed up the entire night reading Duet For Three Hands and unbeknownst to myself, I fell asleep in the middle of reading the book. I literally woke up the next morning with Tyler the Kindle beside me (thankfully, still safe and intact) with no ounce of battery left. I shouldn't have worried about deadlines because, guess what? Duet For Three Hands was the epitome of unputdownable." - *The Bookish Owl*

Miller's Secret

"From the very first page, I was captivated by this wonderful tale. The cast of characters amazing - very fleshed out and multi-dimensional. The descriptions were perfect - just enough to make you feel like you were transported back to the 20's and 40's.... This book was the perfect escape, filled with so many twists and turns I was on the edge of my seat for the entire read." - *Hilary Grossman*

"The sad story of a freezing-cold orphan looking out the window at his rich benefactors on Christmas Eve started me off with Horatio-Alger expectations for this book. But I quickly got pulled into a completely different world--the complex five-character braid that the plot weaves. The three men and two women characters are so alive I felt I could walk up and start talking to any one of them, and I'd love to have lunch with Henry. Then the plot quickly turned sinister enough to keep me turning the pages.
Class is set against class, poor and rich struggle for happiness and security, yet it is love all but one of them are hungry for. ......Where does love come from? What do you do about it? The story kept me going, and gave me hope. For a little bonus, there are Thompson's delightful observations, like: "You'd never know we could make something this good out of the milk from an animal who eats hats." A really good read!" - *Kay in Seattle*

"She paints vivid word pictures such that I could smell the

ocean and hear the doves. Then there are the stories within a story that twist and turn until they all come together in the end. I really had a hard time putting it down. Five stars aren't enough!" - *M.R. Williams*

ALSO BY TESS THOMPSON

CLIFFSIDE BAY

Traded: Brody and Kara

Deleted: Jackson and Maggie

Jaded: Zane and Honor

Marred: Kyle and Violet

Tainted: Lance and Mary

Cliffside Bay Christmas, The Season of Cats and Babies (Cliffside Bay Novella to be read after Tainted)

Missed: Rafael and Lisa

Cliffside Bay Christmas Wedding (Cliffside Bay Novella to be read after Missed)

Healed: Stone and Pepper

Chateau Wedding (Cliffside Bay Novella to be read after Healed)

Scarred: Trey and Autumn

Jilted: Nico and Sophie

Kissed (Cliffside Bay Novella to be read after Jilted)

Departed: David and Sara

Cliffside Bay Bundle , Books 1,2,3

BLUE MOUNTAIN SERIES

Blue Mountain Bundle, Books 1,2,3

Blue Midnight

Blue Moon

Blue Ink

Blue String

EMERSON PASS

The School Mistress of Emerson Pass

The Sugar Queen of Emerson Pass

RIVER VALLEY

Riversong

Riverbend

Riverstar

Riversnow

Riverstorm

Tommy's Wish

River Valley Bundle, Books 1-4

LEGLEY BAY

Caramel and Magnolias

Tea and Primroses

STANDALONES

The Santa Trial

Duet for Three Hands

Miller's Secret

THE INN KEEPER

This book is dedicated to anyone recovering from childhood trauma.
You are not alone.

1

DARBY

My father's verdict came on a Tuesday. I'd just come into the teachers' lounge for lunch. Mike, who taught math in the classroom next to mine, had his tablet open. A quick glance told me he was watching the news. Another glance told me it was news of my father's case. No one else paid any attention. It was just another cop accused of a violent crime against a person of color. They'd played the footage from that night again and again until it felt as if I'd been there myself. I had, in a way. He'd been committing similar acts of degradation and physical intimidation to me all my life.

"A verdict's come in on the Hanes case," Mike said. He wore his straw-colored hair long but pulled into a bun on top of his head. Fixated on social justice, skiing, and craft beer in equal measures, Mike followed stories like this one and anything else that supported what he thought was the truth. As we all did, I supposed. No one ever changed their mind about something political by reading someone's post on social media.

By now, the rest of the table had looked over at him. There were six of us who regularly ate our lunches at this time. Fifth period, as the kids call it, started at forty-five minutes after eleven. We had exactly thirty minutes to eat and relax before heading back into the thick of things. I had a hard job. But for some reason unknown to most, I loved every minute of it. High school students were sweet and confused with hormones that ruled most of their actions. Sometimes, I could get through the walls of insecurities and bravado to reach the child inside. Those were the good days.

At the far end of the table, two older women who had taught at Quinn Cooper High School for thirty years, Mrs. Rigby and Mrs. Sloane, rarely spoke to anyone but each other. From my assessment, they seemed interested in counting the days until they could retire and nothing else. They seemed to dislike our kids immensely. I could have been wrong, of course. I didn't know them well. Other than a few snide remarks during lunch, they kept to themselves, as if afraid I'd corner them and start asking questions about how to survive teaching high school for three decades.

The principal's secretary, Ms. Breen, was there as well. Rumors swirled that she was having an affair with our very married counselor, Mr. Knight, who was also present at the table. I wasn't one for rumors and usually shut them down when I heard the kids talking about them. However, they *were* sitting close to each other. Did they play footsie or stroke each other's thighs, thinking that no one could see, that no one suspected?

The room smelled of Mrs. Sloane's fish sticks. They were strong enough to almost take away the scent of burned popcorn that seemed to permanently live in the small microwave. Sloane kept a box of what passed as fish in our community freezer and microwaved it for her lunch. I had no idea who burned the popcorn or even the frequency. For all I knew, it had been years and only the smell lingered. Anyway, I'd gotten used to it. Nose blindness is a real thing. My first month had been rough, though.

I sat down at the end of the table and braced myself for what was coming. It was a difficult act, this balance between pretending I had no personal investment in my father's trial and maintaining the illusion that I was as interested as the rest of the country. No one knew who I was. Or where I'd come from. I'd taken my dead mother's last name when I'd started college ten years ago. After the night my father almost killed me, I left and never looked back. Until now. I'd learned of my father's crime the same way as everyone else. On television.

And God help me, they'd played that footage from the body camera over and over. Not that I needed a reminder. After seeing the tape the first time, I couldn't stop seeing what he did, even when I closed my eyes. He would not be able to walk away from his destruction this time. The complaints—and I knew there had been many over the years against my father—could no longer be dismissed because of the cameras. Now the whole world knew the truth about Benji Hanes. I was of his flesh and bone. How could it be that I could not kill a spider while he loved to unleash power and violence on whomever he deemed worthless or weak?

I opened my plastic lunch box and waited, holding my breath, for news of my father's fate.

"They found him guilty," Mike said. "Sentencing will be later."

My stomach seemed to fall hard and fast, like a runaway elevator, followed by tingling in my hands and feet. I'd expected it, but the flood of shame and anger was swift and harsh. Why? Why had he been this way? His father had been the same way. He'd learned how to hate from him.

I'd been spared. I took after my mother. She'd loved books and teaching school. All children and animals loved her, attracted to her gentleness and the way she would listen with her whole body to whoever was speaking to her. "Do no harm," she used to say to me. After her death when I was ten, I'd learned to silently chant it as I became the target of my father's rage. Without her to punch and kick, he'd turned to me.

A memory came out of nowhere. I'd been about fifteen and come home from a late-night soccer game to find him in the kitchen. His face had been red from drinking and his eyes fixed on me like a rabid dog. No, I told myself now. I would not think of him. I'd gotten away from him. I was safe.

"He'll go to prison," Ms. Breen said. She was a skinny woman in her forties. For lunch, she had what appeared to be a bag of lettuce with some shreds of carrots. Obviously, she liked the way she looked, but to me, she seemed artificially thin with skin that seemed stretched too tightly over her bones. Defying the laws of nature.

"I wonder what the sentence will be?" Knight shuddered. He wore his thinning hair cropped close. I was pretty sure he regularly spray-tanned. His skin was a shade lighter than rust. A color never seen in nature on a white guy. "A cop in prison. That's not going to be pretty."

I wanted to run away and not think of any of this. My father was sixty years old. I could see from the footage I'd accidentally caught that he'd aged much since his arrest and trial: sloped shoulders, pot belly, large bags under his eyes, and a puffy face. All that drinking and lack of sleep, I figured.

He seemed old and vulnerable.

No, don't feel sorry for him, I ordered myself. *He doesn't deserve your pity.*

"These idiots need to remember they're on camera now," Sloane said before biting into one of her fish sticks. Her black hair was streaked with white, reminding me of a skunk.

"How about they stop committing hate crimes instead?" Mike asked. His man-bun wobbled. Mike was passionate about social justice. He never let anyone forget it, either. Although I understood his feelings and beliefs, sometimes I wished he were less heavy-handed and self-righteous. Perhaps people would be able to take in what he said if he presented things with less rancor. Instead, he made people bristle with his didactic tone.

Should I pull out my own phone and look for the coverage? Did I want to see him that way? Led out of a courtroom in handcuffs to a jail cell? He deserved it, I reminded myself. For the crimes against Russel Johnson and the others he hadn't had to answer for. And for me too, maybe. Without realizing I'd been doing it, I realized I was touching the scar on my neck. The one he'd given to me on the night of my high school graduation. The last one had been the worst.

Mrs. Rigby sniffed and looked over her skinny reading glasses at Mike. "Most cops are good. This isn't a reason to hate them all."

"I don't hate anyone," Mike said. "But I'm not sure I agree with you about most cops. Isn't it the criminal-minded, the power-hungry, who decide to be cops? Men who crave violence?"

No one answered him. I suspected no one agreed with him, either. His venom for my father and what he'd done was obvious.

"Again, I don't hate anyone," Mike said. "But it's a good day when justice is finally served."

As for me, I did hate someone. My father. He'd taught me how to hate him with every punch and shove. Every time he locked me in my room and refused to feed me. But as any child raised by an abusive parent knows, it's not that simple. The line between love and hate was always being tested. Flexed to see where the breaking point was.

I knew only that I was broken. In my brokenness, I'd found purpose. Every day was a chance to make a mark on the world through my students. I could see the ones in trouble. I couldn't always save them, but I could try. Some of these kids had no one.

"You're quiet, Darby," Ms. Breene said. "What do you think?"

I scrambled to come up with an answer that wouldn't give away how I trembled and my heart seemed to pump in my brain instead of my chest. How I wished I could be alone so I could cry for my father and for me and for the man he'd killed with his cruelty.

In the end, I chose to stick to the facts and leave all emotion out of my answer. "I think the case went to trial and twelve jurors believed he was guilty and now he'll have to pay for what he did."

"There's no disputing it," Knight said. "It was all in black and white, so to speak."

Ms. Breene nodded with enthusiasm. "I agree one hundred percent. He was caught on tape. How would they have been able to find him not guilty?"

"They have before," Mike said. "Many times."

"Well, they didn't this time," I said, more dismissive than I meant. I reached into my lunch box and took out my peanut butter and jelly sandwich. Not that I could eat. I'd be lucky not to throw up.

"I, for one, can't wait to discuss this with my students," Mike said.

"You teach math," Mrs. Rigby said. "How is this relevant?"

"It's my duty to teach them how to think, across disciplines." Mike looked over at me as if to get support.

I studied my sandwich instead. Peanut butter and jelly reminded me of my mother. An image played before me. The sun had come in through the windows, warming my shoulders and the top of my head and bringing out the streaks of blond in her brown hair. She'd set a plate with a sandwich on the table before me. The crusts had been cut off, and she'd spread one of the pieces with strawberry preserves. My favorite. Then she'd brushed her cool, dry knuckles against my cheek, her eyes so filled with love that a lump had risen in my throat. "Eat up, young man. You need to grow up strong and tough." A bruise the size of my father's fist covered her forearm. Perhaps guessing where my gaze had gone, she snatched her arm away.

The others continued discussing the case, ultimately getting into a heated argument with Knight and Mike on one side and the older women on the other. Ms. Breene seemed to have given up on the conversation and picked at her lettuce.

The pounding between my ears went on, relentless. I forced myself to eat a few bites of the sandwich and then packed the remnants back inside my lunch box. Maybe I'd be hungry later. I didn't bother to say anything to my companions. They didn't seem to notice me slipping away, or if they did, they couldn't care less. A good political fight was more interesting.

———

HERE'S the thing about only revealing half of your life to people. It's hard to keep the truths from tumbling out. Any time you let your guard down and forget for a moment that you're unlike any of your friends, you're jeopardizing the life you've carefully crafted. My friends knew I was raised by a single father in LA but nothing else. They didn't know he was a cop. Or that he made my life a living hell until I got away and went to college. And no one knew that my father was one of the most hated men in America.

Now he was going to prison.

After work that afternoon, I put on my running clothes and drove down to the riverside park. A nice, mostly smooth running or walking trail that ran up one side of the river, starting at the park and ending out by the old mill, now a museum. As I locked my old beater of a car, I admired Jamie's new inn, just on the other side of the grassy park, looking crisp and quaint with its white exterior and black shutters. After losing her newly renovated Annabelle Higgins mansion to the forest fire that swept through much of our community, she was open for business once again. I'd been happy to be invited to the opening ceremony and had gone to give her my support. It was no longer awkward between us. Enough time had passed since our one-night stand and subsequent surprise to find each other in Emerson Pass. We'd met in Cliffside Bay and had enjoyed a no-strings-attached night together. Since moving here, we ran in the same circle. Our mutual friends often threw us together for one occasion or another. So we'd had to get over our awkwardness and move on. Not that there was anything to move on from. It had been one reckless night, never to be repeated again.

One *hot* reckless night.

I hadn't brought a ball cap, and the sun was still bright in the valley between our two mountains. Instead, I put on my sunglasses. I had my contacts in so I'd be able to see. My vision was terrible without them. This early in September, the afternoons were mostly warm and sunny. They were numbered, which meant I needed to take advantage of them all. Running this trail was my therapy. And I needed it today.

I set out on a leisurely pace, needing a few minutes to warm up. The river was low this time of year but still clear. Water bugs made ripples for the ducks who floated near the water's edge, looking for their dinner in the reeds and grasses. Above us, a flock of geese headed south. The path, which started out as cement, changed to dirt about a half mile from the park. All in all, it was only a four-mile run, perfect for me. I'd been an athlete back in school and missed the camaraderie of team sports. Now I kept in shape not to play sports but for health and vanity. Plus, exercise warded off any gloominess. Or at the very least, dwelling in it for long, anyway.

Soon, the mountains would be covered in snow, and the skiers would come. For now, we had the town mostly to ourselves. Summer visitors were gone after Labor Day. Winter enthusiasts wouldn't be here until after the ski mountains opened. Locals enjoyed our peaceful months when the river park and trails were all ours.

I didn't meet a single soul all the way to the museum. Breaking for a moment to drink water from the fountain outside the front door, I turned back around to head in the other direction. I'd quickened my pace by then and somehow missed a tree trunk, tripping and falling. My head smacked into the hard ground. Sunglasses went flying. I sat up, dizzy. My pride was hurt more than my head. Or at least I thought so until I tried to get up and felt like I was drunk. I reached up to touch a sore spot on my forehead and felt dampness. Blood? Great, I'd cut open my head. What an idiot.

Not the first time I'd split my head. My father had slammed me against a coat hook in the hall. Was it the same spot?

I brought my knees close and rested my forehead on them. A rustling in the grass revealed a squirrel. He sat for a moment, his little cheeks full of nuts and his mouth twitching, just watching me. *What creature is this*, he might have thought, *fallen and bleeding?*

The day's news had cut me off at the knees as surely as the root had.

I looked up when I heard footsteps coming toward me. Oh great, it was Jamie on a run of her own. Here to see my humiliation.

She stopped when she saw it was me. Alarm widened her eyes. She snatched her earbuds from her ears and stuffed them into the side pocket of her tight running shorts. They left nothing to the imagination, I noted. Her thigh muscles were taut and muscular. As was her stomach, flat under a spandex top. Apparently, I could still see. The bump on my head couldn't be that bad.

"Darby, are you all right?" She fell to her knees beside me. Her scent, perhaps heightened from sweat, wafted over me. Jasmine and vanilla and something else. Blue eyes peered at me with concern from a face bare of makeup. Her dark blond hair was tied back in a ponytail.

"You should wear sunscreen," I said, even though her skin was a golden tan. A California-looking girl, I'd thought the first time I met her.

She touched her forehead as if reminding herself of the last application. "Yes, yes, I am. I always do."

"It doesn't look like it." Why had I said that? She looked flushed from her run but not sunburned. Is that what I meant? Good Lord, maybe I'd really hurt my head.

"What? Why are you asking about that?" Pursing her lips, Jamie scrutinized me as I did with my students when I suspected them of mischief. As if I were hiding something, like drugs in my backpack. "Do you have a concussion?" She pushed my hair away from my sticky forehead. "Should I call an ambulance?"

I reached for her hand before she could take out her cell phone, which was nestled in a side pocket of her running shorts. Genius. And lucky phone. I'd never been jealous of an inanimate object before. "No, no, I'm fine."

"There's blood on your hand." She spoke with considerable alarm. Her concern touched me. She was adorable. As always. "Darby, do you see the blood? Is that from your head?"

I looked down and sure enough, she was right. "It's just a little cut."

She placed her hands on the sides of my head, inspecting me. Her ample cleavage was on display inches from my mouth. The sports bra had a nice way of pushing them together. I shut my eyes, not wanting to be disrespectful. Although truth told, I'd already had a nice long look at every part of her. What a night that had been.

I yelped when her fingers found the cut. She scooted around the back of me to get a better look at it. With gentle fingers, she lifted my hair near the wound. "Okay, it's not that bad. Just a little cut. No brains spilling out or anything."

"Brains spilling out?" I felt suddenly faint.

"Here, let's get you more comfortable." She adjusted herself next to me. "Come here. Put your head on my lap." Perhaps the brain injury had me loopy, but I didn't hesitate to follow her instructions.

She sat with her back against a tree and patted her thighs. Staring up at the tree, I rested my bloody noggin with its intact brain on her lap. She had her legs stretched out, and her firm thigh muscles made a nice pillow.

"I'm not sure what to do with you," she said, playing with the front of my hair and brushing her fingers across my forehead in equal measure but almost absentmindedly, as if her mind was elsewhere. Regardless, her fingers felt cool and silky on my warm skin.

"Your eyes match the sky," I said. "I can see it through the branches of this tree. But you probably know that."

"I guess so."

"Don't say it like that," I said. She should own her beauty.

"Like what?

"Like you don't know how pretty you are."

"Oh, well, thank you. That's very sweet. However, I am still worried you have a concussion."

A spattering of freckles decorated her slightly turned-up nose. "I love freckles."

Her hands went still. Above us, an orange aspen leaf floated lazily on its way toward us. "Whoa, you are acting a little weird. Are you sure you're all right?"

"A lot of people like freckles," I said. "You should embrace them."

"I'm not worried about my freckles right now." Her teeth were all white and shiny and even. "Do you know who the president is?" Beads of sweat moistened her forehead.

I blinked, unsure for a second. Then I remembered and told her.

"Okay, that's good," Jamie said.

"Why did you ask me about the president? Did you forget?" I wanted to laugh at my little joke but only managed a raspy guffaw.

"They always ask who the president is in movies and stuff to make sure the person doesn't have any brain damage."

"Again with the brains," I said, quite content to sit like this forever.

"I think you're fine, but maybe we should take you to urgent care?"

"No. No doctors. I can't afford it."

"Can you walk?" Jamie asked.

"I'm a little dizzy, if you must know." I spoke in a posh accent, hoping to make her laugh.

She didn't. "I'm texting Breck," Jamie said, tugging her phone from that lucky pocket. "I want him to come look at you."

"He's a vet. An animal doctor." I floated, suddenly tired. Was it my head or this pretty woman stroking my cheek? She smelled delicious, I thought again. I could spend all day taking in her scent and be a happy man. "I'm an animal, I guess, so that might be all right."

"He'll know if it's okay for you to walk out of here or not," Jamie said.

"Good thinking." I continued to stare up at her. The day's event pushed into my mind. My dad. Going to prison. A cop in prison. Why did I care? I didn't want to. "It's been a very terrible day. If you can believe it, falling and subsequently being found by you is a big step up."

"I'm sorry." She clucked her tongue in a way that seemed too matronly for her. "You were trying to run it out, right?"

"Exactly. But that root bit me."

She smiled. "I think you're fine if you're cracking jokes." She picked up her phone. "Breck hasn't texted me back. He might be with one of his furry patients."

"Good. No Breck then? He'll give me so much crap for this."

"Can you stand?"

"Do I have to?" I asked, only half joking. It was quite pleasant there in her lap.

"Unless you want to stay out here all night, yeah."

I reluctantly rose to my feet. The gash in my head stung, but I no longer felt as if I were drunk. "I'm good."

"Well, let's go back together, okay? That way I can keep an eye on you," Jamie said.

"You'd be a good nurse," I said as we started walking down the trail arm in arm.

"Only if she were naughty." She winked at me, her ponytail bouncing sassily to and fro.

I'm pretty sure she winked anyway. I wanted her to have winked at me, I realized. However, the knot on my head *may* have affected my vision.

I almost tripped again.

2

_____

JAMIE

On a whim, I'd decided to go down to the river for an afternoon run. I'd taken part of the day off, leaving it in the capable hands of my assistant Maisy. Most mornings I ran before going to work, but as the days began to shorten and the sun rose later, I knew I would soon have to change my routine to the gym. For now, I enjoyed being outside as much as I could. The summer had gone by quickly. Between reopening my inn and my friend Tiffany getting married and Stormi engaged, there had been copious gatherings and celebrations, all increasing the pace of my already busy life.

Today, however, I'd decided to take a breather and make a little time for myself. Running along the river was one of my favorite routes. I did not expect to find an injured Darby Devillier lying in the grass. Having seen only his tennis shoes sticking out on the trail, I'd thought for a few seconds that he was a dead body. I read a lot of mysteries, and my imagination had always been a little overactive. Fortunately, as I came fully around the bend in the trail, I found Darby very much alive. Bleeding and groaning, but alive.

Darby's eyes had been glassy, and his usual reticence seemed to have been knocked out of him. In fact, he was saying a bunch of funny things. If I hadn't known better, I'd have thought he was drunk.

Now, as we walked toward the park, he seemed better, although walking at a slow pace. I had my arm in his as we walked, just in case he stumbled. If I had to, I'd call 911. So far, he seemed fine. I understood his desire to stay out of urgent care. My insurance was remarkably lame. When I added in the co-pays and deductibles, it was basically useless.

When we reached our cars, I asked him if he could drive. He assured me he was fine. I decided to follow him in my car back to the apartment building where we both lived. "I'll be right behind you, just in case."

"I'm sorry I ruined your run," he said, dipping his chin into his chest.

"It's no big deal."

Yes, this living in the same building thing. Yet another coincidence. My one-night stand on an impulsive night in Cliffside Bay, California, seemed to be the gift that continued to give. First, to my great surprise, Darby Devillier was living in Emerson Pass, having accepted a teaching position at the high school. Two, I'd rented an apartment in the very same building. And there were only six apartments in the whole place. What were the odds? I had no idea. I'm sure there was some calculation one could do, but that wasn't really my specialty. Ask me what wine to serve with salmon, though, and I was all over it.

I took another good look at him as he leaned against the side of his car. He touched his hand to the back of his head. "No more fresh blood," he said.

"That's good. But I still think you should get it checked out."

"We'll see."

"I know, it's expensive. But teachers have good insurance, right?"

"There's still co-pays. I'm barely making it, and look at this."

He thumped the top of his old Honda. "She's been good to me, but I don't think she's long for the world."

"I get it," I said. "I was just thinking the same about insurance." I was probably as broke as he was, only mine included gobs of debt on the inn. As much as I loved the place, especially now that the rebuild was done, there were at least a dozen times a day when I wondered if I'd made an epic mistake with my life. Since I was a little girl, I'd dreamed of owning an inn. However, I was in trouble. I couldn't afford to have missed an entire year of business. I'd only just opened when the fire took all my dreams away.

I could have taken a nice safe job in an office or even continued to waitress, and life would have remained simple. It's funny about dreams coming true at last. When they do, they come with problems one never anticipated. I mean, I *should* have anticipated the debt and how it would feel as though the weight of the world rested on my shoulders because of it, but I didn't. I was too busy fixating on my goal. I could still see my wish list scratched into my high school notebook. We'd been asked to describe our five-year plan. I was all about it.

I want to own a quaint inn where I will pamper my guests some- place quiet and beautiful.

My teacher had laughed at my specificity and encouraged me to go to college just in case I changed my mind.

I knew I wouldn't, although I did get that degree. But living a life doing what I loved—giving people a respite from the chaos of life, if only for a weekend—felt like a purpose. Providing my guests with a crisp, serene room, delicious pastries and coffee, and wine and cheese in the afternoons had proven as joyful as I'd anticipated. At least I had that, even if the debt felt over- whelming.

I couldn't exactly explain what doing so did to my soul, other than to say it did not seem like work. It was like floating on air, this job of mine. Until I went into my office and opened bill after bill and looked at the schedule and saw that we weren't even half full through the rest of the month.

At those times, I would drop my head onto my desk, filled with regret and worry, and think: What have I done? I was not yet thirty and I felt as if I'd lived two lifetimes since coming to Colorado two years ago. To have worked as hard as I did restoring the old Higgins mansion into an inn only to lose it in the forest fire seemed more unfair than it should have been. Yes, it was true that much worse things happened to others. Still, it hurt. Bad. After all I'd given up, all the saving and scrimping since I'd graduated from college seemed so stupid to me now. Especially when it seemed as if all my friends and family were having so much fun, enjoying being young and in love.

I was young, not in love, and overworked. A good night's sleep had eluded me for years now.

"See you back at the ranch," I said now to Darby.

"You bet." He smiled, and the lines on either side of his mouth creased into half dimples. "But did I ruin your run?"

"No, really. Don't worry. I was on my second round anyway." I explained how I ran the trail twice to get in a good four miles. Sweet of him to be concerned, I thought. He was such a nice guy. Who knew under all that niceness was a beast in bed.

"Good for you," he said. "I usually only do it once."

"I'm trying to exercise enough to sleep better. It's not really working." Was it my imagination or was he stalling? He'd said such cute things. Saying I was pretty and that he liked my freckles and that compliment about my eyes had thrilled me.

His dark eyes were soft, sympathetic. This was not because of the head injury. He often looked this way when talking with someone. This gift of listening so intently probably made him a great teacher. Around town, I'd heard about how good he was and how much the kids respected and admired him. I hadn't attended, but last spring he'd been the teacher voted to speak at the high school graduation. I'd overheard him talking about his speech at a party one night but I hadn't asked him any questions. Even though I'd wanted to. I was drawn to him for some reason. Not just because we'd shared a night of passion, either. There was something about him that made me want to know more. To know everything. Regardless, I never acted upon these feelings. He'd made it clear that he wanted only a superficial friendship. It all worked out just fine, really. We had mutual friends and were part of a group that hung out almost every weekend for at least a meal or drinks and had agreed, albeit silently, to pretend that nothing had ever happened. It was best to keep myself from complicating things further than they already were.

The sun had lowered and tossed rays of light through the surrounding trees. Darby's eyes appeared lighter than they did indoors. He had a neat, well-ordered face, nothing too prominent or overdone. A clean jawline, a small nose, and skin so smooth it seemed as if he wore some kind of dewy foundation. He didn't. Not the type. Nothing wrong with it, of course. If a guy wanted to wear makeup, that was his business. I was all for whatever made people feel good.

He dressed simply, usually jeans and T-shirts, except for work. I saw him leave in the mornings for school wearing khakis or black jeans and a button-down shirt. Each time, his appearance moved me, seeing him so earnest and old-fashioned. One day I'd met him in the apartment complex's lobby and he had on a bow tie and a jacket over the button-down. He'd blushed when he'd noticed my gaze resting on the tie and explained that they'd had an event at the high school for incoming freshmen and their parents. "I wanted to look grown-up. Respectful, I guess. A teacher with whom they can trust their children."

It almost broke my heart, the old-fashioned sweetness of Darby Devillier. He was a man to build a life with, I'd thought in that moment. Of that I was certain. It would be a sad day when he finally found the right woman. A sad day for me, that is. He would be happy. Obviously. Me? I would feel as if I'd missed an opportunity to be with someone special. However, the truth was, he'd never really been mine to choose. He was a one-night stand. A drunken decision made by two lonely people. One who had just been dumped—him. And me, still stung from the rejection of my father and his decision to marry a woman younger than me.

It was a fluke we'd been in Cliffside Bay in the first place. My mother and I had rented an apartment in Cliffside Bay so we could be close to my brother, Trey, while we licked our wounds. Hearing Mom cry in the shower when she thought I couldn't hear her had been reason enough to go back to Darby's hotel room that night. A night of sex with the hottest guy I'd ever been with had been a pain blocker, even if only temporarily.

It was the drink that made me do it. Although we consumed an entire bottle of champagne. A bottle he'd put on ice, intending to celebrate his engagement with the woman he loved. Only she'd broken up with him before he could give her the ring.

I'd been at the brewery in Cliffside Bay the night of his botched proposal, waitressing. The staff had been all aflutter when Darby had come in earlier that day and asked if we could put the ring in a piece of chocolate cake. Some of us, including me, had commented that all the good ones were taken.

But it was not to be. I'd kept a close watch on his table so that I would know when to bring out the ring. However, I knew something was amiss by the sudden sagging of his handsome face. The woman was crying. Even from the corner of the room where I watched, I could make out her apology. At first, I froze, uncomfortable with watching a pain show, but then I remembered the ring and ran back to the kitchen, catching the chef right before he plunged the ring into one of our mini chocolate lava cakes. I'd been right to do so. When I returned to the dining room, Darby had been there alone, shoulders slumped and a look of pure misery in his eyes.

Later, after my shift was over and I stopped into the Oar for a drink on my way home, he was at the bar. I sat down next to him and offered him an ear. I ended up giving him the rest of me, too.

That was two years ago. Now we were friends. And one of us had a hurt head. "Come on, let's go home. I'll text Breck to come by your place if he has a chance."

"I'm fine." He reached out to touch my arm. "I promise."

"I'll follow just in case."

"All right, if you insist." He flashed me a grin before he got into his car, and I hustled over to mine, then followed on the road toward downtown.

OUR APARTMENT BUILDING was in one of the old brick buildings right on Barnes Avenue, the historical section of town. The building where Darby and I had apartments was supposedly where Lord Alexander Barnes, the town's founder, had first conducted his affairs. I wished some of Alexander's good luck and fortune would come my way. From the condition of Darby's car, I'd guess he needed a little luck too.

I followed Darby up the stairs. He kept insisting he was fine and from his steady gait, it seemed to be true. His calf muscles seemed to know what they were doing as well, flexing just right as we climbed the stairs. "This place needs an elevator," I muttered under my breath.

"I know. It would be a lot easier to get a sofa up here. Not that I would know. My futon folded up nicely." We'd reached the third floor by then. His apartment faced the street, while mine was against the alleyway on the other side of the building.

From both angles we could see the mountains through the leaves of aspens that grew on either side of the building.

He unlocked his door and turned to look at me. "Thanks, really. So kind of you to watch out for me like this, but I think I can take it from here."

"How about I come in while we wait for Breck?"

"You don't trust me to take care of myself?" Darby asked, the corners of his mouth twitching and his eyes amused.

"I don't really, no."

"Fine, come on in. We can wait for him together."

He held the door open for me, allowing me to breathe in his spicy scent as I passed through. How did he smell so good after a run? For that matter, how did I smell? The sweat had cooled by then, and I was actually a little chilled. After the summer's heat, it was an unusual feeling. Labor Day had passed, though, and soon the mornings would be frosty and crisp. I loved autumn.

All these thoughts went through my head before I dug my phone back out of the shorts to see if Breck had texted back. He had, saying he'd stop by on his way home from dinner. He and Tiffany were having a meal at the grill but they'd come as soon as they could.

Breck was such a good guy. I'd gotten used to seeing him in the building a lot when he was dating Tiffany, but now she'd moved in with him. I missed having her down the hall but at the same time, I was happy for her. They were madly in love, and being around them made me wish for a coupling of my own. Fat chance of that, I thought. The only eligible bachelor left in town was standing in front of me, and he clearly wasn't interested.

"What's wrong?" Darby asked, drawing me from my thoughts.

"Nothing. Nothing at all." I told him Breck and Tiff would stop by after dinner.

He nodded, seeming suddenly exhausted, and collapsed into

one corner of his futon. I'd been here many times before, but I took a second to look around the bare apartment. The living room had only the futon, a beat-up coffee table, and a cabinet that held rows of books. In the corner, an old secretary-style desk with spindly legs seemed wrong somehow, as if an old lady had left behind a piece of her furniture. Still, the old thing was cool.

I went into his small kitchen, a mirror image of the one in my apartment, and filled a water glass for him. "Here, drink this."

He obeyed without protest, drinking thirstily until the entire glass was empty.

"Where'd you get that desk?" I asked, sitting next to him.

"I found it at a yard sale. The owner said it dates back to the beginning of the twentieth century, but I doubt that."

"Why?"

"Because they wouldn't have been selling it for twenty dollars if it were really an antique. My guess is it's a modern knockoff."

I got up to inspect it further. The details of the flower etchings on the front panel didn't look like the workmanship of some modern knockoff. Mahogany wood shone under the lights. "You did a great job. I could see that kind of piece in the inn."

"You could have it for a price," Darby said.

"Really?"

"I don't think so. What would I do without it? Open it up and you'll see why."

I pulled down the hinged desktop. Inside were cubbies, holding papers and books as well as what appeared to be piles of essays from his students, given the red grades that marked the top of the pages. Everything was neat and tidy, with a generous use of manila folders, all labeled, including one for bills, first period, second period, and so on. "You're very organized." I admired that quality, as I was somewhat obsessed with order myself.

"That's where I keep my life," Darby said. "It's the only thing in this apartment that serves a true purpose. The rest of this junk could go." He swept his hand over the futon's cushion between us.

A knock on the door startled me. I'd almost forgotten Breck was coming over to check on Darby. I told him to stay seated and hurried over to answer the door. Breck and Tiffany stood in the hallway, carrying a large pizza box. "We brought dinner," Tiffany said.

"You're sweet," I said. My stomach growled at the scent of basil and tomato. How had they had time to order this for us and bring it so quickly? "Wait, did you guys cut your dinner short?"

"We'd ordered a pizza and figured why not share it with you guys?" Breck asked.

Once inside, Breck went immediately to Darby and asked to see his wound.

While he did that, Tiffany and I took the pizza into the kitchen. Tiffany knew her way around Darby's kitchen, as we'd had many get-togethers over the last few years. What had started out as casual acquaintances had grown into deep friendships. Darby had become close to Breck and Huck especially. Tiffany, Stormi, and I were tight as well. Although Darby and I were the only single ones left, it hadn't started out that way. We were the only soldiers still standing.

"What's going on?" Tiffany whispered to me. "Did you guys go running together?"

"Don't be ridiculous," I whispered back. "I do not run with other people, especially not him. I found him along the trail. He tripped over a root and smacked his head. There was blood and everything. I insisted I follow him home and talked him into calling Breck. He didn't want to shell out the deductible for urgent care."

"I don't blame him for that." Tiffany had opened the pizza box and set several pieces on each plate. "Do you want to eat here at the table?"

"Um, no." That seemed like a double date. "The living room's fine. I'm going to go home after we eat. I have to work tomorrow."

She raised one eyebrow but didn't comment further. By the time we got back to the living room, Breck and Darby were sitting, talking quietly on the couch.

"Well?" I asked. "How's the patient?"

"Just a nasty gash," Breck said. "I'm going to get an ice pack for him and some painkillers, but he should be fine. I don't see signs of a concussion, so there's no fear of letting him be for the night."

"Really? He was saying some goofy things," I said. "No offense, Darby."

"None taken." He smiled at me, and my stomach did that flip-flop thing. Annoying. "But I told you, it wasn't my head that made me goofy. I am naturally that way. Plus, I was staring up at a beautiful woman while resting on her lap."

"That'll do it," Breck said. "Professionally speaking."

Tiffany giggled. "I didn't know you could diagnose that kind of thing."

"They don't call me the love doctor for nothing," Breck said.

"No one calls you that," Tiffany said, laughing.

Love doctor? Good grief. What did they think was going on here?

"Are you sure someone shouldn't stay with him?" I asked.

"Yes, good question," Tiffany said. "Maybe one of us should stay overnight to look after him." She widened her light blue eyes a little too innocently. I knew better. That gleam meant only one thing. She was scheming. Tiffany thought Darby and I should go on a real date, one that didn't involve nighttime antics but rather some old-fashioned courtship. She'd even claimed to see a glow between us, as if there were some magical spell drawing us together.

She wasn't the only one. Stormi had said denying our attraction was a sure path to loneliness and regret. She added that she should know, given what had recently transpired between her and Huck. Once enemies, they were now in love and rarely out of each other's sight. It was sweet. I mean, if you're a romantic. I was not. My feet were firmly planted in the pragmatic, hard-working ground. Working hard was my romance. Building my dreams. No time for entanglements that would ultimately lead to heartbreak. Men left women like me. It might take two decades, as it had with my mother and father, but eventually, betrayal would come. My mother was now in her fifties, single, and forced to start over after giving her whole life to her marriage and children. I would rather be alone than risk the same fate.

"I'm fine," Darby said. "Really. No one needs to stay and babysit me. Let's have some pizza, and then I have to kick you all out. I have papers to grade."

He must be on the same page as me. Good. That's the way I wanted it. Right?

3

DARBY

When I first took the position at the high school, the principal told me several stories about Quinn Cooper Barnes, including her passion for teaching adult immigrants English. The first winter she lived here, in addition to teaching at the one-room schoolhouse, she taught adults during the evenings. That act of service had fostered a commitment to provide immigrants a safe place to learn or improve their English language skills that had carried on for decades. My principal had asked if I would be willing to teach one evening a week. I knew what volunteer meant. Working for no money.

Still, I was happy to do it. Every Wednesday evening in my classroom, I spent time with whoever showed up to practice their reading and writing. Instead of a lecture or lesson, I taught them individually.

Tonight, I had only two students, Mrs. Lin and Mr. Rodriguez. Both in their fifties, her native tongue was Chinese and his Spanish. Among the three of us, we communicated as well as we could. As a matter of fact, I suspected the two of them were talking outside of class, too. They were both single, and I'd heard Mr. Rodriguez ask in his best English if she'd like to have a cup of coffee or a drink after class. She'd agreed, beaming and giving me a small wave before ducking out the door to accompany him into the parking lot.

This evening, I had them working on writing a letter in English to someone they needed to communicate with for practical reasons. I wanted our time to be useful as well as a learning opportunity. Often, they had a reason for needing to communicate with a company or person. I'd begun to see that this was one of the primary stressors about living in a country where you didn't speak the language fluently. They couldn't ask their doctors specific questions, for example. Mrs. Lin was writing a list of things she wanted to discuss with her physician at her upcoming appointment. Mr. Rodriguez was working on a letter to his granddaughter who had moved away last year and was coming to visit soon. "I'll tell her about all of things we will do when she comes here," he said to me as he picked up his pencil. I had them use pencil so I could give them corrections and they could rewrite whatever they needed to.

They were working away, so I went back to my desk and pulled out a stack of essays from my tenth-grade class. I chose the first one, an essay by Jerome, one of my favorite students. He was a talented musician as well as a mathlete, but he also had a gift for understanding complex literary themes. Small and shy, he sat in the front with the rest of the serious students and shot furtive glances at Shelley Stevens, who had no idea of his giant crush.

From my vantage point at the front of the room, on any given day of the week, my students revealed themselves to me. They didn't think so. My hormonally challenged students thought they kept their thoughts and emotions hidden, but I could see it all. The crushes, the feuds, the mean girls, and the jocks who pretended they didn't care for fiction but sometimes grew misty-eyed when we were reading together from a story or novel. They were good at hiding things, but not from me. I'd been them not so long ago. The boy with the crush on a girl way out of his league or swallowing a knot in my throat while reading something particularly moving.

Now, Mrs. Lin asked me if I could help her figure out the word for what sounded like gee-aye-sing to my English-speaking ears. However, I could see from her writing that she'd translated the Chinese spelling from symbols to *juéjīng*.

"The time of life when it ends," Mrs. Lin said.

"What ends?" I asked.

"The...blood...you know...woman blood...no more."

I had a bad feeling about where this was going. Already warm, I told her I would look it up on my computer.

Ah, yes, thank you, Google Translate, I thought. *Juéjīng* meant menopause. The tips of my ears grew hot, but I told her none-theless, spelling it for her on a piece of paper.

She seemed oblivious to my embarrassment, smiling broadly before writing the word down on her list.

Mr. Rodriguez was busy scribbling away while taking breaks to look up words in his Spanish-to-English dictionary.

I went back to my essays, hoping Mrs. Lin would not ask me anything more about the womanly experience. If she asked me to translate vaginal dryness, I was out.

Fortunately, the rest of the night passed without further incident. At eight, I told them it was time to go home and that I looked forward to seeing them next week.

"I'll have a letter from Sophia by then, yes?" Mr. Rodriguez said. "I have hope."

"I hope so too." I perched on the side of my desk and watched as Mr. Rodriguez helped Mrs. Lin with her coat. "Tonight we have wine," he said to me with a happy smile on his face.

"Have fun," I said. "Practice your English with each other."

"It is all we have between us," Mrs. Lin said. "Good practice."

After they were gone, I tidied up my desk and turned off my computer. Tomorrow would be here soon enough. My head wound stung still, and it was everything I could do not to press on it with my fingers.

When I arrived home, I noticed a light under Jamie's front door. She was home already? Often she was still at the inn this time of night. I sometimes heard her coming into the building around nine. I didn't love that she parked out back and walked in alone after dark. But what was I to do? Offer my assistance by meeting her at her car when she returned back to the apartment building? I would do it if she asked, but she wouldn't.

I DON'T KNOW what got into me as I drove home later that evening, but I decided I wanted to share with my friends the truth about my dad. For some reason, it felt important. I'd isolated myself too much. My friends were loyal, and they would still care about me if I told them about my background. So I sent a group text and asked Huck and Breck to meet me at the grill.

An hour later, the two of them, looking stunned, assured me that nothing from my past could ever make them change their minds about me.

"We're your friends," Breck said. "No matter what."

"I feel ashamed," I said. "So I've kept it from you. That and how bad it was growing up."

"We're here if you ever want to talk about it," Huck said. "Turns out talking is actually good for you. Stormi has taught me that."

"Past trauma can control your life if you let it," Breck said. "But friends and the women we love can help you through."

The women we love. I wanted someone to love. An image of Jamie standing over me on the running trail ran through my mind. Was there a chance with her? Would she consider a real date? I wasn't sure, but I'd never know if I never asked. I put that idea aside and focused my attention on my friends. Tomorrow was another day.

4

JAMIE

My inn was not an exact replica of the old mansion I'd lovingly remodeled. Instead, the architect and interior design by my brother and his firm had added more modern touches, including better plumbing and electrical. My brother had made sure every detail, from the stain of the hardwood floors to the soft gray of the wall and the white trim, was exactly what I'd wanted. Dark floors gleamed against white wainscoting just as I'd imagined it would when I described to them what I wanted. There were twelve rooms in total as well as the common area that served as a breakfast area and hosted the wine-and-cheese hours in the afternoons. Although it was not technically a bed-and-breakfast, in the mornings, I served pastries and muffins from Brandi's bakery and rich, dark-brewed coffee.

The common area included a baby grand piano, which had been a gift from my friend Crystal. She was the widow of a tech billionaire and more than a little generous. In fact, she'd been instrumental in getting our little town back on track for tourism. As a ski town, we relied greatly on visitors. No one wanted to come to a place charred from a fire. She'd worked closely with my brother and his firm to rebuild as quickly as we could.

At the moment, a talented high school student named Gerald Fisher played Chopin, providing a nice backdrop to the chatting among guests. I found this particularly satisfying. Visitors exchanging information about where they were from and what they did for work and how many children they had filled me with joy. I'd already witnessed several couples who had become friendly with others, even exchanging information for when they left the sanctuary I'd created for them. My dreams had come true at last.

I'd just served my last guest a glass of red when one of my staff, Maisy, motioned to me from the doorway. *Please, don't let anything be broken*, I thought. There was no time or money to fix anything. Although a hint of autumn in the air meant that tourist season would curtail before picking back up again when the snow fell and the ski mountain opened, I couldn't afford anything to go wrong.

Maisy had been invaluable in the stressful weeks before the reopening. In her late forties, she'd recently sent her last child off to college. For the first time since she'd started having children, she was free to do as she pleased, she'd told me in the interview. And what pleased her? Working at a beautiful inn putting her hospitality degree to good use. "Finally," Maisy had said, "I can do something besides taxi kids from one event to another." Her husband was a physician, so I doubted they needed the money. I'd asked her in the interview if she would mind working for someone younger. I wasn't yet thirty, after all. She'd joked that I was only a few years older than her oldest child, but yes, she would be fine taking instruction from me.

Thus far, she'd been even better than I'd hoped. Dressed in black slacks and a crisp white button-up blouse, Maisy looked impeccable. She always did. I don't know how she managed to never crease her clothes, even after a long shift. I was a hot mess most days. Every day.

"What's going on?" I asked.

"You have a potential bride waiting in your office. She wants to book the inn for her wedding." Maisy tugged on an earring that dangled just below her precision-cut bob. With silver hair and bright brown eyes, she was actually quite striking.

"Really?" My spirits lifted. Maybe I could pay the bills this month after all.

"And she wants to rent the entire inn out," Maisy said. "Isn't that wonderful? However, she said there's a time factor. She wants to do it the first weekend of October."

That was three weeks away.

Mentally, I ran through my list of booked rooms. If I recalled correctly, I didn't have a single room rented that particular weekend. "This is great," I whispered without hiding my glee at the possibilities before leaving Maisy to head for my office.

I found a tall woman with gleaming brown hair waiting for me in my small office just off the lobby. She stood as I entered and held out her hand. The first thing I noticed was the gigantic diamond on her wedding ring finger. I had no idea how many carats, but it was the width of a nickel and sparkled like the Christmas star. "I'm Arianna Bush. Are you Jamie?"

"I am. Pleased to meet you." We shook hands before I went to sit behind the desk and encouraged her to have a seat as well. I darted a few quick glances her way. She looked vaguely familiar, but I couldn't place where I knew her from.

She crossed her long, tanned legs. Why was it rich people were so often good-looking? I smoothed my plain black skirt over my knees and scooted closer to the desk. "Maisy tells me you're interested in booking the inn for your wedding?"

"Yes, for the ceremony. We'll have some guests staying here and some at the lodge. But I just adore the intimate feel here at the inn. My fiancé wanted to marry at the lodge, but I'm not feeling it."

"Were you thinking inside or outside?" I asked, taking out my notebook to jot down details.

"I have something very specific in mind, actually," Arianna said. "You see, my parents married in this inn—or the one that burned down—thirty-five years ago."

"But it wasn't an inn then." I knew that what had once been a mansion for the famous wedding dress designer, Annabelle Higgins, had not yet been turned into an inn thirty-five years ago. At the time of my arrival, it had sat empty for a few years. The structure had needed a lot of work, thus I was able to buy it for less than its true market value. I'd spent the better part of a year returning it to its formal glory, only to lose it in the fire after only being open a few weeks.

"Right," Arianna said. "My mother had known the people who lived here. When my father asked her to marry him, she insisted the wedding be held here. There was a gazebo then, and that's where I want to marry Rob. Here, I have photos." She rummaged in her designer handbag and pulled out several black-and-white photos.

I took a good look at them, anxious to see what it had been like thirty-five years ago. There was indeed a gazebo surrounded by roses. Standing just inside the gazebo were a bride and groom. "This is your parents?"

"Yes, on their wedding day." She reached back to take the photographs, obviously wanting to keep them close. "It's one of the only things I have left of my mother. She died when I was only five."

"I'm sorry," I said. "That's terrible."

"It was. My father remarried when I was ten to a nice woman, but she wasn't my mother, you know. No one could replace her for me."

"I see. You want to marry in the same location that they did?

For sentimental reasons?" When talking with customers I kept my voice low and calm.

"Precisely. I want it to look just like this." She tapped the photo to indicate the gazebo.

I had no gazebo and no rosebushes. "It doesn't look like that any longer." I explained about the fire and that the gazebo must have been removed long before I ever bought the place. "We have a lot of other pretty locations on the property. If there are none to your liking, we could have the ceremony and reception in our great room inside the inn."

She was shaking her head and her mouth puckered as if she'd tasted something sour. "That's just the thing. I want it to look exactly like it did back then. I want to stand under that same gazebo and marry the man I love just as my mother did thirty-five years ago. It will be on their anniversary. Or what would have been, anyway."

"I'm sorry, but I couldn't possibly build one in time." My heart sank. I couldn't do what she asked. In debt up to my neck, even with the insurance policy replacing most of what I'd lost, I couldn't afford to build anything more. I'd bought the inn after saving every penny I could from the time I was fifteen until just two years ago. Regardless, I still had to take out a mortgage to finance my dream. Now I was looking at losing a very lucrative wedding weekend. What could I do, though? It wasn't as if I could construct a gazebo and put in a stone patio in three weeks' time. "Even if I had the money, which I don't, three weeks isn't enough time." Why the hurry, I wondered? Why not next year instead? "Would you be able to postpone the wedding until next year?"

"No. Rob wants to marry now. He's tired of waiting." Arianna tossed her silky hair behind both shoulders and fixed her gaze on me. I felt a little as though we were playing chicken with our eyes. "I'll pay you a hundred thousand dollars if you do it for me, on top of whatever it costs for the labor and materials."

I almost did a double take, like a cartoon character. "Are you kidding me?"

"Money's no object. I'm a very rich woman marrying an even richer man."

"I see." My mind was scrambling to keep up with her proposal. How would I find someone to build something so quickly? What about the materials? I'd need a good contractor, which was hard to find.

However, a hundred thousand dollars? I could pay down some of the mortgage with that money and actually buy a decent car and still have some to put in savings. "I could try to get it done quickly, but I'm not sure it's possible." Why didn't she come up with this idea before now? How long had she been engaged?

"Can you do it for that?" Arianna asked. She was a woman used to getting what she wanted. That much was obvious.

I cleared my throat, uncomfortable.

"Well?" She stared at me, unblinking.

"I can do my best." This was nearly impossible, but I had to make it happen.

She tapped the photo again. "It has to look just like this one."

"Yes, I understand."

"Good. Well, I'll go so you can get back to work. I'm in town until the wedding. Maisy just booked me a room for the next three weeks. That way I'll be here to supervise."

"What about your fiancé? Will he be here?"

She smiled for the first time. "Not until the week before the wedding. Rob's the CEO of a software company and can't take as much time off as I can."

"What do you do?" I asked, curious. "Because you look very familiar to me."

"I'm an influencer. Beauty products, that kind of thing."

An influencer? Wasn't everyone these days? But what did I care? If she could pay me a hundred grand for a gazebo, then I was in. "That must be it." I held out my hand to shake hers. "I'll let you know as soon as I find someone to do the work. I'm assuming you'll want to see the proposal?"

"I'd appreciate it," Arianna said.

I walked her out then and returned to my office. Where in the world was I going to find someone to do this work in a mere three weeks?

I RETURNED to the wine-and-cheese hour in the common area and mingled with the guests, answering questions about where to dine and what activities were available this time of year, but my mind was elsewhere. Specifically, I silently churned on the subject of a certain gazebo. I knew because I'd just spent the better part of a year rebuilding my inn that carpenters and workers were in high demand here in a town still recovering from a forest fire that had taken out several of our businesses, including mine, and a dozen homes. My brother's firm had agreed to do much of the work for a discount, but there were only so many of them to go around, especially since their home base was in Cliffside Bay, California, not here in Colorado.

After the guests had all wandered off to finish the rest of their evenings, I cleaned up the glasses and almost-empty trays of cheese and crackers. Tiff, Stormi, Crystal, and Brandi were on their way over to enjoy a happy hour of our own. Since reopening, I'd been too busy to see any of my friends. Stormi, who had been busy herself running our new art gallery and taking pictures for our local newspaper as well as being the town's primary wedding photographer, had come up with the idea of a gathering at the inn for wine and dinner. Brandi, who owned The Sugar Queen bakery, had promised to bring sandwiches left over from her lunch offerings. Crystal said she'd bring wine from her cellar. A treat, as her wine collection was substantially better than anything I offered my guests.

I hadn't known a soul in Emerson Pass when I purchased the old Higgins mansion several years before. That I had a friend group still amazed me. Back home in San Diego, I'd had several close friends and had missed their easy companionship when I'd moved away. However, the relationships I'd built with the women here had lessened my homesickness considerably. In fact, I couldn't remember when I'd felt more blessed and full. These women had become like family to me, which I desperately needed. My father and I hadn't spoken since the divorce. When I left Cliffside Bay, my mother had decided to travel the world to get over being left by him for a woman my age. Midlife crises were real. I'd witnessed it with my own eyes.

I still had my brother Trey, though. That would never change. He was as loyal and steady as the rising sun. His wife, Autumn, had just given birth to their second child—another little girl to go with her adorable sister. I hoped they would all come visit soon, but the demands of two careers and two babies kept them busy out in California. I'd moved out here so hopeful about my new life, only to have that dashed with the fire. There had been more than a few times I'd thought of packing it all in and going back to the West Coast. But to where? My mother had sold the home I grew up in. Dear old Daddy was busy with whatever her name was. This was my home now. For better or worse, I was tied to it as long as I owned the inn. The small-town culture I'd craved all my life was more than enough, I told myself on the lonely nights.

My friends arrived around half past six. I'd sent Gerald home by then to eat his supper with his family. He was only seventeen and still pink-cheeked and dewy-eyed and expected home for dinner every night. I envied the simple but loving family he had. Growing up in a wealthy suburb in San Diego hadn't been as wholesome as one might predict.

I took in a deep breath, hoping to rid myself of thoughts of the past. I was here now with my best friends. Being present with them was a gift. One I didn't plan on ever taking for granted.

We were seated on the soft, all-enveloping chairs and love seats my brother had chosen as I told them about the request from my potential new client.

"Wait a minute," Stormi said, fluffing her dark bangs that hung just above her almond-shaped green eyes. "This woman offered you how much?" She looked her usual arty self—dressed in jeans with holes in the knees and a tight black tank that clung to her slender frame.

I reiterated the financial details once more.

"Incredible. I've never heard of such a thing." Brandi poured another slug of wine into our glasses without spilling a drop. She could make a sandwich and brew a double espresso while taking money from a customer all at the same time. I'd never met anyone as competent in my life. She could do anything, including caring for a baby and running one of the most successful businesses in Emerson Pass without breaking a sweat.

"Sentimentality will cause you to do a lot of things that might not seem rational to other people." Crystal crossed her long legs. She wore designer jeans and a silky blouse, both of which probably cost more than my car. Before she'd attended culinary school, she'd modeled on the runways of Milan to pay the bills. This was long before she'd married one of the richest men on the planet, only to lose him in an accident. She was now happily married to Garth and the mother of a sweet baby boy named Huckleberry.

"You know who has mad carpentry skills?" Stormi asked.

"Yes." Tiffany nodded solemnly. Her brown hair was piled on

top of her head tonight, making her light blue eyes stand out from her fair skin. "He would be perfect."

"He?" I asked.

"He's looking for extra work," Brandi said. "So he can buy a house and replace his car."

"Who are we talking about?" I asked.

When I saw them all exchange humorous glances, I knew. They meant Darby. My cheeks flamed with heat.

"No way," I said. "Not Darby."

"He built a patio for us," Tiffany said in her soft voice. "He's detail-oriented, which we both appreciated."

I had to admit, their deck had turned out well. Would it be possible? Or would it be too weird? I mean, we were friends now, so maybe it was fine. "I guess I could ask him."

Again, they exchanged glances, apparently still amused by my embarrassment. "More wine, anyone?" I asked.

"That means she's going to ask him," Tiffany said.

"This is awesome," Stormi said. "You'll be thrown together all the time."

"You ladies should mind your own business," I said, laughing.

"That's not how we roll," Stormi said.

That was the truth.

5

DARBY

I wrote a B on the top of a student's paper with my favorite red pen. I did love my red pen, I had to admit. I loved teaching English, too. Basically, it was a way for me to perpetually geek out over great literature. Sometimes, the kids didn't fully appreciate the talent or skill of Dickens, for example. They said there were too many words.

Dickens might have written for the people and to support his family, but it didn't mean he wasn't great. So what if he wrote in extra detail because he was paid by the word? People had a lot less to do back then. There was no TikTok or Snapchat. My students would have been grateful for a long, character-driven story like *Great Expectations* without the distraction of their screens 24-7.

I'd saved my best student's essay for last, knowing it would give me a boost. Some of the others had had the opposite effect. The assignment had been to compare and contrast Dickens's *Great Expectations* with Kafka's *Metamorphosis*. Yes, it was a hard assignment. And no, nobody reads existential literature for the pure joy of it. I felt strongly that this kind of critical thinking was important, especially in today's world of unreliable news and social media.

Matilda's essay didn't disappoint. I gave her an A and stuck her paper on top of the others. She was captain of the cheer team as well as my best literature student. Polite and bubbly, a student like her was a teacher's dream, but I also enjoyed reaching the kids others had given up on. I could feel them struggling to overcome whatever it was that made them avoid eye contact from the back row.

My second love was carpentry. I'd been able to make a little money building decks or doing light remodel jobs for friends. I'd recently put an ad out in the newspaper offering handyman and carpentry skills with hours in the late afternoon and weekend.

I hoped someone would call sooner rather than later. My car was making a strange noise, and I figured it wasn't long for this world. I sighed and began straightening up my classroom. Instead of a blackboard, I used a an interactive board while I gave my lectures. After I'd shut it off for the day, I wiped the plastic clean and tucked the whole thing into a corner of the room.

I'd just packed up my leather briefcase, a gift from a professor after I completed my Ph.D., when my cell phone rang. A quick glance told me it was Breck. He probably wanted to get together for a boys' night of beer and pizza. I hoped so, anyway. I'd barely seen him since he returned from his honeymoon.

I picked it up on the second ring. "Hey, how's it going?" I asked.

"Good, good. No complaints." He had a slow way of talking that always made me want to close my eyes and take a nap. This was why he was so good with animals; he lulled them into a state of relaxation. "I have a lead for you on a carpentry job. You have room in your schedule?"

"Sure. As a matter of fact, a gig would come in really handy about now. Who's it for?" This wasn't a big town, and highly likely I would know the person in need of a carpenter.

"It's for Jamie. Out at the inn," he added, as if I needed more explanation. I was quite familiar with Jamie, I wanted to say but didn't. Every inch of her. I rubbed my eyes, the image of her wearing nothing but a pair of silky panties played before me. Ever since that night in Cliffside Bay, I hadn't been able to forget what she looked or felt like. Imagine my surprise when she showed up in Emerson Pass. Once I heard about the old mansion she bought to make into an inn, though, it all made sense. She'd told me about her dream during the night I'd spent with her. The hottest night of my life.

However, she'd made it obvious she wasn't interested in anything serious, and I'd stayed away from her as much as one could in a town this size. My friends were her friends, and the group had only gotten tighter over the last year. It hadn't been easy to resist making an embarrassing move on her. I knew where it would lead, however, so I acted cool around her. After what had happened with my girlfriend, right in front of Jamie, no less, I wasn't about to put myself out there to be publicly humiliated.

I squeezed my eyes shut at the memory of that mortifying night. I'd had a ring ready in the kitchen of the brewery back in Cliffside Bay. They'd had the ring and were going to bring it out buried in the dessert. Sadly, I was dumped before I could propose. Jamie had been waitressing that night, and she saw it all go down. When I ran into her later, we started talking and one thing led to another, as they always do in this kind of situation. We'd agreed to one night only and no contact ever again. What we didn't know? In six months' time, we'd both arrive in Emerson Pass.

"Is everything all right out there?" I hoped it wasn't a leak or electrical issue. She'd had a grand reopening last spring, with an invitation to all her friends, including me, for wine and cheese the night before the opening weekend. She'd wanted to thank everyone for their support. After the fire had demolished her dream, it had been hard to try again. But boy had she. I had to admire her for it, too. She did the proverbial brushing herself off and getting right back to work. A year later, she had a brand-new inn, even better than the one that had burned to the ground. Every time I drove past the pretty white building down on the old river road, I smiled.

"Yes, everything's good there," Breck said in answer to my question. "But she needs a gazebo built for a wedding and needs it done yesterday." I heard Tiffany's voice in the background. "Right, yeah. Tiff says the woman's paying for the whole thing plus giving Jamie a chunk of change to get it done in time for her wedding."

"When's that?" I asked.

"Three weeks from tomorrow."

"Oh, that doesn't give me much time. I mean, if I were to accept the job. Why didn't she call me herself?"

"Well, um, I thought I'd run it past you first," Breck said. "In case it felt awkward for you."

"Nah, we're good. You saw us the other night."

"Yeah. I did. Tiff noticed, too," Breck said.

"Noticed what?" That had me curious. Maybe they saw something I couldn't?

"That you two seemed close."

"Well, if by close you mean I embarrassed myself by staring longingly into her eyes, then yes."

He laughed. "Maybe she digs you but is too shy to let you know."

"She's not shy." I got hot under the collar just thinking about how bold and uninhibited she'd been. I'd forgotten all about my ex-girlfriend during the hours we spent together.

"Regardless, why don't you call and see what she needs? Or pop down the hall?"

I was getting the distinct impression that this was about more than just building a gazebo. Were our friends trying to push us together? Married people always thought everyone else should be married too.

"Yeah, I guess I could do that," I said. "But don't get your hopes up if you're trying to get us together."

"No, sure, I understand. It would be a job, that's all. One that pays well. You said you need a new car."

"True enough." I didn't think my old Honda would make it through the winter. She didn't seem to like the cold. "I'll go out there. Worst case, she says no." Even as I said it, I inwardly cringed. The words *she says no* brought me right back to the humiliation of my botched proposal.

"Good. Also, we're thinking of having people out to the house this weekend. My mom's house, that is." Tiffany and Breck were still living at his mother's house while theirs was being built.

"How's your house coming along?" I asked.

"Slow. We're still waiting on countertops and cabinets."

"Those are always slow but especially right now."

"Anyway," Breck said, "give her a call."

"I will. Thanks for the heads-up."

We hung up, and I stared down at my phone. Should I call her? Would it be too awkward? Maybe she'd already found someone. If she'd wanted to hire me, she could have called. All our friends knew I was looking for simple carpentry or handyman work.

"Whatever," I muttered under my breath. I would call and ask her if she still needed someone. I was making too much of this.

She picked up right away. My heart sped up at the sound of her pretty voice. "Hello?"

"This is Darby."

Silence for a few seconds, as if she were trying to place who I was. "Yeah, what's up?"

"Breck called and told me about your project."

"He did?" Her voice went up in pitch. "That was presumptuous of him."

Presumptuous? Weird word to use. "You have someone, then?"

Another hesitation before she answered. "No, I don't. I was going to call you to see if you were interested but then couldn't decide if that was a good idea."

I chuckled. "Yeah, me too. But we're good, right?"

"I mean, I did nurse you back to health the other day," Jamie said.

"You basically saved my life. Which means I owe you."

"Do you think you could do it so fast? This woman is fixated on a certain date. There was no budging her."

"I've built a couple of gazebos before. It shouldn't be a problem."

"Really?"

"I mean, if you're interested." I told her my hourly rate and then held my breath. "No pressure. I could use the work, but I don't want you to feel weird."

She paused to take a quick breath. I could hear her inhale even over the phone and it made me remember her breathing the night we were together. Never mind, I told myself. "Yes, can you come by the inn now?"

"I'm about to head home, so yes, no problem."

I hung up and dropped the phone into the pocket of my khakis. Was this a mistake? Probably, but what the heck? I had nothing to lose. She'd already made it clear she wasn't interested. We were friends, that's all. I'd be there to get a job done and that would be that. Simple. "Don't get your hopes up, buddy," I said under my breath.

THE EARLY-AUTUMN SUN felt good on my shoulders as I walked toward the entrance of the inn. The landscaping in the front was simple but elegant with neatly kept grass and shrubs. Painted white, with modest columns in the Georgian style, the inn seemed perfect to me.

Maisy was at the front desk. I'd had her youngest child, Holly, the year before in my senior English class. She'd been a delightful student and had just left for her first year at college.

"Maisy, are you working here now?"

"Just started." She beamed at me. "What do you think? Do I seem like a career woman now?"

"Your kids must be proud of you," I said.

She grinned and tucked her hair behind her ears, giving her a youthful, puckish appearance. "They're too worried about themselves to even think about me. As it should be, of course. But it's nice to have a job of my own and a reprieve from my taxi duties."

"I can imagine. I'm here to talk to Jamie about a project."

"Are you still paying off those student loans?" Maisy asked. "Is that why you're taking on more work than you already have?" She had slipped into her mother voice with me. I wasn't that much older than her children, so it was understandable. Maisy was a great mother to her own and others. Strays like me, I thought with a pang. There were moments I missed my mother as fiercely as I had when I first lost her. They came in sudden waves like this.

"Yes, I'm afraid so," I said, composing myself. "And there's something wrong with my car."

Her brow creased with worry. "Oh dear. I wish there was something I could do to help."

"You raised wonderful children," I said. "Your debt to society is paid."

She laughed, shaking her head. "Holly's already pledged to a sorority, if you can believe it."

I could. She had been a popular student, pretty and athletic. "I hope she'll be careful."

"Me too. I shudder to think about the parties."

"She'll be fine," I said, immediately sorry I'd brought up the dangers. That was not what a mother who had just sent her baby off to college wanted to think about.

"Anyway, off you go. Knock her dead." Maisy waved me toward Jamie's office. "And don't be afraid to ask for what you're worth. The client's covering all the costs." She pointed to her hand. "Big rock. Don't undercut yourself. "

I laughed despite my inward caving of spirit at the word *worth*. "Will do." I waggled my fingers at her and headed toward the open office door.

Jamie sat behind a modest but pretty vintage cherry wood desk working on a laptop, her slender, manicured fingers clicking above the keys. Her dark blond hair, streaked with golden highlights, was pulled into a high bun with only a few strands left to dangle near her high cheekbones. Between that and the crisp white blouse, she presented a different image than her sporty running look from the other night. Both looked good on her. Darn it anyway. Why did she have to be so pretty? None of that mattered, I reminded myself. This was a job. One that would save my proverbial bacon at the moment.

She looked up and smiled. "Hey, Darby. Thanks for coming by." Formal. Businesslike. Okay, I could match that.

"Not a problem."

"It's probably best if we go out to the back gardens and talk about what's possible." She picked up a square photograph from her desk and handed it to me. The color had faded and the corners lifted slightly from years of being stored away somewhere, but I could see right away that it was a standard gazebo with eight posts and a shingled roof. "She wants it to look like this."

All hope for the job and all that lovely money vanished. "Yeah, so this is totally standard. You could buy a kit and put it together in no time. I can do it for you, but honestly, almost anyone could put it together." This would be so easy I could probably do it in a day.

She tilted her head, looking at me. "She wants it exactly like the old one. No kits. She said that specifically."

No kits. This woman must have way too much money. "Okay, that's a little weird. She knows it'll cost more this way?"

"Yes, apparently. And then there's the rosebushes. I told her those were impossible."

I nodded. "I could plant some but they wouldn't be blooming. If you want them, though, I'm happy to do it for you." I'd never actually planted roses, but I'm sure I could do it. I'd worry about that later. For now, I wanted to see the outside, do some measurements, and put a quote together.

She gestured toward the door. "Let's do it."

I'd like to.

Putting aside my filthy thoughts, I followed her out of her office, doing my best to keep my gaze from drifting to her shapely hips in those clingy slacks. This might prove to be a long job for more reasons than a simple gazebo. Keeping my thoughts from straying toward Jamie would not be easy.

6

JAMIE

We spent a good thirty minutes assessing the garden and doing measurements. I wasn't sure exactly where the gazebo had been before I remodeled the original mansion and gardens. I'd chosen not to put anything out here. I preferred a tidy and sparse garden with manicured shrubs and a few benches. A gazebo had seemed outdated and trite for a modern inn. I wished now I'd had one built after the fire.

Goodness, would I ever stop construction on this piece of property? This had not been what I'd imagined when I dreamed of running my own inn.

Regardless, Darby and I did our best to figure out where everything had been. He was cute, all serious as he jotted down notes in a little pad he'd pulled out of his khakis. The button-up blue shirt paired with the tan pants suited him. He wore his glasses today, and the black frames gave him just a tinge of nerd, which also looked good on him. I'd always loved the way his mouth dimpled at the sides when he smiled. The earnestness in those dark eyes of his had made my stomach do another floppy dive. Darn it all. Why did he have to be so good-looking?

I also remembered the hard muscles hidden under his clothes. I'd felt every inch of them with my fingers that night. Stifling a shiver, I focused on what he was saying. Something to do with digging up the grass and pouring a cement foundation. Whatever. It didn't matter. He knew what he was doing. "As long as you think you can do all this in three weeks, then do it however you need to."

"What about your guests? Will it disturb them?" Darby asked, pushing his glasses farther up his nose. "I won't be able to come until after school each day." He stuck his thumbs through the belt loops of his pants, then seemed to realize what he'd done and took them out. His hands dangled awkwardly by his sides. Did I make him nervous? A fissure of pleasure ran through me at the idea. Maybe he liked me just a little and remembered our night together with the same yearning as me? *No, no*, I warned myself. *Don't even go there. I must stay focused on my inn.* Getting distracted by a man was the very last thing I needed.

"To be honest, I don't have many bookings this week." I sighed, and the weariness made me feel heavy and discouraged. God only knew what I must look like. I hadn't slept well for months and the smudges under my eyes proved it. "If I get any, I'll have to give the guests a discount, I suppose, because of the noise."

"You said the client's paying for everything, right?"

"That's correct."

"Build it into the costs then. I can include it on the proposal."

"What a good idea." I let out another sigh and my shoulders lifted to my ears. "This place is nothing but a money pit."

"You've done an amazing job, though. The inside is stunning."

"That was all my brother. Thank God for Trey. But I'm terrified I'm not going to make this work. We're off to such a slow start, and I have so many bills." Why I was confessing all this was beyond me. Really, I needed to learn to keep my mouth shut.

"I get it. Trust me. Maybe if we pull this off, your rich client will tell all her rich friends to come here?"

I smiled at the idea. "Let's hope so." For some reason, I didn't want him to leave just yet. His presence was comforting and made me feel less alone. "You want something to drink or eat before you go?" Some voice in my head screamed, *don't go yet*. "I have some wine opened."

He smiled and shifted his gaze toward the windows of the great room where the grand piano gleamed in the late-afternoon sun. "That sounds really nice, but no, I have papers to grade and a proposal to put together tonight. I'll email that over to you later so you're not worried about it. After you and the client approve, we'll get started as soon as possible." He placed his fingers lightly on my shoulder. "Try not to worry, okay? We'll make it work. And I promise not to gouge this rich client of yours." He grinned and a hint of his playful side emerged. What was it like to have the weight of the world on you all the time, I wondered? Oh yes, that's right. I knew exactly. We were two people trying to prove ourselves at every turn. We had that in common, among other things. Two English majors making their way in the world.

"You're a lifesaver," I said, meaning it. "Thank you."

"I'm glad for the work. I keep trying to figure out a way to buy my own house, but expenses pile up one after the other."

"I know the feeling," I said.

Our gazes locked for a moment. An unwelcome flutter in my stomach followed. Not good. I had to keep my head. Apparently, my mouth wasn't listening, because the next thing I knew, I was inviting him to dinner at my apartment. "I mean, if you want to pop by later and show me the proposal. Maisy's taking the evening shift tonight so I can have an evening off." I paused as a thought occurred to me. "Since my girls all fell in love, it's lonely at the apartment. We used to have so much fun, didn't we? And now everyone's paired off and I'm...feeling left behind, I guess."

"I've felt the same way since Breck and Huck moved on. We had some good parties and poker nights, and now I'm heating up that frozen pizza all alone watching reruns of *Castle*."

I laughed. "I love *Castle*."

"The weird thing is—I've seen them all but I can never recall who the murderer was, so they're new every time."

"I'm the same way." I stared into his eyes, or rather fell into them, unable to look away. "But to your point, yeah, I hate eating alone now that Tiff moved out of the apartment building and Stormi is busy with Huck. We had a blast these last few years, but I guess that's all over." Why had I added that last part? God, I sounded pathetic.

"It's just you and me left in the apartments," Darby said. "And our frozen pizzas."

"Right? I love to cook, but it's no fun to do for just myself. Everyone keeps telling me that it's important to learn to enjoy your own company or whatever, but I think I've proven myself long enough."

"I love to eat. You know, if you ever want company." Again with that adorable grin of his. How did a man possess both sexiness and boyishness at the same?

"Well, if you're around tonight after finishing the proposal, you could pop over. I mean, we live in the same building. There's no reason we can't enjoy a meal together every once in a while, right?"

He nodded, holding my gaze. "I can't think of any reasons."

My pulse raced. A shiver of desire traveled up my spine. This was dangerous. I knew it but for some reason, I couldn't find it in myself to care. "What do you like to eat?"

"Anything. My father was a terrible cook, so I eat whatever anyone gives me."

"Your father?" He'd never mentioned any family.

"My mother was a terrible cook too. That's why I had to learn how," I said. "Or I wanted to learn, anyway. My father was never home, so I made whatever my mom or brother wanted. It was a way for me to show them I loved them." I flushed, hot in the warmth of the autumn afternoon. "Why am I still talking?"

"I like it when you talk," Darby said. "Sometimes I've worried you clam up when I'm around."

I looked at my feet, noticing that my toenails were in need of a good polish. Had I shaved my legs? *Who cares, you moron*, I said to myself. *You're not rubbing them on anyone anytime soon.* "I was embarrassed to be around you after what happened, but you've always been so nice that it's silly."

"Yeah, me too. I couldn't believe we ended up in the same place. What are the odds?"

"I've no idea. I was an English major, not a math major."

He chuckled, and the shallow dimples on either side of his mouth appeared. "Well, let's not be awkward any longer. We're friends who need to stick together now that everyone seems to have abandoned us." An edge to his voice made me curious. There was weight to the word *abandoned*. I understood that only too well.

"Right." I smiled back at him. "I could make pasta and my homemade sauce. Do you like meat or vegetarian Bolognese?"

"Again, whatever you make, I'll gladly eat." He looked down at the grass for a second before lifting his gaze back to mine. How had we gotten so close together? I could smell his aftershave and see the beginning of a five o'clock shadow on his chin.

"You want me to bring wine?" Darby asked.

"Make it a red?" I should not be this pleased at his suggestion, I thought, but there it was.

"You got it."

We agreed on seven for dinner and then he was off, striding across the lawn on those sexy legs of his.

————

By seven that evening, my Bolognese sauce was simmering happily and filling my small apartment with the scent of tomatoes, garlic, and oregano. I preferred if it cooked all day, but since I hadn't had much time, a few hours would have to do.

I'd changed from my black slacks and white shirt into a pair of soft, loose jeans and a light sweater despite the warmth of the afternoon. The temperatures dropped swiftly this time of year. As soon as the sun went down, a chill slid into the air.

My apartment, always neat and tidy, especially now that I was rarely here, had needed a quick vacuum, which I'd done after I had the sauce on the stove.

My windows faced the northern mountain. I was high enough that I could see over the other buildings in town to the ski runs and lodge. Below us, The Sugar Queen, Brandi's bakery, lent scents of freshly baked bread and sweets starting at 4:00 a.m. I often woke to smells that made my stomach growl.

I'd decorated the apartment with help from my brother. He often had rejected furniture or accessories from his ridiculously wealthy clients and had saved me some choice pieces, including a brown leather couch and two sky-blue chairs. My hardwood floor was covered with a tan-and-blue rug. Books and a few choice pieces of pottery decorated hanging shelves. All in all, I'd created a cozy dwelling for myself. What it lacked in space, brick walls and high ceilings compensated nicely.

A knock on my door came at a few minutes after seven. I opened it to see Darby standing there, smelling way too good. His hair was damp from a shower, and I felt certain he'd shaved. For some reason, this touched me. He was an older-model-type guy from another era, this Darby Devillier.

He had a file tucked under his arm and a bottle of red wine in the other. "I hope you like Spanish wine," he said.

"Sure. You can get some wonderful Spanish wines for a bargain sometimes."

"Agreed."

"Come on in. I hope you're hungry, because I made enough for a family of ten." I stood aside so he could enter.

"I'm super hungry." He handed me the wine. "I could use a glass of this too. Long day."

"I hear you. I'll open this, and you can keep me company while I finish up dinner."

We went into my small kitchen. I'd often thought they should have torn down a wall and made it into a great room, but Trey told me the structure wouldn't allow for it because of a major beam that held up the ceiling.

"Your place looks so much better than mine," Darby said.

"It's all my brother's influence."

Darby sat at the small table stashed in one corner of the kitchen. I opened the wine and poured us each a glass and set one in front of him. From the refrigerator, I grabbed slices of fresh mozzarella, tomatoes, and basil dribbled with balsamic reduction and set it on the table. Then, remembering the bread, I used a mitt to take a baking sheet with thinly sliced baguettes brushed with olive oil from the oven. "Good, I thought I might have had these in a minute too long." They were toasted perfectly, with a tinge of brown. If they were overcooked, they became too brittle, but these would have the right amount of crunch. "Nibble on these while I cook the pasta?"

"You don't have to ask me twice." Darby's eyes lit up at the sight of the toasted pieces of thinly sliced baguette. He scooped some of the cheese and tomatoes onto a piece of the toast, looking like a child with an ice cream cone. An appreciative half groan as he chewed nearly distracted me from the boiling pot of water waiting for the pasta. I remembered similar noises coming from him in a different circumstance.

We chatted about his work while I put the finishing touches on dinner. "The year's been going well so far," he said. "I have a great group of students. Other than a few knuckleheads, but those come with the job. Helicopter parents, too."

"I never asked you why you became a teacher." I leaned against the sink and sipped from my wine glass. "Did you always want to be one?"

"Yeah, ever since tenth grade of high school. I had a teacher named Mr. Ferris. He was absolutely phenomenal and watching him in action—the way he could bring literature alive and make grammar fun—I was inspired to do the same. Not that I had much choice. After I finished my work and came out of graduate school as an expert on Dickens, there wasn't much else to do but teach high school English."

"Why not teach university?" I asked.

"No way. Too easy." He laughed. "I'm kidding. I didn't want the pressure of publication and believe it or not, I love high schoolers. There's more of a chance to influence them for the better in the high school setting. With college classes, they come and go quickly. I get to keep them for a whole year."

"Any regrets?" I asked, taking the pot of pasta from the stove and dumping it into a strainer I'd set in the sink. He was totally adorable. A genuinely good person.

"None. I love what I do. If I made a little more money, I wouldn't be sorry. It's hard sometimes to have to say no to stuff with the guys because I'm always the only one without the funds."

"I get it. I've been lucky because Tiff and Stormi have been as broke as me. Now, though, everything's going to change. It'll just be me on a budget."

"Yep, I get it. I mean, not that they try to make us feel bad, but there's no way I'm going to Vegas for a bachelor trip. That kind of thing is hard. I'm complaining. I hate whiners." He shrugged, looking chagrined. "I sound like a complaining little boy."

"Not at all," I said. "There's no reason to pretend things are perfect on my account."

"Well, regardless, I'm lucky to live here and to have a steady job and so many nice friends. And my students, of course."

"What does your dad do?" I asked.

"I haven't seen him since I graduated from high school." The firm set of his mouth told me he wasn't interested in speaking about it further.

"Oh, I'm sorry."

"Don't be. What about your family?" Darby asked, a little too quickly. He wanted to get past his family and move to mine. "I know your brother, obviously, but what about your parents? They're divorced?"

"Yes, kind of recently, actually. My dad just up and left my mother for a woman my age. So stupid. He's a mess. I've pretty much washed my hands of him. Trey has too."

"I'm sorry," Darby said, echoing me.

"Don't be," I said. The hardness that accompanied any thoughts of my dad was reflected in my tone of voice. "I'm better off without him. He's one of these people who only loves you when you do exactly what he wants."

Darby nodded, a flush creeping up his neck. "Yep, I know all about that."

"What about your mother?" I had to ask. Curiosity had taken hold. Had she left them? Died?

He took another piece of bread from the platter but didn't eat it, instead setting it on the small plate in front of him and studying it as if there were words written there. "She died when I was ten."

"That must have hurt so much." Tears pricked my eyes. What a tragedy for a little boy.

"It wasn't the best, no. My dad was…is…a pretty terrible guy. But I had books. They never let me down."

"No, they never do."

I put together our plates and then asked him to pour us more wine. I'd completely forgotten about the project proposal. That could wait until after wine and pasta. Priorities.

7

DARBY

I couldn't stop eating the pasta and homemade sauce. Afraid I'd have to unbutton my pants if I ate any more, I finally pushed away my plate. "That was truly amazing. How did you learn to cook like this?"

"It's a passion of mine." She picked up my plate and then hers and headed toward the sink. "But I'm not a professional or anything, just a foodie." I reached to turn on the sink's faucet for the dishes. These old apartments didn't have dishwashers.

"No, you don't. The cook shouldn't have to do dishes too."

She smiled and sank back into her chair. "You know what, I'll take you up on that. My feet hurt this time of day."

I'd have liked to offer a foot rub but figured that would come off way creepy. Plus, I didn't want to ruin what was turning out to be a pretty awesome evening. We had an easy way between us. We'd had it that night several years back when I'd met her in Cliffside Bay. It had occasionally occurred to me in the years since that there might have been something between us if we'd been in different places in our lives. I'd just gotten dumped. She was focused on saving and planning for her inn. Was now a better time for both of us? An inkling of excitement tickled the back of my neck as she opened a cabinet to fetch us water glasses, exposing her tanned, lean stomach. Not that I needed the reminder about her fitness level. I'd often seen her running in the mornings and knew she attended a Pilates class at the YMCA during the same time I did a Spin class. Forcing myself to look away, I got busy on our dishes.

I washed the plates and scrubbed the saucepan, then set them in the drying rack. When I was done, I poured us each a little more wine. "You want to go over the proposal in the living room where you can put your feet up?"

"You're speaking my love language." She got up and followed me out of the kitchen. We settled on the couch and I pulled out my estimate, going through each point, including fees and delivery dates.

"Looks good to me," she said. "I'll send the numbers over to the bride right now and make sure she's willing to pay what you've asked."

Jamie texted rapidly into her phone. It often amazed me how fast some women could type into those things. I didn't use mine enough to get that fast.

"Well, there we go. Let's see what she says." I caught a whiff of her jasmine and vanilla perfume as she leaned back into the corner of the couch and spread her legs out on the coffee table. "This is nice. I haven't felt this relaxed in ages."

I didn't know if she was referring to our evening or resting her legs, but I kept the question to myself. "It's interesting, isn't it?"

"What's that?" She turned her head to look at me, pressing one cheek into the back cushion.

"This rich bride and her need to recreate her parents' wedding," I said. "What drives us to do things like that? I mean, humans, not us specifically."

"Loss, for one," Jamie said. "She wants to feel close to her mother. Do you ever feel that way about your mom?"

"Sure. I wish she would have lived to at least see me grow up. Not a day goes by I don't wish for that. She was a teacher when my dad met her, so what does that tell you?" I was surprised at how easily the conversation flowed tonight. My guardedness seemed to have retired for the evening.

She made a clucking sound with her tongue. "It tells me a lot. What happened to her?"

"Car accident. I don't know that many details." That was a lie. I knew she had left the house in a rush to escape another beating from my father.

"Again, Darby, I'm so sorry."

"I'm good now. There, now you know everything about me."

"I have a feeling there's a few more layers or secrets inside that head of yours," Jamie said.

I grinned before lifting my glass to my mouth.

"You know what, Darby Devillier? There's something I want to know."

"Shoot," I said.

"Why did we agree to never see each other again? After our night together, that is."

"I'd just gotten dumped. I don't know what your reasons were, but I suspected you were not in the space for a relationship," I said, answering honestly. "I was pretty shattered. For months after that, I was in bad shape and wouldn't have been emotionally ready for anything to start up between us." I held up a hand. "Not that you would have been interested, I just mean it's the only time in my life I ever had a casual night like that with a virtual stranger."

"Yeah, it wasn't my usual thing either," Jamie said. "But there's something about Cliffside Bay, isn't there?"

"True enough. The scent of the sea is my guess."

She continued to look at me from the other end of the couch. "What did you think when you found out I was here in Emerson Pass too?"

"Surprised, to say the least. But then I thought about it and realized it wasn't mere coincidence. Stone Hickman told me about this place. His buddy Rafael and Lisa got married here, remember?"

"I didn't know him then, but yeah."

"He told me Emerson Pass was looking for high school teachers," I said, recalling the conversation we'd had at the local watering hole, the Oar, a few days after my ill-fated proposal. "Stone had fallen in love with the place and said I should check it out. I needed a big change, so off I went."

Her expression went from curiosity to sudden understanding. "Oh my gosh, now that you mention it, Autumn and my brother had been at that wedding and told me it might be a good spot to look for property. I'd told them I wanted to live in the mountains, far away from my father."

"So it wasn't really a coincidence at all," I said. "We just happened to know the same people."

"It's weird we've never really talked before now," Jamie said.

"I've been embarrassed. You saw me on my worst night, and then I let myself get carried away with you. Like I said, I'm not the one-night-stand type of guy."

"I was in a pretty vulnerable place myself," Jamie said. "I act fine and tough, but under all that I'm a hot mess."

"You don't look like a mess to me. Not then or now."

She flushed. "Thanks. That's sweet."

A ping from her phone took our attention away from each other. "That might be her." Jamie picked up her phone and read whatever had come through from her client. She nodded and smiled. "We're good. She didn't have any problems with the fees."

"Wow. Okay. I came in on the high side, too." I felt a little sheepish about it, but if this bride wanted to waste her money that way, who was I to turn it down?

"This is fantastic," Jamie said. "You've no idea how badly I need this money."

"Oh, I do."

We shared another smile and clicked our wine glasses.

"What's the name of this rich bride, anyway?" I asked, having made the proposal to Jamie and not the client.

"Arianna Bush. Doesn't the name sound rich?" Jamie asked, laughing.

It was like a boulder came crashing down over my head. I instantly sobered. It couldn't be. I'd heard her wrong. "What did you say?"

"Arianna Bush? Don't tell me you know her?" Jamie's brow wrinkled.

I knew her all right. Arianna Bush was the woman I was ready to pledge my undying love to. Until she dumped me on the night I was going to propose to her. I covered my eyes with my free hand. "This can't be. Impossible."

"What is it?" Jamie asked, sounding concerned.

I dropped my hand to meet her gaze. "She's my old girl-friend. The one…you know."

Jamie's mouth fell open in a look of surprise that would have been comical had I not been under such duress. "Oh my God, I thought I recognized her." She tapped her fingers to her forehead. "That's it. I couldn't place her. She has long hair now. Wasn't it short then?"

"Yeah, just to her chin," I said.

"It's been bugging me, but now I remember where I'd seen her before."

I nodded, miserable. The entire restaurant had seen my humiliation that night. "Did she say who she's marrying?" I braced myself, knowing the answer.

"She said his first name—Rob—but not his last. She said he's the CEO of some software company."

"I introduced them," I said, woodenly. "He was a friend of

mine. My best friend from high school. She didn't tell me the night she broke it off that it was because of him. She'd been sneaking around with him behind my back. Said they were madly in love and how sorry they were. Via text, I might add."

"What? Oh for God's sake. Does she know you live here?"

"I don't know. I ceased all contact with her after she dumped me that night."

"Wait, you don't stalk her online?" Jamie asked, sounding incredulous.

"I don't do any social media. Mostly because of my students. I don't want them knowing anything about my personal life. That said, even before I took the teaching job, I deleted all her contact information from my email and phone. I didn't want to get drunk one night and decide it was a good idea to text her at three in the morning."

"I can't believe this. I'm so sorry." By this time, she'd taken her feet off the table and had tucked them under her legs. "I can call it off. Tell her it's impossible to get done and that the contractor took a different job."

I was tempted to take her up on her offer, but pride and my commitment to Jamie kept me from doing so. "You already told her we could do it. And I couldn't do that to you." I'd just have to suck it up and pretend I was fine. Maybe I wouldn't run into her.

"But the money isn't worth you feeling awful," Jamie said softly. "We're doing fine without it right now. We'll be fine."

I rounded my shoulders and rubbed my eyes. "Talk about coincidence."

"No kidding," Jamie said.

I set aside my wine and buried my face in both of my hands. An image of that night came to me. Arianna had shaken her head, as if she knew I was about to ask for the staff to bring out the dessert with the ring. Her eyes had been glassy as she looked across the table. "Darby, no," she'd whispered. "It's not right. It's not even us."

"What's not us?" I'd asked, completely befuddled.

"It's not supposed to be you and me."

I was too stunned to think of anything to say and had watched helplessly as she picked up her bag and left the restaurant. I'd gotten the text the next afternoon, explaining that she'd fallen for Rob. "Rob Wright," I muttered under my breath. His name sounded rich too, now that I thought about it. Maybe they did belong together? "Rob freaking Wright. The lying snake. We hadn't spent that much time together since high school, but he came over one night for dinner. I should have known. The way she lit up around him. He'd just made a bunch of money at his start-up. Some high-tech software that I didn't understand. According to him, he'd made his goal of becoming a millionaire before he turned thirty. She loved that kind of thing. I was really stupid."

Jamie moved closer to me and rested her hand lightly on my thigh. "Darby, what can I do?"

I looked up at her. "Nothing. I'm fine. It's somewhat humiliating. She told me that we were too different—came from different worlds. Meaning, she's rich and I'm not. Her family had a ton of money. And now she's marrying into even more."

Disgust flashed in Jamie's eyes. "You should see the size of the ring on her finger."

"Yeah, that sounds like Rob. I'm the one who asked him to come over and meet her, hoping it would help her to make some connections. She was interested in this influencer nonsense, and he knows a lot of up-and-comers, so to speak. Which, in hindsight, might not have been the smartest move. They clicked right before my eyes. After she told me about them, I started thinking about things and putting it all together. He took her away from me, and I didn't even notice he was doing it until it was too late." The first dinner turned into another a few days later, with Rob picking up the tab for an expensive meal by the water. Over oysters on the half shell and a bottle of champagne that cost more than my weekly salary, they'd talked about business strategy and marketing. I'd glazed over, uninterested. I should have felt like a third wheel, but I was too dumb to see it. I explained all of this to Jamie, ending with the kicker of the night. "She picked a fight with me when we got home, saying I was too quiet and why hadn't I participated in the discussion and that I'd embarrassed her."

"What a witch," Jamie said.

I smiled, grateful for her solidarity. "I guess she had a point. In hindsight, anyway. She said she had big plans for her life and that people like Rob could help get her there, but not if I behaved like a child. I didn't know what I'd done to make her feel that way, but needless to say, I felt terrible about myself."

"Whoa, wait a minute." Jamie put her hand up like a traffic cop. "Big plans? What did she mean by that? Wasn't she already rich?"

"She meant getting in with the right people. Her father has money but no connections to the world she wants to be part of. You know, TikTok Hollywood people." I shook my head. "I don't even know what that means, but I know she did."

"Jeez, Darby. I'm sorry." She moved her hand from my thigh to brush her knuckles across my cheek. And just like that, we were in a bubble of intimacy. I could see her and she could see me. "Let's just tell her no, all right? I don't want to put you through this. No one should have to make a dream wedding for their ex-girlfriend."

I sighed, touched by her offer but knowing we had to go through with it. "If I know her, she won't take no for an answer —even if I thought that was the right thing to do—which I don't. We already committed. Anyway, I don't have to see her. She doesn't even need to know the contractor's me."

"Darby, are you sure? Because I've never made any decisions in my life based on money. My need for it or otherwise."

I had to laugh. Her pretty eyes were so sympathetic, moving me in a way I hadn't thought was possible. I'd been soft and sentimental before Arianna dumped me, but since then I'd made a concerted effort to harden myself. However, Jamie was such a forthright woman, so fun to be around, I felt my curated barriers melting away. "It's not the whole wedding, just the gazebo."

"Yes, but I don't know. It seems like a situation ripe for disaster." She pinched her bottom lip with her thumb and finger, obviously thinking through what to do.

I ran a hand through my hair. "She'll see me for what I am and know she made the right decision."

"What are you?"

"A teacher who needs extra money to replace my run-down car and is forced to moonlight as a carpenter. Can you imagine what she'll think? What I'll seem like next to Rob?"

"Well, I don't know this Rob person, but anyone who steals another man's girlfriend can't be all that great. You have your pride and integrity. Don't ever let people like that make you feel differently."

I nodded, amazed by her clarity, but also knowing it didn't make me feel any better. "You're right, but it's not that easy."

"Oh, I know. Trust me, I do."

"If I had a girlfriend or wife or house or something, it would help," I said. "Instead, I'm alone and still driving my 1997 Honda."

"Hondas are good cars," Jamie said in a serious tone. "I mean, 1997. A car that lasts. There's something to be said for that, right?" She jumped to her feet. "I have the perfect song to play for you." She headed toward a cabinet next to the television with her hard-heeled gait. A woman with purpose, I thought. I'd noticed that the very first time we ever spoke. She wasn't a woman who needed a man or authority figure to tell her what she should do or how she should act.

She yanked open the cabinet to reveal a vintage record player and stacks of records. "Have you ever heard that Guy Clark song—"

"'Stuff That Works,'" I cut her off, unable to contain myself. "I love that one. My mom left me all her old vinyl records, and I listened to them to feel close to her, and then I fell in love with the music."

She froze, her expression distraught and empathetic. "That's really sweet. And sad."

"Yeah, I know," I said. "But at least I had those records after she died. I was so lost and lonely."

"A little boy who lost his mother at ten? No wonder," she said.

We locked eyes for a moment before she returned to the records. She flipped through the covers until she found what she was looking for and deftly put the old vinyl record on the turntable. Guy Clark's gruff voice filled the room. The man could stir all kinds of emotions in me. I'd always thought if we met in real life, he'd understand my love of Dickens perfectly. Maybe he'd even see their similarities in storytelling?

"I've never met anyone else who knew this song," I said. "Under thirty anyway."

"I love *Dublin Blues*—the whole album is to die for." She tented her hands as if paying homage.

"That one has 'The Cape,' right? One of my all-time favorites."

"Oh yes. And this one too." Jamie held up another album to show me: *Old No. 1* from 1975. "'L.A. Freeway' reminds me of how happy I was to get out of Southern California. I needed to breathe, you know, and the smog and those brown mountains. Ugh."

"How did you find Guy Clark?" I asked, unsure if I was really understanding this correctly. "It's unusual for someone our age, is what I mean, not that you're incapable of recognizing good music."

Her expression softened and her eyes grew dreamy. "My grandfather. Pop Top."

"Pop Top?" I asked.

She laughed. "Yes, Pop Top, like the lyric in 'Margaritaville.' When I was little I thought Buffet was saying Paw Paw and I couldn't understand why he was singing about my grandfather. Once he explained to me that I'd heard the lyric wrong, he said I should call him that from now on. Which, obviously, I agreed with. Pop Top introduced me to Jimmy Buffet and a lot of other things my mother thought were inappropriate. Not that she didn't adore her father, even though they were so different. She's very buttoned-up and he was more of a flip-flop-wearing margarita lover. Their relationship was never the same after she married my father. She told me just recently that Pop Top had tried to talk her out of marrying him, and thank goodness he hadn't or Trey and I wouldn't be here."

"What didn't your grandfather like about him?" I asked, curious.

"Pop Top thought my dad was a cheater and a liar and treated my mother terribly. He was right."

"That sucks." I was surprised to find that I'd forgotten all about Arianna and her stupid gazebo and Rob. This woman in front of me was a wonder, and I found no room to feel bad in her presence. I wanted to bring the conversation back to something she'd said earlier. "About California and getting out—I felt like that too. Which is one of the reasons I came here. Like I said before, I thought I might never get out of there alive." I laughed to show her I was joking.

"Do you want me to start this from the beginning?" She gestured toward *Dublin Blues*, which had finished with "Stuff That Works" and gone on to a song about Hank Williams.

"Sure." I couldn't help but smile back at her. She was adorable. "I didn't know you liked music so much."

"I do. Almost as much as books, even though I have no talent of my own." Jamie joined me back on the couch. "I bet there's a lot we don't know about each other."

"I think you're right. Why haven't we done this before?"

"Pride. Awkwardness. Embarrassment." She said this with a totally straight face but then laughed, the hearty kind that seemed to come directly from her stomach.

"Well, we shouldn't let that night ruin what could be a great friendship," I said.

"Agreed." She drew her legs up under her and grabbed her glass, took a sip, and then set it back on the table. "You know what I think we should do?"

"What's that?" I was almost afraid of her answer. She was the type who shifted the very plates under which one built a life and home. An earthquake that changed everything forever.

"We should pretend to be dating. You know, in front of Arianna and that cheat Rob. It galls me—what they did right under your nose. I don't want to give her the satisfaction of thinking you've just been pining away for her."

"I haven't." I hadn't, not really. But a blow like that takes a while to get over, even if you know it was right to have parted.

"Of course not. I didn't mean to imply that her callous dumping of you had any effect on you at all," Jamie said, teasing.

"Anyway, go on," I said, drily.

"You want her to think you're living it up out here without a worry, right? And this job you've taken is because I begged my boyfriend to do me the favor. Get where I'm going here?"

"I do. I most definitely do." It would be nice to have Arianna think I was in love. And Jamie Wattson? She was beautiful and sexy and very accomplished. A man like me would be lucky to have her in their life. "You'd do that for me?"

71

"Heck yeah. We're both Guy Clark-loving underdogs. We have to stick together."

"What would we tell our friends?" I thought about my buddies and their new affinity for marriage. Would they get carried away and hope we would get together for real?

"They won't have to know what we were up to," Jamie said. "But if they do discover our little lie, who cares. They'd totally be on our side anyway."

"Good point." I grinned at her, feeling light-headed. It might have been the wine, but more likely it was the woman next to me. "Let's do it. We get what we want from her and I save face."

"Boom." She made a fist in the air. "She'll be there tomorrow afternoon. When you get off work, come on over and we'll act all lovey-dovey in front of her and I'll pretend to be surprised that you two know each other."

"This is a little goofy, but I kind of love it. I kind of love *us* right now," I said.

"Me too. She'll get to see what she's missing." Jamie pointed at me. "I don't care how rich he is, there's no way he's as handsome or as smart as you."

I thought about that for a second, flattered by the compliment. However, Rob was a good-looking man—blond and tanned. Plus, money made people better looking. "He looks like Ken."

"Ken?"

"As in Ken and Barbie."

She made a gagging noise. "Give me a break. You have to get over the feeling of, 'I'm less than this guy.' You know that, right?"

"Easier said than done."

She cocked her head to the right, watching me, clearly trying to figure me out. "If you could see yourself as I do, you'd never feel bad again."

I couldn't speak for the lump in my throat. "That might be the nicest thing anyone's ever said to me."

"If so, you need better friends and family."

I laughed. "Maybe so."

Then her eyes lit up. "I have an idea. Let's take a cute selfie for my social. Maybe I can friend Arianna and she'll see my cute, fake boyfriend and eat her heart out."

"I doubt there'll be any of that but sure, why not?"

Jamie grabbed her phone and sat next to me on the couch. "Try to look like you adore me," she said.

"How do I do that exactly?" It wouldn't take much acting on my part, whatever the pose. I did adore this woman. I had from the beginning, I realized, remembering how we'd connected about books. How sympathetic she'd been about my plight. And I could honestly say, for the few hours she was in my arms, I hadn't thought about Arianna. Strange, now that I thought about it. I would have guessed that I'd have felt odd, touching someone else after all the time with Arianna. However, it had felt natural and good. Oh so good.

She turned to face me, her blue eyes lively. "Let's do one with you kissing my cheek as I snap the selfie. Totally cheesy. Which is perfect."

I leaned closer and pressed my lips to her cheek. She raised the phone above us and snapped a photo. I gasped when she turned her face to mine and kissed me on the lips.

Everything went black for a few seconds as this unexpected peck lingered into a real kiss. Was she still taking photos? I couldn't care less. I kissed her back, sliding the tip of my tongue into her soft, warm mouth before I realized what I'd done and abruptly drew away from her. "I'm sorry," I said. "I didn't mean for that to happen."

She brought the phone to her lap, avoiding my gaze. "It's all right. I started it."

"Well, it's practice, in case we have to kiss in front of Arianna," I said, making light of it.

She lifted her gaze to mine. "If this is acting, then I'm a natural."

"You mean because it felt so…?" I didn't know what word to use for the way she was both familiar and fresh, exciting yet comfortable.

"A little magical," she whispered. "Right?"

I nodded, unsure what to do next. Fortunately, she decided that for me.

"You should go home now before we get carried away," Jamie said. "And have another night we regret."

Regret? I wouldn't have called it that. Complicated maybe. I'd never been sorry for the night we'd spent together. Strangely enough, her assessment crushed me. I deflated like a suddenly popped balloon. I kept my voice even though, thankfully. "Sure, you're probably right. Plus, I have a big day tomorrow." I got up from the couch and brushed the front of my jeans, thankful I'd changed from khakis to the thicker denim material of my jeans, thankful nothing embarrassing was evident.

It wasn't until I was back in my own apartment that I realized she hadn't done anything with the photographs. Would she post one of them? Was Arianna out there, only a click away?

I leaned against the door and touched my lips, still feeling Jamie's on mine. The taste of her was still in my mouth, a mixture of red wine and something sweet, like honeysuckle. She'd been right to send me home. I'd have liked to stay, but I certainly wouldn't want her to feel regretful of my presence in her life as it seemed so many did. Living down the hall from her might be dangerous if I didn't keep myself in check.

8

JAMIE

The next morning, I found myself smiling all through my Pilates class. So much so, the teacher probably thought I'd taken up some kind of happy drug overnight. Instead, it was the evening with Darby that had me grinning like a loon. Since the inn burned down and all the stress and hassle of rebuilding, I hadn't had a night where I didn't think about work. It had barely crossed my mind last night.

When I was a kid, my father often said the most successful people were those obsessed with something. He meant a career and not relationships. If one met him, one knew immediately that his career as a high-powered attorney dressed in thousand-dollar suits was his top priority. It certainly wasn't his children. When Trey and then I had rejected his way of life and his chosen profession, the only parts of him that were connected to his children were suffocated, leaving us with the knowledge that some parents love conditionally.

I hadn't spoken to him since before my brother Trey married Autumn, which was before I'd come here to buy and rebuild the former Annabelle Higgins mansion into an inn. However, my father's lessons endured for both Trey and me. We were both obsessed with our work. Trey had fallen in love with design in college. I'd loved cooking and taking care of guests, if only in my mind, for as long as I could remember. While some little girls played school or family, I played innkeeper. Mom says it was after we visited an inn back east when I was three that I became obsessed with the idea of opening one of my own. In my journals from high school, there are all these notes about what I would do when I owned my own inn, including the details that made it into reality.

I'd studied English in college but minored in hospitality and also took cooking classes and sommelier workshops to learn everything I could about creating elevated experiences for the wealthy. Why? I don't know for sure, other than making something delectable or beautiful gave me great pleasure. Taking my father's philosophy of life, I'd decided early on that I would find a way to own my own luxury inn. I hadn't wanted to run a resort or spa like some of my classmates but rather an old-fashioned quaint inn, located in a rustic, touristy setting. Emerson Pass and the Higgins mansion had been perfect for me. That is, until the fire ripped away my dreams.

For months afterward, I walked around in a haze. All my attention and energy had gone into transforming the faded interiors into a marriage of dark wood and light walls, with antique dressers and beds in every room. I'd scoured antique shops to find just the right pieces and had happily had them placed in what I felt were the right rooms. In a trunk in the attic, I'd found faded, thin paper patterns of some of Annabelle's creations as well as bits of fabric and lace, all of which I'd had framed for artwork in the rooms and hallways.

All was lost in one terrifying night. I was happy for my life and that none of my guests had been harmed, obviously. But it hurt.

Since then, I'd hunkered down and started over. My father

might be a stubborn, selfish man, but he taught me how to work for what I wanted. I supposed I should be grateful to him for that.

When I got back from my exercise class, I showered, still smiling. After I'd blown out my hair, it occurred to me that I hadn't posted the photographs I'd taken. In fact, I'd been so shaken up after that kiss I hadn't trusted myself to even look at them for fear I'd be down the hall knocking on Darby's door before I could come to my senses.

Now I picked up the phone and pulled up the photos. I'd snapped several of him kissing my cheek but only one of our full kiss. I hadn't even realized I'd captured that moment, so overcome with the taste and feel of his expressive mouth. Good Lord, he was hot. The line of his jaw would have looked snobby and aristocratic if it weren't for the adorable cleft in his chin. The two of us pressed together like that was also pretty hot. I liked the way my straight blond hair contrasted with his thick dark waves.

The hour was getting late, and I really needed to get to work. But first, I wanted to post the photo on my Instagram. I'd have to tell the girls what was going on via text or I'd have four calls come through all at once. Actually, I should do that first before they saw it and freaked out. And got their hopes up. These romantics would immediately run away with the idea of Darby and me finally getting together. *You have no time or inclination toward any romantic notions*, I reminded myself, as I gazed once more at our kissing photo. Even I didn't believe myself.

I texted our group chat, which consisted of Tiffany, Stormi, Brandi, Crystal, and me.

Don't get excited over the Instagram post with Darby and me kissing. It's a ruse to make his old girlfriend suffer a little.

As expected, various texts came back. I'd have to answer them later. Or appease them anyway. I wrote back: *I'll explain everything later. Nothing to get hopeful over. Just a friend pact. I'm still the group spinster.*

After shutting that down, I pulled up Facebook and Instagram and sent a friend request to Arianna. She accepted almost immediately. The life of an influencer, I supposed. They lived online. Once I knew she'd be looking at my feed, I posted one of the photographs of him kissing my cheek and what I hoped told Arianna exactly what I wanted her to think.

This guy. My everything. #luckiestgirlever #dreamscometrue #mytruelove #myheart #lovewins

Feeling pleased with myself, I donned one of my favorite dresses—a silky lavender dress that was appropriate for work—and tried not to think about whether Darby would think I looked nice in it. *Keep your head, girl*, I warned myself.

I took special care with my makeup before going to work. It was already ten by the time I arrived. Maisy was at the front desk talking on the phone. Hopefully, booking a guest, I thought, as I flipped on the light switch. I'd no sooner opened my emails when a knock on the door stole my attention. It was Maisy with Arianna right on her heels. That didn't take long. She'd seen the photograph.

"Sorry to interrupt," Maisy said. "But Ms. Bush needs a minute."

I motioned for her to come on in and stood to greet her. "Hi, Arianna. What can I do for you?"

"Well, I came by to give you a heads-up on something." She stood awkwardly in the doorway.

"Come in," I said. "Have a seat. What's up? Is there something in the contract that's bothering you?"

"No, not exactly. It's just that, well, this is such a weird coincidence but your boyfriend—he and I used to date."

"Sure, he mentioned it. Briefly. He said it was not a big deal —just a blip in his life." I don't know why that particular thing came out of my mouth, other than this overwhelming urge to hurt her as she'd hurt Darby.

She paled slightly. "Oh, well, that's strange because we were together for several years."

"Yes, but you cheated on him with his high school friend. Isn't that right? Which would make you an unfortunate time in his life. But he's moved on, obviously. That's what healthy people do when they've been wronged. Put it behind them and move onto something better."

She paled further. "Um, yeah, that's right. I didn't want it to be awkward if I happened to run into Darby here at the inn. I mean, since he's your boyfriend, he might stop by a lot so I thought I should warn you." She was babbling, which made me quite happy.

"You won't believe this," I said. "But he's also the contractor we've hired for the gazebo. I'm sure that won't matter to you, but since we're taking so openly, I figured I should mention it."

"He's Dickens Construction?"

"That's right."

She appeared gob-smacked for a moment, staring down at the floor. I could almost hear the machinations of her mind as she put it together. Finally, she looked up at me, her composure restored. "I should have figured it out. Who else would name their business that?" She narrowed her eyes. "And you didn't know I was his ex? It doesn't bother you?"

"After I asked him if he could do me a favor and use his extraordinary talents to help a client, he said yes, of course— he'll do anything for me." I was really laying it on thick. "He's so sweet and supportive. I'm sure you remember how he treated you. Anyway, when he told me who you were, he thought you might not want to hire him but I felt sure you wouldn't care. It's been several years, after all."

"That's right." She tugged on a dangly topaz earring that matched her eyes. I disliked her quite a bit for those eyes. "It might be better if we found someone else. You know, someone who didn't have a past with me. I mean, he would essentially be helping his ex to make the perfect wedding day."

"There's no one else," I said flatly, enjoying myself a little more than I should.

Her forehead crinkled, and a pinch of irritation pursed her mouth. "That seems unlikely."

"This town lost a lot in the fire, and every good contractor's booked up."

"I thought Darby was a teacher now." She seemed uncertain, perhaps wondering if she had the right to ask questions about him. As people do when they wronged someone and then disappeared from their life, I thought to myself.

"He is. A very popular teacher, actually. He was the graduation speaker last year." Although I hadn't been there to hear his speech, Brandi had said he'd killed it, merging the perfect amount of humor and serious life lessons. "Like I said, he's doing me a favor, and if it's not him, then there's no way I can make your dream day a reality."

She shifted in the chair, crossing one leg, then the other. "What did he tell you about how things ended between us?"

"He told me the whole story. You cheated on him with his best friend from high school and broke his heart." Apparently, I had a mean streak. One that enjoyed torturing women like Arianna. "You really hurt him, but he's good now. Better than good." I fought the urge to lick my lips as if we'd had great sex that morning. Laying it on too thick could backfire.

"That's nice to hear." She tugged on her earring again. A nervous habit, I thought. She shouldn't play poker.

"Anyway, I don't think this is a problem." I spoke with my best hostess assurance. "He's long past all that. We'll get your gazebo built, and you'll have the day you've dreamed of."

"Good. Yes, I feel better now." She tossed her hair behind her shoulders. "I'm glad I came by. I felt, well, unsure what to do when I saw your photograph this morning. I had no idea he was here in town or I wouldn't have been so insistent on getting married in Emerson Pass. He disappeared after we broke up. I couldn't reach him by phone or email. He blocked me, is what I mean to say." She paused, staring past me toward the window. "I didn't mean to hurt him, you know. It just happened—this thing between Rob and me. My feelings for Rob overpowered everything. I knew I had to break up with Darby or hurt him worse by continuing to lie to him. It wasn't until I'd already told Darby I wanted out that I realized he was about to propose. I don't know how I missed it, to be honest. Thinking back, it was obvious that's what he was planning. I felt like the worst person in the world. But sometimes, one has to save oneself before they can be any good to others."

I tried to find a little sympathy for her, but nothing came. Instead, I found some understanding. Arianna Bush was the type of woman who hadn't had to struggle for anything ever. She'd been born rich, beautiful, and intelligent. However, it was not my right to judge her. If she'd fallen for another man, breaking up with Darby had been the right thing to do.

Arianna stood, smoothing her hands over her high-waisted linen pants. She was tall and slender and looked good in those pants, darn her. My curvier petite stature was not flattered by these high-waisted jeans and leotard shirts, thus I never wore them. But she looked amazing in them. "Thanks for letting me come by." She held out her hand. "I hope you'll give Darby my best. And let him know I'd love the chance to see him if he'd be open to it."

"I'll pass that message on to him. He'll be here around four this afternoon with some of the materials. He'll be working after school." I shook my head. "I don't know how he does it. Such loyalty to the kids and then his girlfriend requests a gazebo."

"Ex-girlfriend," Arianna said, obviously mistaking my meaning.

"His current girlfriend, that is." I smiled to take the edge off, sorry to embarrass her. Sort of.

"Of course." She flushed. "What an idiot I am."

"Not at all." I gestured toward to door. "Let me walk you out."

"That's not necessary. I know you're probably busy." She gave me a stiff smile and turned on her four-inch heels toward the door.

When the clicking of her stilettos faded, I got out my phone to text Darby. To my surprise, there was one from him.

I saw the photo of us on Breck's Instagram this morning. He came before work to show it to me and asked me a lot of questions. You've caused quite a stir in the friend group! I had to talk fast to fill them all in on what we're up to. I hope you're having a good day. I'll see you later. Looking forward to it. Very much.

I smiled into the phone, knowing I would have to explain it all in detail to the ladies. For now, I texted back to Darby.

Lots to tell you but SHE WHO SHALL NOT BE NAMED came by just now. In brief, she saw the photo and came down to the office. Almost immediately afterward and the plan is working perfectly. I'll tell all when you get here this afternoon.

I waited for a response, but none came. He was probably in the middle of morning classes. It was only ten, and already I was counting the minutes until I could see him.

DARBY SHOWED up a few minutes before four with a load of wood in the back of his truck. I went out to the parking lot to greet him. The afternoon was one of our perfect autumn days, full of sunshine and a freshness in the air. He wore faded jeans, a T-shirt, and a baseball cap with "Cliffside Bay" etched across the top. Sunglasses covered half of his face and it wasn't until he ripped them from his face and grinned at me that I knew all was fine between us. "There you are. My coconspirator."

I breathed a sigh of relief. I hadn't heard from him after my last text. Had I made a mistake to post the photograph without speaking to him first? But all those fears dissipated when he reached for me and swung me up into his arms, twirling me around in a circle. "I can't tell you how good that felt this morning—seeing the photo and knowing she came running over here," he said when he put me back on my feet.

"I was worried you were mad." My voice sounded more vulnerable than I expected. I didn't like that, but I didn't seem to have much control over myself with good old Dickens-loving Darby.

"Why would I be mad?" His brow furrowed as he gazed at me with curiosity in his eyes. "We agreed to the plan last night."

"Yes, well, I didn't hear from you today so I wasn't sure."

"Ah, I see." He brushed my shoulder with his fingertips. "You're that type."

"What type?"

"Like me. You worry about stuff and overthink everything."

"Yes, that about sums it up," I said, chuckling to hide how he'd touched me. *He gets me*, I thought. *And seems to like me anyway.*

His eyes roamed up and down my body, causing quivers in all the right places. "You're dressed too nice to help me unload this wood, but I'm dying to hear about your conversation with Arianna."

I didn't like hearing her name from his mouth. What was wrong with me? I truly needed to get myself together.

"I've got to go inside and get ready to do the wine-and-cheese thing or I would help." I scanned the piles of wood in the truck. "You don't have a truck." I hadn't thought about it until just now. "Where's your car?"

"Well, that's a sad story that I'll tell you later. Breck lent me his truck for as long as I need it. He's so cool that way."

"He is. Tiffany too. They'd give their friends the shirts off their backs if they thought we needed it."

"Agreed. What time will you be done inside?" Darby asked. "I'm planning on working until dark."

"Now that I have more staff, I usually head home around eight. I have someone scheduled to man the desk for late check-ins and ensuring all the guests are settled for the night." I'd have liked to have someone stay through the night, but I couldn't afford it. Instead, I just made sure guests knew when they checked in that no one would be at the front desk past ten.

"I could make you dinner tonight." Darby's feet made a crunching sound in the loose gravel of the parking lot as he shifted his weight from one foot to the other. "If you don't mind frozen pizza and beer."

My chest expanded and hummed. He wanted to see me tonight. "No, come to my apartment. I'll make us something quick and easy."

"You sure?"

I smiled at him, noticing the way the rays of afternoon sun illuminated his eyes, making them appear more green than hazel. "I'm sure. I'll see you around nine?"

"I'll be there." He turned toward the truck. "For now, I need to hustle. Where's the best place to put all this?"

I asked him if he could store it outside the little fence that surrounded my grassy lawn where the natural grasses and flowers had grown over the summer. I'd enjoyed seeing the greenery return, but a gazebo and some additional grass around it would give everything a more finished look. All in all, it would be a good addition. Hopefully my current guests would look past the construction and focus on the river that glistened in the late-afternoon sun.

He agreed and then waved me away. "Go on. Go pour your wine."

I said goodbye and made my way through the loose gravel to the front porch of my inn, hoping my butt didn't look too big. In case he was watching, that is. When I turned back to see for myself, he was reaching for a stack of two-by-fours. Well, that's that, I thought. *Don't get too excited about this guy. He's only interested in being my friend. I must remember that and rein in my romantic notions.*

Good luck with that, a voice whispered to me.

9

DARBY

I started unloading the lumber and stacking it neatly where Jamie had asked before getting out the drawings I'd done at lunch. Tomorrow, I'd bring out some cement to anchor the platform. Tonight, I would dig the holes in preparation.

Jamie had asked that the gazebo be made just outside the white fence. Once I had it built, then I would put in a gate. This way I didn't have to mess up any of the pretty landscaping. The ground was flat and smooth. Fire had destroyed all the natural plants, but small shoots and grasses had come back up, not defeated for long. Just down the path, guests would arrive at the river. From here, I imagined I could hear the flow of water over rocks, but it was only in my mind.

I shook my head, astounded the fire had jumped the river to take down the inn. We'd all hoped Jamie's newly opened business would be safe. We were wrong. The girl had gumption, I thought for the hundredth time as I hauled another load to its temporary position.

After measuring carefully, I dug a good foot down into the dirt for the four main posts. Knowing the snow and harsh weather we often had in this part of Colorado, I wanted to make sure the posts were secure. I'd just begun digging the fourth hole when my shovel hit something hard. Probably a large rock, I thought, as I set aside my digging tool and got down on my knees to inspect further. The sun had gone down by that time, leaving me in a dim light. I dug both hands into the soil, seeking whatever had stopped my shovel. Soon, I found it with the tips of my fingers. It was something hard, but not a rock. I dug until I saw metal. A box of some kind? Maybe someone had planted one of those time capsule boxes.

My heartbeat sped up as I realized that it was indeed a box. Made of a silver metal, most likely stainless steel, and the size of a boot box. A lock held it closed. One that required a key, I noticed, rubbing away the dirt to see better. How long had this been there? They wouldn't have found it when they put in the new landscaping because Jamie had left this part wild, clearing it of debris and smoothing the soil but without the manicured feeling inside the fence.

I brushed as much dirt off the box as I could and set it aside. Regardless of what was inside, I needed to finish before it grew too dark to work. My muscles ached already, but I must keep on. Jamie was depending on me, and we both needed the money. I would not think too much about the reasons for the gazebo. Arianna was the past. Was Jamie the future? I put that question aside and got back to work.

However, this stirring in my belly whenever I was near Jamie had me discombobulated. All day at school, I'd thought of her and the kiss we'd shared. Would there be another tonight? Or had that just been part of our ruse and meant nothing to her?

Dig, you fool. Just dig.

Between school and working on the gazebo, I'd managed to keep my mind off my father. Grateful for that and the dinner with Jamie to look forward to, I put any thoughts of him out of my mind. I'd been doing this for years and years. His absence from my life was normal. Seeing him on television had not been.

I managed to clean off the stainless steel box at home in my kitchen sink before presenting it to Jamie. After a good washing, I made out the engraved initials: *ACH*. Annabelle Higgins, I assumed, although not sure what the *C* stood for. "It has to be hers, right?" I asked Jamie.

We were sitting on the floor of her living room staring at the box. "Has to be. But how do we get this lock off?"

I rose to my feet. "Not a problem. I brought a hammer." The latch, although metal, was thin and rusted. I'd have no problem breaking it using the claws of the hammer and pulling hard. "I didn't want to do it without your permission."

"That was very thoughtful of you," Jamie said, a little huskily. "I do feel a kinship with her. Sometimes I swear I can feel her presence at the inn. Especially in the area of the house that used to be her studio."

Using the hammer, I easily broke the latch. "Do you want to do the honors?" I asked Jamie.

She was looking at it with the eyes of a child standing at the candy counter. "I can't wait. But will you do it? I'm afraid of spiders."

I laughed. "No spider got through here, I don't think." The box was a small fortress and heavy. They didn't make things like this nowadays. Good Lord, I sounded like my grandfather. An image of him flashed before my eyes. He always wore overalls and smelled of pipe smoke and sometimes of gin. His silver hair had thinned by the time I knew him, and he often wore a cap. He'd been good with his hands too, building and repairing his house up in Oregon. I'd only been able to visit him once a year.

My dad wasn't interested in maintaining a relationship with his father-in-law after my mother died. I couldn't blame him for that.

I had plenty of other things to blame him for. Regardless, those summer weeks in Oregon were the best of my childhood. My grandfather wasn't much of a talker, but he loved reading as much as I did. During the day, I followed him around the property helping him as best I could. In the evenings, he would make us what he called a bachelor's feast, usually eggs or peanut butter sandwiches. On Sundays, after church, we had cheese melted between two corn tortillas with mounds of his homemade salsa. He'd been a widower since before we lost my mother and seemed to have no interest in remarrying. The only thing he ever said to me about their deaths was one of the saddest things I'd ever heard. "I am only glad your grandmother died before her daughter. It would have killed her."

Now, I had to tug to get the lid open but finally, it came up, and I pushed it as far back as it would go, then set it all in front of Jamie. She was still on the floor and peered into the box as she clasped her hands together under her chin. Quite adorable, I had to admit.

I sat next to her. "Do you want me to look in case there are any bugs?"

"I thought you said it was too tight?"

"I'm just teasing you." Whatever was in there had been covered with a piece of finely knit lace in a flower pattern. The material had yellowed with age but was remarkably intact. I lifted it. Inside was what looked like a leather-bound book of some kind. I pulled it out and handed it to Jamie. "A journal?" I asked.

She opened the first page. "Yes, it says 'The property of Annabelle Cooper Higgins. All intruders beware.'"

"I hope she didn't put a curse on it," I said.

"It's dated, too: 1928." Her eyes sparkled. "This is amazing.

It's the diary of Annabelle Higgins. But why was it in the box buried in the yard?" She pulled out a long, narrow box like one a necklace would come in. At least in modern times. I had no idea what kind of jewelry men used to give to their women back then. She popped it open, but it was empty. Only a yellowed cushion where a necklace would have been displayed remained. "This must have been a special piece of jewelry. I wonder where it went and why this box is in there without it?"

"All good questions, detective," I said.

Next, she drew out several letters and a faded, sepia-toned photograph of a woman sitting in a wide chair dressed in a simple dress and a straw hat over what seemed to be masses of hair.

"This is Annabelle," Jamie said. "I recognize it from the other photos I had before the fire. I had them displayed all around the inn. All that was lost, obviously."

I inspected the photo carefully, curious about this woman from the past. Since the photo was in black and white, I couldn't make out too many details, but it was obvious she had been a beautiful woman. She had a round, merry face, a small waist, and curvy hips. I remembered seeing a photograph of Clive Higgins that Jamie had had hanging on the wall of the inn before the fire. He had been broad-shouldered with a face as square as his wife's was round and wide-set eyes that seemed to stare at the camera as if he expected something bad to leap out of the contraption and kill them both. "I'm remembering you had Clive's photo up on the wall."

"That's right. Their wedding photograph as well." Jamie tapped the end of her nose with her index finger. I'd noticed she did this when she was thinking. "I always thought they seemed like an odd couple."

"How so?" I asked.

She shrugged. "I'm not sure how to explain it. She seemed worldly and sophisticated and he was kind of big and rugged.

Obviously, they were in love and were married for a long time, so what do I know?"

"Why do men in old photos always look wary?"

"I don't know, but I totally agree." Jamie peered more closely at the photo. "She was a redhead, but you can't see that in this picture." She looked up at me and said, as if I'd asked her how she knew all that, "I read anything I could find on her when I bought the inn. Clive was already here when she arrived to live with Quinn Cooper Barnes. Alexander Barnes had sent for her and Quinn's mother. They'd been in Boston, practically starving."

I nodded. This was all Emerson Pass folklore around the high school, which was named after Quinn Cooper Barnes. The history of our little town was simple but sweet. Lord Alexander Barnes had come from England and transformed a town ruined in a fire into a thriving ski community. He'd had five children before his first wife passed away and was raising them on his own until he met Quinn. She'd been hired to be the town's first schoolteacher. They'd fallen in love and married, adding two more daughters to Lord Barnes's five. "Trapper's dad has a lot of information on the history as well. He let me look at some of the old letters and journals one time."

"Lucky."

She sounded so genuinely envious that I laughed. "I'm sure he'd let you take a look if you asked," I said. "He's proud of his Barnes family heritage."

"I would be too." She sighed and touched the silver heart that hung around her neck. "It's all like over-the-top romantic. Don't you think?"

"Indeed." I couldn't help but grin back at her animated expression.

She drew from the box a dull silver pocket watch and handed it to me.

The hands had stopped forever at four minutes to five. What

day, I wondered? "This is beautiful. If we polished it up, it would look like new."

"Does it work, do you think?"

"We could wind it and find out," I said.

"Not yet. We don't want to mess up the last recorded time."

"Agreed." I turned it over in my hand to see a small etching on the back. *To my love. Forever yours. A.* "She must have given this to Clive for a present."

"It's weird she put it in the box," Jamie said.

"Or any of this stuff."

"Maybe after Clive died she put it all in here? She wanted to keep it safe?"

"Could be," I said, thinking out loud. "It could be a way she dealt with her grief. Who knows? Maybe she only meant to put it out there temporarily and then died before she could bring it all back in the house?"

"If that's the case, then she was way more eccentric than what I've ever read about her. She was, by most accounts, passionate about her work and family, including all the nieces and nephews the Barnes family gave her."

"But where's the jewelry that was in here?" Jamie held up the skinny box and shook it. "Why is the watch here but not whatever this was?"

I looked at the small stack of letters, tied together with a red ribbon. They were addressed to Annabelle Higgins. The return address had no name but was listed as Canal City, Florida. "I think that's about an hour south of Tampa," I said. "Who did she know there?"

"Maybe a bride?" Jamie asked as she opened the journal. A separate piece of paper slid to the floor. She picked it up and said, "Oh, this is interesting. It's like an intro to whatever's in the journal."

"Read it immediately," I said.

"I'm with you." She began to read.

This is Annabelle Cooper Higgins. Wedding dressmaker. The year is 1924 as I write this. I have a secret. One I cannot hold inside me another moment. I cannot tell anyone what I've done. Not my husband, obviously. Not even my beloved sister, Quinn. We have never kept anything from the other but my shame keeps me from telling her the details of my heart. If I don't write it all down and confess, I shall perish. So I'll put it all here in the contents of these pages and then I'll lock it all away. All of it. The jewelry and letters. The watch Bromley returned to me. The one gift I gave him he could not bear to keep. Not after we'd agreed to walk away. Within the pages of this journal are the details of my indiscretion. I've included all the letters we exchanged as well. Per my request, Bromley sent them all back to me. He understood my need for control. My desire to pretend it never happened.

This is the burial spot for our love and my betrayal. By burying it all here under my favorite spot in the garden, I hope to finally put this love affair to rest and go on with my life. Such as it is.

I have come so often to sit on this bench in the shade. Thoughts of him always accompanied me. But they can no longer do so. I must let go or hurt the man who has stood by me through everything, who has loved me beyond measure. I must be present in the here and now with my Clive. My first love. My husband.

I keep my hands busier than ever, hoping hard work will erase the memories of Bromley and the love we walked away from. "We must do the right thing," I'd whispered to him. "I must go home."

"Yes, you must," Bromley had replied. "But it will feel like death to me."

I've tried to push away thoughts of him. But it is no use. He is always with me. I cannot let him go. Not all the way. But in truth, all I have left of him is the regret and angst about the impossible choice I had to make.

If only my creations could make me forget. Although there had never been secrets between us, I've been of two minds. Should I tell Clive what's distracted me for these past months? Or, would it only hurt him to know the truth? Perhaps, it's bad enough that I know it already. Whatever I decide, I cannot run from my grief or longing. It is ever present. Perhaps this is my punishment for betraying my husband?

Yes, I've deceived my beloved husband. Not in body, mind you. No, I couldn't allow that to happen. Only once did I come close to allowing him to kiss me. That is the night I decided I must walk away and come home. In my mind, though, my heart, it all belonged to Bromley. It was not my intent.

I'd like to think it was only vanity that drew me to him. No man had fallen at my feet in such a way. I was thirty-four years old, after all. Beyond my best blooming years of youth to be sure. Yet he fell for me. Nor was it the lifestyle he represented. I never became caught up in his life of glamour and wealth. It might have been intoxicating to other women. Especially for one who grew up hungry as I had.

No, it was all him. Bromley Hunting.

It began with an invitation to make the dress and gowns for the wedding of Cordelia Hunting. They asked that I come to Florida to design a custom gown.

Who would have ever thought such a request would come? Not me. The Hunting family was as rich as the Rockefellers and Vanderbilts.

All my life, I've tried to emulate my sister Quinn. I truly have. She is loyal and nurturing. A mother figure to all who meet her. I've failed miserably at being anyone but me. A dreamer and a romantic with the ambition of Lady Macbeth. How can all three of those qualities reside in the same woman and not do herself harm? I don't know the answer, other than I am broken. I'm destroyed by the intensity of my feelings. I cannot simply carry on as if I am not changed by love. It would be impossible.

The ruin of two hearts, Bromley's and mine. Now I must protect Clive. He must remain unhurt and innocent. He's done nothing wrong except choose the wrong woman to be his bride. I am the one who must pay the penance, not him.

My story remains inside this journal. No one but God and myself knows the truth of my feelings. How ripped to bits I am. I must bury all my feelings and move on with my life. That is all I can do.

"Wow," Jamie said, looking up at me with wide eyes. "Can you believe it?"

"Barely," I said.

"Me either, but you can bet I'm going to find out more if I can."

I had no doubt about that.

1 0

JAMIE

As obsessed as I was over the mysterious box and its contents, I was perhaps more so with Darby. I'd have spent the rest of the evening reading the journal and letters, but I didn't want to waste time doing so when I had Darby alone. Plus, I had to feed the poor guy. It was almost nine by the time I got up from the mystery box and my dinner date to put the steaks on to broil. I'd stopped after work to pick up groceries, including two large potatoes to bake, which were already done and smelled terrific. The steak was a tough flank cut, but I'd beat the crap out of it before putting some meat tenderizer on it.

Darby opened the bottle of wine he'd brought with him. While the steaks broiled, I quickly put together a salad. As I worked, we continued with theories about our friend Annabelle.

"What I know," I said, "is that Annabelle left Emerson Pass for good in 1937. Clive died in 1936, unexpectedly." I'd read that during my research of the house. "The year after his death, she sold the house and moved somewhere else. The people who built the gazebo lived there for decades after that. I think anyway. They only lived there part of the year and according to their kids had refused to sell it. When they died, the kids left it abandoned for long enough that it needed almost a complete overhaul. But the old place had good bones, as they say." I paused to take a sip of wine. Berries and tobacco.

"Is the wine okay?"

"Yes, it's good," I said.

Darby winced as he sat in one of my kitchen chairs. "Sorry, a little sore from today."

"I hope you're not going to permanently hurt yourself," I said.

"Nah. I'm tough. If you'd seen how I was raised you wouldn't be worried."

That made me curious, but I decided to let it go for now. I found myself wanting nothing more than to hear everything about him.

"I wonder where she went?" I asked Darby. "Do you think she went to Bromley after Clive died?"

"It's certainly possible. I don't know if we'll ever understand the whole story."

"There was an old chest in the attic, left over from Annabelle's time there. Or, I assumed so, because it had her name carved into the side. You know, one of those old steamer trunks."

"Where is it now?"

I laughed at the glitter in his eyes. He was as into this as I was. "At the time I didn't think it was my place to go through it. Once I realized they were things left behind by Annabelle, I took them out to Mr. Barnes—Trapper's dad. I figured they belonged in their family. He was kind enough to bring me a few photographs that he thought I might like for the walls. I wish he hadn't now, because they're gone."

"Do you think he'd let you look at what was in the trunk? If you gave him what we found?"

"I'm sure he would. He loves to talk about the history of this town." I leaned down to pull the steak from the oven and waved away the smoke. "Don't worry. They're not burned."

"I wasn't worried." He gazed at me for a moment, head cocked to the side. "I know I'm in good hands with you."

We sat down to eat, enjoying the food without talking much. He scarfed his down, which meant I'd practically starved him with all the excitement over Annabelle's things. When I was done, I pushed away my plate and told him to eat the rest of the steak.

"You sure?"

"Go for it." I poured more wine into my glass and leaned back in the chair, crossing my jean-clad leg over the other. It felt good to be out of my work clothes, especially the shoes. "I wonder what ever happened to this Bromley guy?"

"Maybe the journal will tell us. I'm going to be itching to hear about what you find out." Darby cut into another piece of meat and brought it to his mouth and chewed. I liked the way the muscle in his cheek moved.

"I'll go out and see Trapper's dad tomorrow if I have a break at work. Maybe he'll know more."

"Be sure to take notes." He grinned and pointed his steak knife at me. "And now, you promised all the gory details about your talk with Arianna. I want everything."

I laughed. "I completely forgot about her. Let's see. Well, I wasn't very nice. I was evil, actually." I recounted as best I could the conversation. "I laid it on a little thick but held myself back from going on too much about how great you are."

"I'm surprised you could think of much." His eyes held both vulnerability and a marked lack of self-esteem. I could relate.

"Why would you say that?" I asked, curious what he would say even though I suspected I knew the stories he told himself all too well.

He lifted one shoulder. "You don't know me that well."

I caught his eye for a moment. "I'd like to. What do you think? About that idea," I finished lamely. This putting oneself out there wasn't for the faint of heart. As much as I'd told myself I wasn't interested in opening myself up this way, here I was, compelled toward him like metal to a magnet.

His forehead wrinkled and in the hesitation that followed, I feared the worst. He was not interested in anything other than friendship. There was someone else. Another teacher maybe? He spent a lot of his life at school. Or maybe he still had feelings for Arianna. Ones that would keep him from exploring a new relationship for fear it would hurt whoever was on the hopeful end of the rope.

Finally, he spoke, taking away my fears but giving me something mysterious nonetheless. "I'd like to get to know you better too. Tonight and last night, I've really enjoyed myself." A pink flush smeared his cheeks and jawline like strokes of liquid blush.

"I have too." I braced myself for whatever was next, already sweaty and embarrassed and wishing I'd kept my big mouth shut. In my life, the "but" had often come from the man I was trying to connect with, starting with my father and continuing on with the men I'd dated.

"I'm not sure if you knew me better that you'd feel that way," Darby said.

"Try me?" Darn, I was being brave tonight. Maybe it was the wine or being so tired or the romance of the silly metal box.

"It's just that, well, I'm broke, and I have no intention of being anything else but a teacher. I love it. I can't compete with guys in suits, you know."

"Yeah? So what? I already know that anyway."

He watched me, eyes glittering in the dim light. "Growing up, my dad was…harsh."

"How harsh?" I held my breath, knowing that whatever he said next would change how I perceived him. He would no longer be just a hot, sweet guy I liked, but someone complicated with layers. Complexities that could lead to dysfunction and betrayal. Like my parents.

An image of my mother after my father left played before my eyes. She hadn't come out of her bedroom for two days. Desperate and worried, I'd gone into the room to check on her. She'd been curled in the fetal position. The shades were drawn, and the room was overly warm and stuffy. When I'd yanked open the shades, she hadn't opened her eyes. For a split second I'd been worried she was dead, but a slight moan informed me differently. I'd sat next to her, stroking her dirty hair, coaxing her eyes open. When she did open them to look up at me, the utter defeat and despair filled me with a darkness I'd never felt before. One I'd not fully shaken since then.

She was doing much better now. Life had returned to her eyes and her spirit. However, a shadow remained. One that made her cautious and guarded. I doubted she would have the courage to try love again. As for me? The same shadow lurked over me as well. I must remember what he did, I thought now, in the presence of this beautiful man before me. Men leave once the bloom of youth is gone. They find a younger version of their wives in an attempt to recapture their own youth perhaps? Or was it purely man's instinct to seek the young, with their firm thighs and taut skin? Was it purely physical? I didn't know and probably never would. My own father would certainly give little insight. Especially since I hadn't spoken to him in years. I hadn't even recognized myself in the blowout we'd had. The venom that spewed from my mouth was not only for what he'd done to our family with his desertion but the ways in which he'd undermined us all when he presented the model husband and father to the outside world. Total hypocrite.

I returned my attention to Darby and immediately melted. He had such a strong yet vulnerable presence—an openness to him that drew me to him and weakened my defenses.

"Beatings for the smallest things, like placing the knife in the wrong direction at dinner. He was very controlling. Very precise. And violent." Darby's shoulders lifted and then drooped. "He was also a cop. A corrupt cop, as it turns out."

"No, really?"

"Yes. He's the one in the news recently. I'm sure you've seen the story. Benji Hanes." He said this casually, as if it weren't a big deal.

This confession was a punch in the stomach and drained me of breath. "Oh, Darby. I'm sorry." How had I not known this? Did anyone in our circle know?

As if I'd asked the question out loud, he said, "I hadn't told anyone who I am until recently."

"Who have you told?" I was surprised to find that I wished I was the only one he'd confessed to. Selfish, I know, but I'd felt such intimacy with him. As if I were special to him. The only one he trusted. I tossed those selfish thoughts aside and returned my attention to him.

"I told the guys. Just recently. It felt like my secret was keeping me from true friendships. Do you understand what I mean?"

"A thousand percent." How could we expect to truly connect with others if we didn't share where we came from and how it had shaped us? Yet, there seemed to be an instinct in most of us to show people only what they wanted to see or that we thought they could handle. When, in fact, the only way to achieve closeness with others was to show them who we really were, flaws and past hurts and demons. Authenticity, perhaps, was the secret to intimacy. Why then, did we run from it? Fear, I thought. Of not being enough or weak or simply too damaged to be lovable.

"I haven't spoken to my dad since I left for college," Darby said. "When I turned eighteen, I officially took my mother's maiden name." He looked away from me, his eyes glassy. He was remembering the past, I thought. All the hurts and scars from those days were suddenly apparent to me as if they were physically visible.

Without thinking, I reached across the table and took one of his hands. "It must have been so hard to keep all this in, to not let anyone know."

"It wasn't hard until his picture was splashed all over the news for the last year. I've tried to ignore it all and live my own life, but it's not as easy as it sounds."

"I understand. My dad's not in the public eye, and I still find it hard to let go of him and just be. There's this anger and bitterness that just sticks to me, no matter how hard I try to focus on the positive."

"We've built lives, you know," Darby said softly. "Made our own way without them."

"Yeah, but they're still in here." I tapped the side of my head. "I can't tell you how often I hear his voice criticizing my choices. He never hit us, but he could pack a mean punch with a few choice sentences. He's a lawyer." As if that explained everything. There were plenty of good lawyers out there. Not all of them used words as weapons. "He has a way of making me feel small the moment he opens his mouth."

"Yeah." Darby nodded, his mouth downturned into a frown. This was not a natural state for him. He should be smiling, showing off those half-dimples. I'd like to make him smile, I realized. Tonight and all the ones after this. *No, no. Don't get caught up thinking you could save him or that he would even want you to*, I silently told myself.

"I'm glad you told me," I said, taking my hand back to my lap. "Is there anything I can do to help?"

"No, there's nothing to do. It's all on me. I have to figure out a way to live with who I am and where I came from."

"His behavior is not who you are. You're nothing like him."

"Most days I feel that way." He placed his knife and fork onto his empty plate, making them into an X shape. "But sometimes I wonder if he's in here and just not come out yet."

"That seems unlikely. You would know by now. Maybe you would have chosen to be a cop instead of a teacher, for example."

His mouth twitched into a smile, but his eyes remained cloudy and troubled. "He ridiculed me when I told him I was going to be an English major and teach school. You can't imagine the things he said."

"I can, actually. My dad said the same kinds of things to Trey and me when we told him what we wanted to do. Dad seemed to assume that Trey, at least, would become an attorney and a partner at the firm, working twenty-hour days like he had when we were young. I don't think he ever thought highly enough of me that I'd be anything other than a wife and mother. He said that once about my cooking. What a good wife I would make to a high-powered man, creating a home and lifestyle that would be the envy of all his friends. That was how he saw me. An accessory to a man. One whose only goal was to make her husband look good. Not that there's anything wrong with that. If that's what a woman wants, then she should go for it, but I have to have my own way of making money, my own business that's separate from a man."

"So that what happened to your mom doesn't happen to you?" Darby asked softly.

"Yeah, I can't ever let that happen. I can't ever give the power over my life to someone else." I pushed back my hair. "But we're not talking about me. We're talking about you."

"There's nothing else to say. You know the truth now." He rose to his feet and cleared both our plates, putting them in the sink.

"Did you think knowing who your dad is would make me dislike you?" I asked.

He slowly turned from the sink to face me. "Not dislike

exactly. I was afraid you might see me in a new way. The son of a person like that—maybe you wouldn't want that in your life."

"From what I can see, you're nothing like him. Anyway, you're you, not him. Who raised you makes no difference to me. It's what you did after you got away from him that matters."

He was quiet for a moment before striding across the kitchen toward me. I froze, unsure what was about to happen. His eyes seemed to seek answers in my face. It was too intense. I had to look away.

He leaned his backside against the corner of the table, standing close to my chair. "You're killing me here, Jamie Wattson."

"I am?" What did that mean?

"Yes. You are. You're so much more than I thought. So much more."

"What did you think before?" I knew it was dangerous to ask, but I couldn't stop myself.

"I thought you were a California girl. Blond, tan, and careless."

"Careless? Why are California girls careless? I don't get that." I narrowed my eyes, pretending to be mad but failing and laughing instead.

"I just meant that the girls I knew in California never seemed serious about anything but their designer purses. They had the potential to hurt me with their haphazardness and the way they shone with glitter and smelled of coconut."

I sputtered with laughter. "You do have a way of putting things. Glitter and coconut?"

"You know what I mean. That stuff women put on their skin that makes it all shimmery?"

"I *do* know. And I'm not careless. Not at all. Sometimes I wish I was—about something, anyway. Just one thing so I'm not weighed down all the time with self-doubt and this restless feeling, like I'm waiting for my life to start. Everything has always seemed dead serious to me. I've been this way from the time I was a kid. Driven and ambitious and perfectly sure of my path. Until lately. The fire put me back a bit, I have to admit."

"Of course it did. It was a terrible loss after all your hard work. To see your dream quite literally go up in flames." He said it so simply but with such earnestness that darned if it didn't make me feel seen and validated.

"Like you said, I'm still here," I said. "It didn't beat me. You're here too, Darby. No matter what your dad did. Living your life on your own terms, giving the gift of yourself to those kids every day. You have nothing to be ashamed of."

"My father called me overly sensitive," Darby said. "Always thinking too much, he'd say. As if thinking were a bad thing. It took me a long time to realize he was wrong about that. Wrong about me."

He wore an expression I couldn't quite place. Uncertainty? Anticipation?

"Would you like to dance with me?"

I blinked, sure I'd heard him wrong. "Um, dance?"

"Yes, dance." Darby smiled and nodded toward his hand. "I'm a very good dancer."

"You are?"

He laughed. "Why the face?"

"I've never known a guy who likes to dance, let alone someone who's good at it."

"I'm old-school. I should carry a handkerchief," Darby said. "And wear a three-piece suit."

"You'd look good in a suit."

"You think?" He put his hands around his neck, pantomiming a high collar. "One of those shirts that comes up to my jawline? What do you think? Could I pull it off?" He lifted his chin and sniffed, as if he were high society.

"I need to get you some contemporary fiction," I said, teasing him. "And give you a new perspective. Modern men don't act like you."

"Maybe I was born in the wrong time." The corners of his eyes crinkled. He held out his hand again. "Will you do me the honor, Miss Wattson?"

"If you insist, Mr. Devillier." I rose to my feet.

"Have I ever told you how pretty you are?"

"I think so." I flushed, embarrassed and pleased at the same time. "But I thought it might be the bump on the head talking."

"No way. That's all me." He led me into the living room. "Put on one of those records and let's dance."

"What kind of dancing are we doing?"

"The slow kind." He grinned and gestured toward the stereo. "I know you'll pick just the right song."

"Now you've put me on the spot. I'm stumped, but I'll do my best." I went to my stereo cabinet and flipped through my records, choosing James Taylor's greatest hits, and put the needle on the first track.

"Classic choice," Darby said, holding out his arms. "Come here."

A shiver of desire went through me. I almost tripped over my own feet as I went to him. He folded me into him, with his arms around my waist. I came to his chest. "You're tall."

"Did you not notice before?"

"I never thought about it much." Avoiding his eyes, I focused on the artery in his neck, which pulsed with the beat of his heart and seemingly in time to the music.

"Is this a date?" Darby asked, his mouth against my hair.

"I've no idea," I said, and moved closer to him, nestling my face into his neck, which smelled spicy and of fresh soap. He was substantial, muscular, and graceful. "You were right. You are a good dancer."

"I have other talents too."

I giggled. "I remember."

"Jamie?"

"Yes?" I drew back slightly to look up at him.

"Would it be all right, even though this may or may not be a date, for me to kiss you?"

"Yes, it would be fine." I smiled up at him. My pulse raced, and my body ached for him.

He leaned down and captured my mouth in his, kissing me until I was breathless.

"I want you," I whispered in his ear. "Stay with me?"

DARBY

"I cannot stay. I shouldn't stay," I said to her.

"But why?" Jamie's cheeks and neck were flushed, and her hair fell around her shoulders. I knew exactly what she would look like without her clothes.

God, I wanted her so badly.

"Because we have to do this the right way," I said. "Get to know each other in a different way than just sex."

She stopped swaying to the music and looked up at me with big blue eyes. Eyes that melted my resolve. "Is that what you want? To get to know me better?"

"Yes, without sex getting in the way. I'm an old-fashioned guy, remember."

"Your kiss made me forget that for a moment," she said in a wry tone.

I smiled and traced her swollen lips with the pad of my thumb. "I want to stay. Trust me. I'd love nothing more than to take you into that bedroom and do everything I'm imagining. However, I respect you too much for that. We agreed to erase that night from our current situation, right?"

"Did we?" Her forehead creased.

"Yes, we did. Which means we need to date properly before we get back into bed together." My self-control was precarious at best. If she only knew how badly I wanted her. Because as much as we claimed to have put that night away, I remembered it. I remembered her. Every inch of her.

"Leave it to me to find the last old-fashioned guy on the planet." Her breathing had returned to normal. I didn't know if I was glad or not.

"Would you like some more wine?" I asked.

"That's not what I want, but sure."

"We can read more of the journal," I suggested, knowing she would like the distraction.

She brightened. "You get the wine and meet me back here."

WE WERE LIKE AMATEUR SLEUTHS, the two of us. I hadn't been as excited to read something in a while, and that was saying something. I opened the journal to the page after the one we'd already read.

"You read this time," Jamie said. "I'll listen."

"Yes, sure." As a teacher, I was used to reading out loud. Yet now, in the cozy living room of the girl I was starting to fall for, my tongue seemed to have tripled in size. Regardless, I began.

September 20, 1924

The Hunting family sent for me only two weeks ago, asking that I come to Florida to make the wedding dress for their eldest daughter, as well as dresses for the bridesmaids and Mrs. Hunting, mother of the bride. I didn't want to go so far away. Florida! The swamp. No, my husband said, you must go. It will be a chance to see the ocean. I begged him to go with me, but he said he couldn't leave his brother to do all of the work at the shop. Since my business does not fully pay our bills or for the fine house we had built, I understood his logic. But I also knew that he was a simple man. One who did not want to leave the comfort of his own home and community. He had not left since his arrival as a young man and probably won't again. As much as I adore him, this frustrates me a little. We're not exactly newlyweds. I could bear to be apart from him for a month or two. Or could I?

I thought my sister Quinn would try to talk me out of it, but she, too, thought it was a grand idea. An opportunity to meet the kind of people willing to pay for my craftsmanship (or woman-ship in this case) would open up another world to me. Knowing they were both right, I plucked up my courage and am now sitting on a train on my way to Florida. The woman next to me is snoring rather loudly. Not that I could sleep anyway. I'm already homesick, and I miss my husband.

"It's not the life I thought I would have," I'd told Quinn. "I thought it would be a traditional life with a husband and children."

"Alas, the Lord has provided a different kind of life altogether," Quinn said. "There's no use to fight against it. You must go where the fates take you. Look at me."

She often mentioned how her life had changed and fallen into the right place when she came to Colorado. My sister took on the raising of five of her widowed husband's children and then had two more of her own. A happy seven. Whereas I have none. We tried, of course. The pain of it takes my breath away. I've thrown myself into my work, growing my business year after year until now I've been summoned to Florida by the Huntings. What awaits me? I cannot know. I must only fulfill the promise I made to Clive and Quinn—to be brave and do my very best.

I looked up at Jamie. She was on the couch curled up in one corner. "This is a great mystery. Do we have time to read one more?"

I nodded. "But after that, I should head home. School starts early."

"Okay, just one more."

She was so cute, like a kid begging for another chapter

before going to sleep, that I wanted to kiss her again. I held back, however, practicing that annoying self-control once more.

I've arrived in Florida and have been shown to my room in this giant house. Only the head of housekeeping was here to greet me. The family was out at a neighbor's beach but would be back in time for evening cocktails. I was instructed to dress for dinner and that we would enjoy our meal on the terrace that overlooks the sea. This house! I've no idea how many square feet, but it seems as large as a resort.

The Hunting estate is built on the beach. It's ungodly hot, and I've opened the windows to allow the ocean breeze into the room. My view looks out to the blue water and the white sand. From here, I spotted large-beaked pelicans and a few other birds I didn't recognize.

I'd been picked up at the railroad station by one of their staff, apologetic that no one from the family was available to greet me. I assured him that it was no matter. I was only one of the staff, really, here to do a task.

"And what a great one it will be, Mrs. Higgins." I don't know what he meant by that, but I'm trying not to be worried. I can handle whatever comes my way. My needle and thread have never let me down.

Palm trees line the driveway toward the house. I was sweating in my dress and thankful for the open top of the car, even though I had to hold on to my hat for fear it would become loosened by the intense jostling as we bounced down the dirt driveway.

Then we came upon the estate. Oh my goodness, it's beautiful. The house looks like a painting, all white with pillars holding up a long front porch. Beyond that, the sea.

I unpacked and changed into a sleeveless cotton dress. Happy to be done with them, I discarded my stockings and stood under the shade of my patio awning watching the waves roll gently into shore. It was not like the ocean had been in Boston, cold and frightening at times. This was a gentle beast, with waves small and harmless.

The air, albeit hot, felt good on my bare skin. Dinner was still hours away, and I was contemplating a walk on the beach. I longed to put my feet into the water, which the housekeeper told me was warm here on the Gulf. I'd told her about the cold, clear waters of our creeks and rivers, and she'd said the thought of them made her thirsty.

Deciding I must be brave, I risked being seen in my bare feet and stockingless legs to head out to the beach. The sand was hot under my feet and so fine that it felt a little like walking on air. I hustled to the shore, anxious to cool my toes in the water. The water was not a disappointment, warm and smelling of seaweed and brine.

"Excuse me? What are you doing here?"

I jumped at the sound of a man's voice and turned to see who it belonged to. Flushing at the sight of him, I stammered an explanation. "I'm here by the family's invitation." He wore nothing but a swim outfit, his skin tanned and golden. He was golden all around, actually, with yellow hair and blue eyes that matched the sea behind him. Saltwater crusted on his skin and made the bleached hair of his arms even whiter.

"And who might you be?" He looked at me with cold, suspicious eyes.

He might look angelic, but his personality didn't match his appearance.

"I'm Mrs. Higgins. The wedding dress designer." My straw hat wavered as a sudden gust of wind brought an intense scent of fish.

"Designer? Is that what you call it? I thought you were merely a seamstress."

I lifted my chin, annoyed by this rude man who didn't know the first thing about what I did. Obviously, by the way he was looking at me as if I were a joke of some kind. "I design the patterns as well as sew them, so yes, I am, in fact, a designer." I glared at him, hoping I looked defiant instead of intimidated, which was the truth.

"I stand corrected." A slight smile tugged at the corners of his full mouth. I couldn't be sure, but he seemed to be around my age of thirty. No wedding ring on his left hand, I noted, but there was a white, untanned spot where one would have been. Had he recently lost his wife? "I'm Bromley Hunting. Uncle of the bride."

"Oh, well, yes, it's nice to meet you, Mr. Hunting."

"It's actually Dr. Hunting, but you may call me Bromley." He peered down at me. His eyes were the most extraordinary color. Blue without a speck of anything else—no yellow or green spots for Bromley Hunting. He was too well-bred for such imperfections.

"What kind of doctor are you?"

"The medical kind," Bromley said. "I was a medic in the war and came home to become a doctor."

"What a good thing to do." His family was rich. He'd not needed to become a doctor for the income, I suspected. But then again, neither had my nephew, Theo. Some men were drawn to healing, I supposed.

"It's my medical opinion that you're going to burn under this sun." Bromley gestured toward my fair skin. It was true. I could already see freckles popping up on my forearms. "And is it red hair under that hat?"

Self-consciously, I touched my low bun with the tips of my fingers. Drat, my hair. Always such an attention-getter. I wore it long instead of bobbed like the younger women, and right now it felt hot and thick on my neck. "Not that it's your concern, but yes. I'm a redhead." I decided right then to give him some of his own cheeky medicine. "And you know what they say about redheads?"

"No, what do they say?"

"They say the devil gave us red hair so people would know we were coming. And not in peace."

A burst of laughter rose from his chest. More of a chortle than a laugh. Regardless, it made me flush hotter. "I see. We have a feisty one here. Indeed, your red hair suits you."

Instinctually, I moved closer to the shore, hoping a wave would break near me and splash my legs and arms. In addition, it was extremely uncomfortable to be in the presence of a man wearing only his bathing costume. I could see almost every part of him. Every bronzed, muscular inch.

"Is your wife with you?" I asked, hoping to distract myself from the scandalous thoughts his sunbaked skin evoked.

"No, she's not. In fact, she's no longer my wife." He rubbed his *thumb over the spot where his wedding ring must have resided not long ago. "We are divorced, as of a few weeks ago."*

Divorced. I couldn't believe it. I'd never known anyone to get divorced.

His eyes had darkened. I imagined a cloud covering the sun, even though it was bright in the sky. "It's a long story," he said. "Of scandal and humiliation. She found someone she preferred more than me, and now she shall have him."

"I'm sorry," I said, not knowing what else to say.

"Would you care to take a swim?" Bromley asked. "You seem hot."

"I am hot. But I've no bathing costume." Why hadn't I thought to bring one? I'd not imagined the beach to be this pretty or the temperatures to be this warm.

"No matter. I'll have Elsa find one for you. Unless you'd like to design one yourself?"

That made me laugh.

I didn't swim with him because about then the rest of the family appeared, walking through the sand from the northern direction. They carried umbrellas and picnic baskets. An older gentleman with a thick mustache dangled a straw hat from one hand while linking his other one through that of what must be his wife. She was a grand lady, dressed in white and wearing an enormous hat with a scarlet ribbon that danced in the breeze. A younger woman, slim and graceful, clad in a yellow linen dress and small-brimmed white hat, trailed slightly behind. No shoes, I noticed, feeling thankful I wasn't the only one. Perhaps they did that here in Florida?

"The rest of the clan," Bromley said. "Perfect timing, as always."

I was introduced to Mr. and Mrs. Hunting and their daughter, Cordelia. The bride. She was as pretty as her surroundings. Slim and petite, she would be easy to design a dress for.

I'm now back in my room and preparing for dinner. They've kindly sent a maid to help, but I told them I was accustomed to dressing myself. I'm apprehensive of dinner and hope that Bromley won't be there.

The entry ended there. "That's it for tonight." I shut the journal, wishing I could keep reading.

Jamie had picked up her phone and was staring at it intently. "Looking up the Hunting family," she said as if I'd asked. "I found them." Her lips moved as she read whatever it was she'd found. Finally, she looked up, triumphant. "I thought I'd heard of them before. They were early developers in Florida. The company is still run by the family. They build custom homes, it looks like."

"She fell for this Bromley guy," I said. "And what about poor Clive? He doesn't stand a chance."

"No, she comes back, though," Jamie said. "She comes back to Clive. We know that because of the photos I found in the inn. They were together after 1928."

"Until he died in 1936, right?"

"Yes, that's right," Jamie said.

"So she came home and did the right thing," I said. "Even though it cost her."

"It appears so."

"Can you love two people at the same time?" I asked. "It doesn't seem like something I could do."

Jamie smiled. "Not you, no. But maybe Annabelle."

1 2

JAMIE

D arby kissed me before he left, and for a moment, I imagined us on the beaches of Florida, falling in love as I was sure Bromley and Annabelle had.

"Good night, beautiful," Darby whispered in my ear before leaving me.

I stood inside the door, listening to his steps down the wooden hallway to his place. What had we done? Opened ourselves to hurt? Or was there something here? A connection that went beyond the physical? I didn't know.

Although late and the morning would come too soon, I decided to read just one more journal entry.

It is my second day here in Florida, and I began my day by measuring the bride-to-be. She is a slim, flat-chested young woman and has asked if I could make a dress to flatter her lack of curves. I assured her that the modern dresses with the drop waists would make her seem more substantial than she really is. I will use lace on the bodice to distract the eye from her small bosom as well.

I finished with her and went back to my room to sketch out a few designs to show her. I'd promised at least three options for her to choose from. Whatever I don't use, I'll be able to save for future brides or to use for patterns.

My stomach growled at midday, so I wandered downstairs to the dining room. Elsa, the housekeeper, had told me that breakfast and lunch were informal meals and served buffet-style so not to expect to have to sit down with the family. She'd rolled her eyes and muttered something about unruly hooligans and the beach.

Thus, I didn't expect anyone to be there when I went into the dining room. I was wrong. Bromley Hunting was already seated, facing the large picture windows that looked out to the sea.

He greeted me with a nod of his golden head. I said hello and then went to help myself to cold sandwiches set out on a tray as well as a lump of potato salad and a glass of lemonade. I would not starve here, I thought, even if the food wasn't as good as Lizzie's.

I joined him at the table. "I'm sorry to have missed dinner last night," I said. "But I was tired from my journey and happy to have something in my room."

His blue eyes sparkled at me from across the table. "I'm sorry you weren't there. You may have saved us from a family fight."

"Oh, dear. I'm sorry." A family fight? What did these people have to fuss about? They were rich and lived by the sea.

"My niece and her mother don't always agree about the wedding plans." He lifted his sandwich and took a bite from the corner. "I'm beginning to regret my extended stay." He explained that he'd come for six months. "I needed to get away for a while. You know, the nasty end of my marriage and all."

"Where do you live when you're not here at the beach?" I asked.

"I'm up north. In Boston. Most of the time."

"That's where I grew up as well." I told him of my childhood in south Boston and the move to Colorado when I was in my late teens. "My sister had married a man with five children and sent for Mother and me. We were very poor. Quinn, my sister, went out there to teach school and save our family. My father had died, leaving us in dire trouble."

"I'm sorry to hear that."

We reminisced about Boston for a few minutes, then moved on to what life was like in Colorado. "My husband was already there when I arrived," I explained, before describing the butcher shop he runs with his brother. "It's a simple life but a good one. We've only just built a new house. The one of my dreams."

"Because of your business?" Bromley asked. "You've been very successful. I've learned just how much since we met yesterday."

"It was the patterns that did it mostly," I said. "I can only sew at a certain pace, but they allow me to sell my product to more people."

"Very smart business mind, I see." He possessed qualities that made me nervous. I couldn't quite understand it, other than the way he peered at me with those intense eyes. I had the feeling not much got past him. He saw everything.

I tried to imagine what his former wife was like but couldn't summon anything. Who had enticed her away from him? "What are your interests?" I picked up my lemonade, careful to keep it between my fingers instead of sliding away and spilling, or God forbid, breaking the glass.

"I like to practice medicine and help people. I enjoy golf and swimming in the ocean and listening to music. Anything outdoors is of great interest to me."

"And your wife didn't share your interests?" I asked.

"She preferred everything shiny. Balls and dances and nightclubs. The man she left me for is much better suited to her." He looked out to the ocean, seeming to drift far away from me for a moment. "She was always looking for a party." He turned back to me. "Don't pity me, Mrs. Higgins. I'm better off without her. The embarrassment of it all seems to be the gift that continues, however."

"How often do you come here?" I asked, changing the subject.

"Usually in the winter when Boston is miserable. I've made myself useful here, offering my medical services for free to anyone who requires help."

"Why would you do such a thing?" I asked this not in an accusatory tone but one of true curiosity.

"Do you see all this?" He waved his hand about. "I did nothing to earn it other than to be born into a family of great wealth. I've found that I crave significance, not because I'm rich but because I have skills that help people."

"What about your practice in Boston? Do you have a partner?"

"I do. A family man who prefers to be at home. When I'm here in Florida, he takes care of our patients, such that they are."

"What do you mean?"

"We only provide care to the wealthy. House calls—even in the middle of the night, I might be called to care for someone. It's fine, but I like to be of use to those who really need us for at least part of the year."

"That's very noble of you."

"Do you think so, Mrs. Higgins? Because I think it's only a selfish need on my part to feel as if my life means something."

"Surely it does." We locked eyes for a moment, and an understanding passed between us. "I have my work, which keeps me apart from a lot of other women in my town. And I have no children. Without them, what significance do I make?"

"Your business? You've done a remarkable thing, building it to such a scale."

"My sister has seven children, and I often think how much more she's doing to make the world more beautiful than I."

"Why don't you have children?" Bromley asked. "Was it a choice?"

"They've never come," I said flatly. "Perhaps God knows I'm too selfish and ambitious to have them?"

"Doubtful. More likely, it's a medical reason."

I flushed, shamed. There was nothing worse than knowing I was flawed somehow. That other women could get pregnant without trouble and I was barren year after year.

"I'm sorry," Bromley said. "I've hurt you. That was a thoughtless thing to say."

"No, it's quite all right. I'm sensitive about it, that's all."

"My apologies. My sister-in-law says I have no bedside manner."

"I'm sure that's not true." I smiled back at him. "And no apology necessary."

We finished our sandwiches, talking about our lives and getting to know each other better.

"What about you?" I asked. "Did you and your wife have children?"

Another shadow passed through his face. "I wanted to but it was not to be." He looked back at me, a blankness in his eyes I hadn't yet seen. "I wonder sometimes if we had—if it might have changed the outcome of our marriage."

"You can't know, I suppose. Perhaps it would have made everything more painful." I couldn't believe we were talking as if we'd known each other for a long time. He felt close to me, much more than our brief encounters would suggest it should.

"In hindsight, it probably would have. Then, I would be mourning the loss of her and a child I loved. And the man who stole my wife would have stolen my son and daughter as well."

For some reason, we started to laugh. Completely inappropriately, I might add. But the giggles had taken control of us and wouldn't let go.

Finally, I wiped my eyes with the handkerchief I kept in my pocket. "We are bad people."

He sobered and wiped his own eyes. "Perhaps we are. But not bad enough. I would love to be the type of man who would suggest a love affair with a beautiful dress designer but alas, after being the one who was left, I can never do that to another man."

I stared at him, dumbfounded.

"I'm joking, of course," he said.

"Yes, of course."

His words touched me in a strange way, a way that made me feel as if I might catch fire. I'd never felt such a thing before in my life.

*"Would you care to take a stroll along the beach?" Bromley asked.
"I can show you where my favorite birds reside."*

"I'll have to get my hat," I said. "The sun, you know."

"Make it a wide-brimmed one."

The passage ended there. How could she leave me with such a cliffhanger? But I was yawning like my head might break in two and knew I needed to sleep. The journal would have to wait until tomorrow.

———

I WENT to bed and woke the next morning excited for the day. Darby would be at the inn later, and I'd get to see him. To my surprise, I found Arianna Bush waiting for me.

She was standing at the front desk talking to one of my staff but straightened when I came in through the front door.

"Jamie, I'm sorry to bother you, but I had an idea." Her eyes sparkled almost as bright as her enormous diamond. "My Rob surprised me and is in town early. He said he could work just as easily here as at home. He may have been just a teensy bit worried when I told him Darby was here. And that's just the thing that gave me the idea. I'd really like to see Darby and tell him how sorry I am, and that I hope we can be friends, and that he and Rob can find their way together again. Rob wouldn't have to be jealous if he saw how happy you and Darby are together. We could go to dinner together, all four of us. What do you think?"

Dinner? The four of us? The idea almost made me laugh, but I kept it together. "I'd have to check with Darby. I'm not sure how he'd feel about all of this."

"Yes, yes, of course. It's so awkward, this whole thing, and I figured it would be better to address it head-on. That's my way, you know. I see a problem and just have to fix it."

"Sure. Like I said, I'll ask Darby when he comes by after school."

She tented her hands and looked as if she might say something else but didn't.

"All right, well, I should get to work," I said. "I'll give you a call later."

"Wonderful." She gave me one of her influencer smiles and sailed out the door. I watched as she got into her red sports car. What was I doing wrong? Slaving away at an inn when I could have done makeovers on TikTok and become an influencer, and then I'd be driving around in a red sports car instead of trudging into my office.

———

AT LUNCH, I read the last entry in Annabelle's journal, forgetting all about the sandwich I'd made.

The morning of my departure I went down the spiral staircase to the foyer where my bags were waiting to be loaded into the car. My chest ached so much I could barely breathe. Mrs. Hunting and her daughter were there to say goodbye, each of them hugging me and thanking me for making such beautiful pieces for the wedding. Cordelia's eyes grew glassy as she kissed my cheek. "Thank you for everything."

"You're very welcome," I said.

Just then, Bromley appeared, his driving gloves in hand. "I'm driving you to the train station," he said. "I have errands to do in town anyway."

"How kind of you." My pulse quickened. Alone with him in a car seemed dangerous. Not because of the driving but my desires. He would sit only inches from me. I had not seen this coming. Yet I knew I wanted to say goodbye. To remind myself and him of our decision.

We didn't speak on the way to the train station. The top was down on his car, and the wind blew the ribbons of my hat this way and that, tickling the sides of my face. When we reached the station, he took my bag from the back of the car and then came around to help me to the ground. It was a relatively mild day for Florida and a slight breeze cooled the bare skin of my arms and face.

"It seems there's always more I want to say to you," Bromley said. "But we've run out of time."

"Yes, we have." A painful lump in the back of my throat threatened to suffocate me. A life without him, that's what I must accept. "I'll never forget you."

"Nor I you," he said. The straw material of his hat gave his skin a lattice pattern. "If only we had two lives."

"I'd choose at least one of them to live with you." Tears gathered at the corners of my eyes. "This is silly, isn't it? We've known each other for two weeks."

"Not long enough to upend our lives?"

"It's Clive. He deserves better than betrayal. And I love him."

He nodded. "Yes, I know. I would never ask you to betray him. You know that."

"I do," I said.

"Even though it's killing me to send you away."

"Well, this is it." The train was pulling into the station. From then on, the sound of the steam engine and clanking of metal brought me back to this moment. To the afternoon I had to say goodbye to my Bromley. The man I'd fallen in love with.

I lifted my cheek. "You may kiss my cheek before I leave."

He scooped under the brim of my enormous hat and brushed his lips against my skin. I caught the spicy scent of him, a mixture of cigar smoke and leather. The smell of a man, I thought. My man. No. My man waited for me in the foothills of our town.

"Goodbye, Bromley Hunting."

"Goodbye, Annabelle. Have a good life. Do what we've talked about. Everything you want, you can have." His voice caught at the end, and he waved his hand in front of his face. I gave him one last squeeze.

Not everything, *I thought as I turned away and headed toward the train that would take me home. For we cannot live two lives, only one. We must make choices of which way to go. Stay or go. I had to go, of course. My sweetheart, the man who had loved me when I was young and foolish, waited for me there. And I could not break his heart.*

I shut the journal and swiveled in my chair to look out the window. Now that I had read to the end, I knew it was time for me to deliver this to the Barnes family. It belonged to them more than to me. The Barnes roots in this town went way back. Trapper's family were direct descendants of Alexander Barnes. Mr. Barnes had taken on the role of family historian, keeping journals and letters safe at his house. He would want to see all of this right away.

After a quick phone call to Mr. Barnes and an explanation of what I'd found, he asked if I could bring it out right away. The excitement in his voice was contagious. The staff could handle everything for a few minutes without me, I decided.

I parked in Mr. Barnes's driveway, admiring the mums in the pots displayed attractively on the porch. This was the original Barnes estate where Alexander and Quinn had raised their seven children. I stood at the bottom step for a moment, contemplating what it must have been like to live back then. How I wished I could go back in time.

Mr. Barnes answered right away and ushered me into the house and back to the kitchen that looked out on the lawn. If I remembered correctly, this room had originally been the formal parlor, and the kitchen was downstairs. But it was all modern now with an exquisite remodel that included a gorgeous white-and-blue kitchen.

"My wife's out this morning, but she left some lunch for us. Do you want a piece of quiche?"

On cue, my stomach growled. I'd been so anxious to talk to

Mr. Barnes I'd forgotten to eat my sandwich I'd brought from home.

"I'd love one."

He hustled around putting two pieces on plates and pouring glasses of lemonade before joining me at the island. "I'm dying to see what you found," he said.

I let him look through the box while I ate the delicious quiche. "Nice crust," I murmured under my breath.

"Old recipe left from Lizzie Strom," Mr. Barnes said.

My friend Brandi was a direct descendent of the original cook and butler of this home. She'd told me they'd found some of Lizzie's letters and learned a lot of interesting things.

"Annabelle Cooper Higgins," Mr. Barnes said. "Strangely enough, we know less about her than we do anyone, given that she was kind of famous."

"Whatever happened to her, I wonder?" I told him what we'd learned so far. "All we know is that she fell in love with a man who was not her husband."

"I'll be darned."

"We're assuming she stayed with Clive Higgins," I said. "But I don't know what happened. There's not much to the journal, so I'm not sure we'll get many answers."

"Hang on a minute. Let me get something." Mr. Barnes, not having touched his quiche, got up and disappeared down the hallway. By the time he returned, I'd finished my delicious lunch.

He carried a manila folder with him. "This is what I have of family death and birth certificates. Marriage licenses too," he said, setting it on the table. "Let's see what I can find for Annabelle."

He riffled through the papers, muttering to himself. "Nothing in here. Let me get the family Bible. They recorded things like that in those days."

He scurried off again and returned with a tattered leather-bound Bible. "Yes, here she is." He showed it to me. Annabelle Cooper's date of birth was listed, as was Quinn's. "This was the Coopers' Bible," Mr. Barnes explained. "Their mother brought it with them when they moved here from Boston."

I looked down the list. "Here it is," I said, pointing to the entry with Annabelle and Clive's wedding date. But they were not mentioned again. "Clive died in 1936," I said. "I wonder if she remarried after his death?"

"I didn't know much about her," he said. "She's the one member of the family I haven't been able to learn much about. She had a child in 1925 who only lived a few months. As far as I can tell, she spent most of her time and efforts into her business."

"How sad. It must have been heartbreaking to lose a child after trying for so long."

"Yes, although sadly, a lot of women lost babies in those days."

I nodded, my heart aching at the thought of Annabelle's lost child.

"She moved away from here sometime after Clive's death in 1936 but returned later. I'm not entirely sure when. Regardless, I think she owned the house all that time but may not have lived there. Let me look through what I have from Quinn and see if there are any clues in there." His eyes gleamed. "Do you mind leaving this with me?"

"Technically, it belongs to your family," I said. "I've been having fun reading the entries and am intrigued by the mystery, but I wanted you to have it."

"Tell you what—give me a day or two with this and I'll see what else I can dig up. It may give us more questions than less after we make our way through the journal and letters."

"I hope not. I like to know how a story ends, don't you?"

"Very much so. But I've discovered as I try to piece together my family's history that there are some things we will not ever know."

I said goodbye then, knowing I needed to get back to the inn. He promised to call if he found anything interesting.

I could hardly wait. This was better than a favorite television show.

I LET Darby work for an hour that afternoon before I went out to greet him and ask him about this double date idea of Arianna's. Whatever he wanted was fine with me. I had a feeling it would be too painful to have dinner with his former friend and girlfriend. However, I was curious to meet this millionaire Rob, stealer of girlfriends. I'd simply tell him her request and be sure not to give away my own desire to accept their offer.

I brought him a cold glass of lemonade when I went out to the construction area. It was a warm afternoon, and he was working in a short-sleeved shirt and faded jeans. A baseball hat covered his head and protected his face from sunburn, and a leather work belt hung low around his hips. Today he was working on the platform part of the gazebo. I watched him for a moment. He was leaning over a section, hammer in his hand and several nails between his teeth. Such nice teeth, all straight and white. Sexy, sexy, sexy.

He straightened as I approached and dropped the hammer, which hit the side of his foot. If it hurt, he didn't say so. "Hey there," he said, still holding the nails in his mouth.

"Hey." Why did I feel suddenly shy and tongue-tied and about thirteen? I hadn't felt that way last night when he was kissing me, now had I? Warmth spread throughout my body just thinking of his kisses.

Darby stuffed the nails into his work belt and nodded toward the glass in my hand. "Is that for me?"

I handed it to him. "I thought you might be thirsty. It's warm today."

"That's sweet of you, and I am thirsty." He took a swig from the glass, then wiped his mouth with the back of his hand before taking off his hat and laying it on top of the pile of wood. I could see him as a boy just then, bashful and a little nerdy. I would've had a crush on him, I felt certain. Unfortunately, the way sweat dampened his dark hair and chest muscles showed through his T-shirt, I was developing one right at this minute. Or was it more than that?

"Why is it that everything you make is better than anything else I've ever had? You have the magic touch," Darby said. "This is great lemonade—perfect balance of sweet and tart."

I didn't want to ruin his opinion by telling him we used concentrate from a can to make our pitchers for the guests. If he thought I had magical ways, then so be it. But I must remember why I was here. "So, Arianna stopped by this morning."

His expression darkened. He picked up his hat and stuffed it back on his head. "What did she want? Let me guess. She's changed her mind about something."

"No, not that. She wondered if we wanted to go on a double date."

"You're kidding?" His eyes blazed with a mixture of anger and amazement.

"Not kidding. She thought it would be healing. Or burying the hatchet. Something like that." I moved closer, taking his empty glass. "It's totally fine—whatever you feel comfortable with. I'm there for you either way."

"We'll have to play up being a couple," he said at last.

"Yes. We might need to share more information about our lives," I said. Was that just an excuse to spend more time with him? I didn't know, and at the moment I didn't care.

"Do you think we should do it? Have dinner with them, I

mean." His gaze fixed on me, his eyes earnest and trusting. He truly wanted my opinion.

I would tread carefully. Whatever he chose, it should be because he was 100 percent sure, not because of my influence either way. "Depends. What would you get out of it? Or, what would you want out of it?"

A flash of humor sparked in his eyes. "Revenge?"

I laughed. "That's good enough reason for me."

He sobered and looked up at the sky. The late-afternoon sun sent slivers of gold through the trees. "I would like her to think I'm doing well, I guess. Both of them. That I didn't sit around crying from their betrayal. Even though I did."

I wanted to reach for him and fold him into my arms. I hadn't known a man, not even my brother, to be as honest about his feelings as Darby was. It touched me and endeared him to me in a way that felt sticky. The kind of affection that lasts through time and space. "They don't ever need to know how hard it was for you. We can pretend we're happy and in love and you can politely let them know you're thrilled with the way things turned out. That without her choice, you wouldn't have found me."

He nodded, seeming to think through what I said and coming to the conclusion that I was right. "Yes, let's do it. We can get together later and talk through some of our past. Facts and all that. Knowing Arianna, she will grill us and want to know every detail. Any crack in our story and she'll find it."

"What if they want to go to the lodge for dinner?" I blurted out. "I can't afford that kind of meal."

"Nor I."

"I could offer to cook," I said. "Really show off my cooking skills."

He gave me a gentle, grateful smile. "You're a good one, Jamie Wattson. The type of friend a guy like me needs in his corner."

"I'm here for you. I hope you know that." A friend? Why did that word suddenly taste bad in my mouth?

"I'm grateful," Darby said.

"Did you ever see those pictures in children's magazines that ask what isn't like the others?"

"Sure."

"I think we're like that. All our friends are happily in love and starting their lives together. We're lone wolves, so to speak."

"Not tomorrow night, we won't be," he said. "Tomorrow we're a pack."

I liked the sound of that. Pack had potential. Packs were family, connected forever.

13

DARBY

That night I texted Jamie and told her that I would take care of dinner and she should come to my house. I stopped on the way home and bought several frozen pizzas and one of those salads in a bag. Hopefully, she would forgive my philistine ways in the kitchen. I couldn't have her cooking for me every night after working a full day. Over the last few days, I'd gotten the feeling that Jamie didn't take good care of herself, pushing so hard at work and sacrificing everything for the inn.

She agreed to come by around eight after she returned from work. I'd left the building site when the sun had set, leaving a narrow window to shop and shower.

I was in the frozen food aisle when I saw Huck and Stormi picking out ice cream. Calling out to them, I pushed my small cart toward their large one, filled with copious domestic, nest-building items. Wouldn't it be nice to have someone to share the ordinary events of the day? Grocery shopping, cooking dinner together, watching TV, or reading.

"Hey, guys," I said, suddenly conscious of my dirty clothes

and the fact that I probably didn't smell too good. "Sorry. I just came from the job site."

"You look fine," Huck said. Ever since he fell in love, Huck was downright charming and positive. Two qualities that had previously eluded him.

"Frozen pizza?" Stormi asked, sounding mournful. "You need to come out to the house for dinner soon."

"Our house," Huck corrected her.

She laughed. "Right. Our house."

It was obvious they were thriving together, which delighted me. Stormi had never looked more beautiful, with a glow that could only come from being in love. I might not have recognized her without my contacts in. Her usual ripped jeans and combat boots had been replaced with a conservative black skirt and silk blouse and black pumps. She must have just come from the art gallery.

Huck, however, looked the same as always except that his permanent scowl had been replaced by a lightness of expression. A man recently freed from jail, I thought. Whatever it had been that tortured him had been pushed aside by Stormi's love.

Yes, from my vantage point, it looked as if they were giving each other a new lease on life, a lightness that comes from knowing someone always has your back.

I asked about the gallery. Going well, according to Stormi, who then asked if I was coming to their party next weekend. I assured her I would be there.

"You can bring a date," Stormi said, looking at me from just under her fringe of dark bangs. "Or a pretend date, as the case may be."

"You know about that?" I asked, sheepish.

"She told me the whole plan. Jamie's such a ballbuster, right?" Stormi asked. "Like in the best way."

"I agree," I said. "We're going out to dinner tomorrow with my ex and my ex-friend."

Stormi's eyes widened, and she laughed. "Jamie told me about that too. I hope the ex suffers a little when she sees you with Jamie."

I smiled, pleased. "Jamie is so pretty, isn't she?" She was the prettiest girl I'd ever been around. A beauty fueled by inner strength and intelligence and a sense of humor and passion. She would age well, I thought, because there was more to her attractiveness than her outer appearance. "I just hope I can keep up the charade. I'm not that great an actor."

Stormi's green eyes watched me, carefully. "Maybe you won't need to act that hard?"

I flushed and looked down at my nearly empty cart. These women told one another everything. I needed to remember that. "We've been spending time together."

"And?" Stormi continued to watch me. Would she report back my answer? I should be careful. But I didn't feel careful the last few days. I felt brave and a little reckless. A loosening of my tightly held heartstrings had begun and seemed to be continuing with every interaction I had with Jamie.

"I'm enjoying my time with her," I said. "She's special."

"What's changed?" Huck asked. "You were always adamant that you had no interest in getting involved with her."

"Or anyone," I said. "But it seems things change."

Stormi punched me lightly on the shoulder. "Good on you. Be careful with her heart, though. It's as big as the Colorado sky."

"I know," I said. "It's probably my heart we have to worry about. After my last relationship, I've been cautious for a reason. Arianna broke me."

"Well, now's the chance to show her how well you're doing," Stormi said. "New girlfriend, great job, and awesome friends."

"I do have awesome friends," I said, grinning.

"Excuse me. That's my phone." Huck lifted his cell phone from his pants pocket. His thick eyebrows shot up. "Sorry, something just came in from the Associated Press." Huck owned the local newspaper. He didn't often include stories outside of Emerson Pass, but it seemed that he was still connected to breaking news.

"What's it say?" Stormi placed a hand on Huck's arm.

"The judge sentenced Benji Hanes," Huck said.

It was as if a fist knocked into my middle. I stumbled backward, letting go of my cart. "Tell me." I wiped my sweaty palms on the back of my jeans.

"Twenty-five years to life," Huck said, shaking his head. "What a waste of two lives."

"It's sad," Stormi said. "But justice has to come at some point."

"I hope the victim's family feels some relief," I said. But what about Hanes's family? I was the only one left, the only one who would care at all. Nothing came, though. Not relief or sadness, just a hollow numbness.

"We should pray there won't be any further violence after the sentencing," Huck said. "This has been such a tumultuous time for the country. We don't need more."

I nodded. Utterly drained, I made an excuse to leave. "I have to go, guys. Good to see you. I don't want to be late."

"Have fun," Stormi said.

"Thanks," I mumbled before wandering down the aisle, heart pounding between my ears. *Twenty-five years to life.*

I went home, showered, and changed into clean clothes. All the while deliberately pushing aside what I'd learned about my father's fate. This was nothing to me, I kept saying over and over in my head. Nothing to do with me. Ten years had passed since I'd even seen him. He was out of my life. I would not be sucked in. After the oven was preheated, I washed the dishes that I had left in the sink that morning and put them away. From what I'd observed, Jamie was a very good housekeeper. She liked everything beautiful and just so. I liked that about her. I liked a lot of things about her, for that matter. All day I had warned myself not to look too far ahead. This was a friendship that could develop into more, but there were no guarantees. But deep down, I am a romantic. It was impossible to be in her presence and not fall in love a little bit more each day.

At precisely eight, a light tapping on the door told me that Jamie had arrived. My stomach fluttered, as if I were a teenager about to pick up my prom date. If my students felt half the way that I did about their crushes, it was no wonder they were such a disaster. They were a mass of hormones and uncertainty. I would remember that the next time one of them did or said something ridiculous or obnoxious.

I yanked open the door. She stood there, holding a box from Brandi's bakery. "I had a few pastries left from this morning. They might be stale."

She took my breath away. A rush of adrenaline coursed through my body. "Pastries? Great." My voice was a little loud. Too much enthusiasm for possibly stale pastries. They weren't what really excited me. It was the woman in front of me.

A pink blouse paired with denim cutoff shorts showed off tanned, muscular legs. Her long hair fell in soft waves down her back. Sparkly earrings dangled against her long neck. My gaze wandered to the curve of her collarbone, so delicate under her tawny skin. "You're beautiful," I blurted out, then flushed, embarrassed to have uttered out loud what I couldn't stop thinking. "You want to come in?"

"Sure, and thanks. It took me a long time to decide what to wear tonight. Stupid, right? It's just dinner at home."

"I appreciate the effort. It's nice to be a man. I just threw on whatever was hanging on the back of my chair."

She laughed and stepped inside the apartment, closing the

door behind her. "You should make a habit of hanging up your clothes at the end of the day."

"Don't be a show-off," I teased.

The timer chimed from the kitchen. "That's our pizza."

"You made pizza?"

"Don't sound so excited. It's a frozen one from the store." Why had I gotten a frozen pizza? I should have made something special. The kind of dinner that would impress a woman like Jamie. But what? I didn't know the first thing about cooking something elegant or elevated, as they said in foodie land. A man has to work with what he has. Which, in this case, was a last-minute purchase at the grocery store.

She gazed around my apartment, as if seeing it for the first time. When in fact she'd been there for many parties. Somehow, though, my place looked different to me tonight, and not in a good way. Jamie's presence made everything look shabby and drab. When one shines as brightly as Jamie Wattson, even the sun wouldn't stand a chance.

The alarm rang again, this time with what seemed like more urgency.

I rushed to the kitchen. Had I burned the pizza? I opened the oven and let out a sigh of relief. The pizza had not burned and actually had crisped up nicely and browned on the top. Cheese bubbled, and the aroma of tomato and garlic wafted through the apartment.

Jamie had followed me into the kitchen and now closed her eyes and sniffed dramatically. "That smells really good. My stomach's been growling for the better part of an hour. I got really busy at work and didn't have time for my afternoon snack." She waved her hands, laughing. "Yes, I usually have a snack, courtesy of Maisy. She brings them from home for both of us. 'Once a mom always a mom,' she told me the first time she broke out the granola bars and juice boxes."

"Smart woman," I said, pulling out the pizza and setting it on a heating pad I'd left on the counter. "I'm not much of a cook, as you probably figured out. Frozen pizza is about the extent of my repertoire." Where had I put the round pizza cutter? I knew I had one in here somewhere, I thought, as I rummaged through the drawer where I kept spatulas and serving spoons and a mess of other items I rarely used.

Just then, I had an awful thought. I was letting her see into my life. My real life, all the messiness of my apartment. The identity of my father. I pushed aside the thought of him going to prison. He would not ruin this night for me.

The worried thoughts continued. Was it too much? Would she think my drawers were disorganized enough that she would rule us finished before we even started? Would she think we were incompatible? Judge me for being unorganized and a little on the sloppy side?

No, no, I told myself. *Don't let the voices in your head destroy the little bit of self-confidence you've managed to build over the years.* The old Saboteur Darby wanted to get out and wreak havoc on the evening so that I would be safe but ultimately alone and miserable. I wouldn't let him. Not tonight. I found the pizza cutter at last and held it up in triumph. "Haven't used this guy in a while. I'm more of a frozen burrito kind of guy."

"A pizza cutter?" Jamie asked. "How sophisticated of you."

"I got it at a yard sale."

"I love yard sales." She'd wandered over to the refrigerator and peered at a photograph of me with Breck and Huck last summer hiking along the river. "But no to the frozen burritos."

"Are you serious about yard sales?" I asked. We had so much in common. Regardless of my cooking skills or organizational rituals.

"Dead serious. You can get a lot of good things, but you have to get up early. Yard sale types are enthusiastic."

"Yeah, and they're early risers." I grabbed two wine glasses, one wide and short and the other tall with tapered glass, also mismatched and attained from a yard sale.

"Frozen burritos, though? Absolutely a hard no," she said.

"But why?" I asked, pretending to be crushed. "That was going to be dessert."

She laughed. I loved it when I made her laugh. I was a king then, not a yard sale collector. Not an insecure son of a criminal.

A murderer.

Turning away from her, I shut my eyes for a moment and took in a deep breath. I was fine. I was safe. He could not hurt me.

"The biggest offense of the aforementioned frozen burrito," she said in a solemn voice, "is the way they're scalding hot from the microwave yet soggy at the same time."

"You have to put them in the oven." I lifted my chin and spoke in a high voice, doing my best imitation of a fussy, snobby chef. "For exactly six minutes at four hundred degrees Fahrenheit."

Smiling, she leaned against the counter and folded her arms. "Do you know what I think?"

"What's that?" I poured, or rather, opened the spout on the box of wine and filled one glass and then the other. I gave her the good one with the tapered sides.

"Eating a frozen burrito with you is preferable to eating a steak with just about anyone else in the world."

That stunned me. I was actually speechless for a moment. I swallowed, flustered and shy and completely unable to take a compliment of that magnitude with any kind of grace. "That's sweet. Really sweet."

Her face fell. "Sometimes I'm a little *extra*," she said apologetically. "I embarrassed you. I'm too bold. I push men away because of it."

"No, it was not too bold. It was nice and it made me feel

good. And if pressed, I would admit to feeling the same way about you. That said, I hope this pizza isn't terrible. It's all I could think of to make on short notice." It was hard to court a beautiful young woman on a budget. "I could have ordered one, but they're so much more expensive than this."

"It looks just fine to me. You shouldn't feel like you have to be a gourmet cook around me. I like hot dogs as much as the next girl."

"Hot dogs good. Burritos bad. Got it." I pretended to write that information onto a list. "I'm a philistine, if you haven't noticed."

"A philistine who likes to dance? If anything, you're an enigma." Jamie settled at my rickety kitchen table in one of the mismatched chairs. They, too, were bought at various yard sales. I'd gotten the one with the red velvet cushion first. The second was Amish style and sat slightly lower than the other. At the time, I hadn't thought I'd need more than two. Really, more than one was one too many. Tonight, though, I had the prettiest girl in town sitting there smiling at me.

"People are complicated. I'm frugal and love to dance and painfully aware of how my apartment must look to you." I gestured toward the living room.

"I like that you're frugal," Jamie said. "You reuse things, which is a great quality, especially in these times of 'newer is always better.' Most people have too much stuff they don't use. As far as your apartment goes, you're a single man with a busy job and a tight budget. How else is it supposed to look?"

"That makes me feel a lot better. I've been looking around and seeing only flaws."

"Ah yes, the old 'what do they see' and 'why didn't I see it and fix it before people came over' thing."

"Exactly." We grinned at each other before I broke away to cut our pizza.

"Although next time, I'll make you some of my homemade pizza. I can guarantee you'll like it."

I like you, I thought. *So much.*

WE'D FINISHED our pizza and were sitting on the couch going over some of our backgrounds and pasts in preparation for our double date the next evening. So far, Jamie had told me about her one brother, Trey. He lived in Cliffside Bay with his wife, Autumn, and their growing family. They now had two little girls, only a few years apart, and living the good life. I'd already told her my story about my father and that I had no siblings. We covered college—she went to San Diego State. I went to Santa Cruz for my undergraduate and UCLA for my graduate studies. She'd grown up in the same house all her life until her mother had to sell it after the divorce. "Traumatic but necessary," Jamie said. "Now my mom's in Cliffside Bay. We were renting an apartment but after I left, she found a house to buy. I think she has a boyfriend even though she won't say the word—calls him her friend Ray. They're in Europe right now."

"Suspicious," I said.

She placed her hand against one cheek and cocked her head to the side. "Hey, I saw the sentencing."

"Oh, yeah. I saw that too."

"Are you okay?" Jamie asked. "Do you want to talk about it?"

I glanced out the window. The daylight had completely faded by then. Lights along Barnes Avenue sparkled from the trees. They kept them up all year. In snow or rain or warm summer nights, they cheered me. "I don't know what I am. Numb, mostly."

"I can imagine."

She sat on one end of the couch and I on the other. I crossed my legs and tapped my bare ankle. I hadn't worn socks and now wished I had. Why hadn't I? Shoes were what grown-ups wear. Jamie needed someone sophisticated. My bare feet with faded jeans and a T-shirt with last year's Emerson Pass Summer Festival logo displayed on the back wouldn't be considered such.

"Did I lose you?" Jamie asked.

"No, my mind was wandering."

"Avoiding thinking about him?" Jamie asked.

"Yeah. It might all hit me later. In the middle of the night, probably. It'll wake me from a dream, this black hole type of feeling, and I won't be able to think of anything else but him going to prison and what might happen to him there." My voice cracked.

"I'm sorry." She swung her legs to the floor and scooted nearer to me. "What can I do?"

"You being here is a great distraction. I keep reminding myself that I'm not even in contact with him. He's not part of my life. Or even my last name."

"But it's hard to separate. He's your father."

I nodded but didn't say anything else.

"As much as I hate my dad, if he were going to prison, I wouldn't be able to think of anything else. I think, anyway. Or maybe I'd think—he finally got what he deserves. He's a lawyer, you know. God only knows what kinds of unethical things he's done."

"Not murdered someone." My voice broke all the way this time. Tears pricked my eyelids. I pressed my fingernails into the palm of my other hand until it hurt.

"As far as I know," Jamie said lightly. "Who knows what kinds of bodies are buried in the backyard." She moved to sit right beside me, putting her hand on my knee. "It's okay to feel bad, even for him. Or the situation or whatever it is that you feel."

"The victim, you know. And his family." Tears flooded my

eyes, making Jamie blurry. "I can't forget that when I'm imagining him going to prison."

She moved even closer and before I knew what was happening, she'd crawled onto my lap. Smelling better than a woman should. She melted into me, soft and warm. I draped my arm over her thighs and let my head drop to her shoulder and closed my eyes.

"It feels better when you're here like this," I said, thick and hoarse.

"Good. Because being here I can do. Whenever you want. Whenever you need me. I'm only right down the hall or across town. In a moment's notice, I could come to you."

We kissed, ever so gently, without the urgency spurred by lust. This was affection and support and friendship.

Jamie's phone beeped with a text, causing us both to jump. She picked it up from the coffee table. "It's Mr. Barnes. He's here in the building and wants to tell me what he found out about Annabelle."

I laughed at the delight on her face. "You're enjoying this a little too much."

"I know. Aren't I awful? This was an actual person. A real-life woman who had troubles and heartache, and all I can focus on is the mystery of it all."

"I don't think you need to feel guilty about that," I said. "Tell him to come on up to my apartment. I want to hear this too."

She did so and a few seconds later, Mr. Barnes was at my door.

14

JAMIE

M r. Barnes declined a glass of wine and settled instead into Darby's shabby armchair. He had the metal box with him, which was now sitting on the coffee table, staring at me like the eye of a hurricane.

"I read what was in here," Mr. Barnes said. "Then I went through some of the other material I have from the family. I have some information but not all. I've brought it back to you in case you wanted to read through the rest of it yourselves. But the gist of it as best I can tell is this—after her husband Clive passed away, Annabelle Higgins went to Florida to see the man she'd fallen in love with twelve years earlier. The details of which are all here." He tapped the top of the box. "From what I can tell from looking through the family letters and journals, she came back to Colorado and left only after Clive died."

"This is a great mystery," Darby said.

"It is indeed," Mr. Barnes said. "I thought I knew all the family stories, but this one seems to have been buried away."

"Do you think Quinn and Alexander disapproved?" I asked, feeling defensive of Annabelle. She'd come back to her husband, after all. What more did they want from her?

"Her wedding dress designs were famous by then," Mr. Barnes said. "From family folklore I know she spent a lot of time in Paris after the Second World War and was considered one of the finest wedding dress designers in the world." He gestured toward the plastic file folder on the desk. "I brought the only thing I could find from Quinn's things. A letter from Annabelle, dated 1937. Would you like to read it?"

I nodded and waited for him to pull it from the accordion-type file holder. When I had it in hand, Darby asked me to read it aloud.

March 7, 1937

Dearest Quinn,

By now you'll have discovered my departure. I'm sorry I didn't say goodbye. I feared if I told you where I was going and why, you would try to convince me not to go. You would probably have been able to do so, for up until the moment the train pulled away from the station, I wavered between going or staying.

In the year since I lost Clive, my life has been tattered and hapless, like a ripped hem of a dress. I have been breathing and making dresses and spending time with all of you, but part of me has been absent. It was like this after we lost our little Mary. I thought I might not be able to go on but all of you, my beloved family and Clive, kept me upright until I was able to return to my work.

You know all this, of course, having been by my side then and recently. Thank you for all you've done for me. I couldn't have made it through without you and Alexander and your unwavering support.

The reason for my sudden trip has roots that began thirteen years ago. Do you remember my trip to Florida in 1924? The Hunting family hired me to design a wedding gown for their daughter, as well as the bridesmaids and mother of the bride. The brother of Mr. Hunting, Bromley, was staying at the house and we became friends. He was unmarried, divorced actually.

We spent time together, Bromley and me. Our relationship remained chaste, I can assure you. Nothing either of us said or did compromised our families or my marriage. However, I felt a deeper connection to him than I've ever felt for anyone else, my husband included. It was as if Bromley knew me as well as I knew myself. He understood my nature and what I wanted for my life. I know, I was married and should have felt this about my husband. I wish I had. For this, I am sorry. I do not feel shame, though. We did not act on our feelings, as hard as it was. The discretion came only from my imagination. But as we know, this too is a sin. My unexpected rush of feelings shook me to my very core. Bromley and I agreed that we must never see each other again.

I left him and returned to Clive. To home, where I've belonged. At the time, it felt as if I'd only narrowly escaped with my life.

To this day, I've kept that promise. But the longing, dear sister, was almost the undoing of me.

Last month, I received a letter from Bromley. He had read of Clive's death in the newspaper. It turns out you were right about that, too. I am moderately famous, as his death was noted in the New York Times, not as a partner in a butcher shop but as my husband. That would have made him smile. He was always so proud of me.

Bromley's correspondence was a surprise indeed. As was his news. I'd thought for certain he would have married again by now. I was wrong. Bromley's been alone all these many years, living in Paris and throwing himself into his art, he told me.

He finished his letter by asking me to come to Florida, the place we first saw each other. I pondered it for a month, wondering if it were wise to open up such a wound. I'm not sure it's a good idea. My hand trembles writing this. Yet I'm still alive. I'm relatively young. Clive would not want me to hide away and concentrate only on my work. He knows more than anyone how heartbroken I was to lose Mary. He was there by my side through all of it. If anything, the loss of our baby brought us closer together. My time in Florida faded somewhat in the years afterward. Clive and I clung to each other. Our devotion deepened, as it sometimes does when tragedy appears. I've devoted myself to my marriage and have had no regrets for having done so.

But a new season has come to my life. Perhaps it's time for me to be free, to see if the love I felt all those years ago was true or only a figment of the sea air and warmth of the Florida sun.

Lately, in the middle of the dark night when I no longer feel the bulk of Clive next to me, I wonder if his early death was my fault. He was so good, so true and loyal. Although he never fully understood my ambition or obsession with design, he let me be myself and never asked that I make myself smaller to fit better with him. On his deathbed, he asked me if I'd been happy married to him. I told him yes. This was the truth. We had a good life together, even after losing a child. A day does not pass that I do not think of him or our little Mary. I will miss them the rest of my life.

Still, there was this small part of me, even loving Clive as I did, that I left behind in Florida. I buried the memories best I could, after writing it all down. (As a side note, you were right that the exercise of recording our thoughts and stories allows us to move forward with our lives.)

I'll be in touch, dearest. Please do not worry about me. After all, I'm a woman in my forties, no longer the impulsive girl I was when I married Clive. Or when I stepped off the train with Mother all those years ago to see about this life you'd made for yourself in the foothills of our glorious mountains. I do not know what will happen once I arrive, only that I will return to you and Alexander and the family you've made and allowed me to borrow all these years at some point. I cannot promise when or if I will come home alone or in the company of Bromley. I suspect it will be alone. These kinds of feelings surely do not last almost a decade? I'm quite prepared that he will seem ridiculous to me and I to him.

Much love,

Annabelle

P.S. Do not be angry at Delphia, who was the only one privy to my plan. She understood that it is something I must do. She had to be brave enough for both of us. Right now, I am shaking with fear of what is to come. Isn't the unknown always the most frightening?

THE LETTER FLUTTERED to my lap. "I wonder what happened?"

"Is there any way to find out?" Darby asked Mr. Barnes.

"I have some ideas. Once I find out more, I'll let you know."

We escorted him to the door and then turned to each other. "I hope it worked out," I said. "Do you think they got together at long last?"

"I don't know. Do people really have happy endings? People like us?"

"Do you think they're like us?" I asked.

"We had one night. They had two weeks."

I stared at him, trying to decipher what he meant. "Except we didn't fall in love that night, did we?"

"I'm starting to wonder about that." He glanced up at the ceiling. "I wasn't able to let it in. The enormity of our attraction scared me to death. Not after what had happened with Arianna. But I wonder if we'd met later—what would have happened then?"

"We're here now," I said. "Now is later."

"Yes, we are." He stooped down to kiss me. "And there's no reason why we have to say goodbye."

"What about Arianna?" I asked.

"What about her?" His forehead creased.

"Do you still have feelings for her?"

He took too long to answer before stuttering something about time healing all wounds.

This was a test, I thought. The next evening would give me a chance to observe him with her. I would be able to tell if he'd truly let her go and if there was space for me in his life.

"Don't look that way," Darby said. "She's in the past."

"Sure, I know."

"Whatever happens tomorrow, we go home together, all right? You and me."

I smiled, feeling slightly better. Still, my insecurities were raging like a teenager with hormones. This was an emergency situation. One that required my girlfriends.

———

THAT AFTERNOON, Stormi was sprawled on the bed while Tiffany looked through my closet and pulled three different choices out to show me. I was perched nervously on the end of the bed, sitting on my hands to keep from biting my nails.

The first was a summer dress with ruffles, very feminine and romantic.

"She wore that one to your wedding," Stormi said. "So it's out."

"A guy won't remember what I wore to a wedding," I said.

"Disagree." Stormi sat up and crossed her legs, pointing to the closet. "Darby notices Jamie, no matter what she wears. Plus, he's the sensitive type who pays attention to what's happening around him. What else do we have?"

Tiffany grabbed the pair of skinny jeans and a sleeveless silky lavender blouse. "How about this?"

"It could work," Stormi said. "I wonder what this Arianna will wear, though? How fancy is she?"

"Pretty fancy," I said. "And we're going to dinner at the upscale restaurant at the lodge."

"We need a cocktail dress, not wedding attire or what you'd wear going out with the girls." Stormi gestured to my closet. "Do you have anything sexy like that?"

I groaned, thinking this might have been a mistake to get Stormi involved. Of the three of us, she was the most unconventional in her clothes and everything else. She could pull off combat boots and a summer dress, for instance. I could not.

Tiffany scurried back into the closet. The sound of the hangers being slid one after the other, followed by a bark of triumph. "I've got it." She came out holding my little black dress. My mother had bought it for me when we went to a charity auction back in California before my dad left and she could still afford to go to events like that. A halter top paired with a pencil skirt, it could be dressed up or down depending on shoes.

"I do like that dress," I said. "I haven't had anywhere to wear it really."

"Put it on," Stormi said. "To make sure it still fits."

"Very funny," I said, but stood to take it from Tiff, then slipped into the bathroom to change. Fortunately, it did still fit well, hugging my hips and showing off my toned arms and shoulders. All in all, I liked what I saw. I had a pair of strappy sandals I could wear with it.

I went back to show the ladies, and they were enthusiastic enough that we knew it was a winner.

"Okay, now we just have to do something about your hair," Stormi said. "I'm thinking you should wear it down with beach waves."

"I can do those for her," Tiffany said. "I've had to step in a few times to help my brides when they've had hair disasters."

Tiffany could do pretty much anything.

"What about makeup?" Stormi asked. "Something subtle but striking."

"Can those be pulled off at the same time?" I asked.

"Totally," Stormi said. "Right, Tiff?"

"Sure," Tiffany said, already rummaging through my makeup drawer. "Come sit, Jamie. We're going to get you prom ready. Not that I went to prom, but you know what I mean."

She'd been raised in a cult. No proms or any other dancing allowed.

I took the dress off and put my bathrobe on instead and obediently sat down at my dressing table. The bathroom in this apartment was too small for doing much besides showering and using the toilet, so I always did my makeup and hair in the bedroom.

Tiffany started combing through my blond strands, assessing me with the gaze of a professional. Stormi had plugged in the flat iron and was looking at my assortment of shadows. Once she'd settled on something, she began by brushing concealer under my eyes. I hadn't gotten enough sleep lately, I thought, noticing the purple smudges.

While they worked on me, I endured a barrage of questions about the nature of my relationship with Darby.

"So, you're pretending to date to impress this Arianna Bush," Stormi asked. "But you're also kind of dating for real?"

"That's about it," I said. "So much for the fake boyfriend idea. Apparently, I'm susceptible to suggestion."

"How was the kissing?" Tiffany asked, then blushed. Our formerly innocent friend still got embarrassed by any hint of sex. Even though she'd told us how happy she and Breck were in that capacity, it still made her uncomfortable to talk about it.

"The kissing was good," I said. "Just like the night of hot sex we had way back when."

Tiffany colored a deeper shade of pink. "I keep forgetting about that part."

"I don't." Stormi stood back to look at her work and seemed to like what she saw, because she picked up a smaller brush and dipped it into a champagne-colored base blush. "I totally thought you guys would end up in bed together after one of our parties. I'd almost given up hope."

"Do you like him?" Tiffany licked the end of her index finger and dabbed at the flat iron to check if it was hot. "Beyond the kissing."

I thought about her question as an image of Darby's grinning face appeared before me. "He's warm and sensitive and yeah, I like him. A lot, actually. I'm not really thrilled about it, since I don't think he could ever like me long-term."

"Why would you say that?" Tiffany wound a section of my hair around the flat iron. "He'd be lucky to have you."

"I don't know," I said. "He's got some issues, and so do I."

"Don't we all? Huck and I have a lot between the two of us. I mean, gobs and gobs." She paused, looking philosophical as she picked up the blush brush. "But we help heal each other of past traumas every day we're together."

"Same with Breck and me. Well, he doesn't have issues really," Tiffany said. "He's kind of perfect. Other than he lost his dad when he was a teenager, he's so well-balanced and steady."

"Lucky him," I said. "And lucky for you, Tiff."

"What do you know about Darby's issues?" Stormi asked. "Like are they the kind that will keep him from being a good partner to you?"

I had to laugh. Since she and Huck fell in love, Stormi had become focused on relationships and what made them work.

"I mean, look at me," Stormi continued. "I had to teach myself how to trust him and that he would be there every night without fail. Which is what I need, given my chaotic childhood with a million stepdads."

"What do you think you need, Jamie?" Tiffany asked.

What did I need? "A guy opposite of my dad."

"What does that mean?" Stormi asked.

"My dad was controlling and passive-aggressive—any hint of that and I'm out of there," I said.

"Darby doesn't seem like the controlling type, does he?" Stormi asked, and didn't wait for a reply before telling me to close my eyes.

I did as asked and held my breath as Stormi applied eyeliner to my upper lids. When she was done, she stood back slightly to get a good look at her work.

"It doesn't seem like it," I said. "Not yet, anyway. But I wonder all the time—is he the leaving type? I need a man who I can relax with, knowing that he won't just suddenly up and leave when I get older, like my dad did. And someone who really likes me the way I am and won't try to change me."

"That's a good list," Tiffany said.

"And someone who makes me laugh," I said.

"Well, Darby doesn't seem funny at all," Stormi said. "Or witty."

"He is funny and very witty," I said before realizing she was teasing me. "We have a lot in common and like the same things." I told them about our mutual love of vintage country music. "I mean, that's pretty weird, right?"

"What's weird," Stormi said, "is that it took this long for you two to figure it out."

"I don't know," I said, the doubt creeping in again. "What if he's still hung up on Arianna?"

"You'll be able to tell tonight." Stormi handed me the mascara tube. "You have to do your lashes. I'm afraid I'll tear your cornea or whatever it is."

"Keep your eyes wide open," Tiffany said. "Like Stormi said, if he still loves her, you will know it."

"And if so, run, don't walk, out of there," Stormi said.

THAT NIGHT, we drove to the lodge in the orange glow of sunset. Darby's car had been released from the shop and seemed to be running well. The valley between the two mountains had never looked prettier to me. I reached over and gave Darby's knee a squeeze. "I feel nervous for some dumb reason."

"Are you?" He glanced my way and smiled. "You sure about this? Because we can tell them you or I weren't feeling well and go back to your place."

"As tempting as that sounds, no, we have to go through with it," I said. "Unless you don't want to?"

He was quiet, contemplating my question. I'd learned this

about him over the last few days. He often took his time to answer, as if organizing the words in his mind before speaking them out loud. Given my impulsive mouth, I appreciated this quality. Being with him made me feel like a delicate porcelain bowl resting in his capable and steady hands.

"I want to," he said at last. "Just to show them how great I'm doing. Or, at least faking it."

"Should we hold hands during dinner?" What a stupid thing to ask, I chastised myself. What was wrong with me, practically begging him?

His forehead creased as he seemed to think through the details of his answer. "It's been such a long time since I've been part of a couple, I don't know. Whatever you think. I'll let you take the lead. I'm afraid I'm going to freeze and just stare at them like a startled deer confronted with a lion."

"Do lions eat deer?"

"I think so." He grimaced, chuckling. "Or antelope, maybe? I don't think we have lions in Colorado."

"Maybe a bobcat then?"

"That works. My metaphors aren't too great, huh? I just teach English, not write it."

I looked out the window. We were out of town now and traveling along the road toward the historic lodge. Late-blooming flowers and tall grasses grew alongside the road. The northern mountain, where the ski runs had long dominated the greenery of the trees, was pretty against the pink sky. In the side mirror, I could see that the southern mountain stood proud, although the fire had taken out a swatch of trees, leaving her partially bald with a feathery dusting of green from new foliage. Soon, snow would cover up the seedlings and saplings that had sprouted in the dead spots last spring. We might not have many more weeks of good weather, but tonight was glorious, with golden aspen leaves fluttering hello from the foothills. "It's pretty, isn't it?" I asked. "I'm still in awe of it—amazed I live here."

"I took my fifth period outside today, figuring I should let them soak up the crisp fall weather for as long as they could. If they get off their devices for long enough, they can still see the beauty of the world. Even more so than those of us who have been around longer. Youth see the world with fresh eyes."

"We're hardly old," I said.

"No, not really." He chuckled and turned into the driveway that led to the lodge.

"But I know what you mean. When I'm with my little niece, who's not even three yet, she sees everything with such excitement that it's contagious. Except when she's pulling the cat's tail just to see what she'll do."

"Poor kitty."

"Is that why you love teaching?" I asked, serious.

"Seeing the world with fresh eyes, you mean?"

"That and being around when someone discovers something for the first time," I said.

"Seeing the kids learn and take in new ideas gives me a huge high. I cannot lie." He glanced toward me before scanning the lot for a parking spot in front of the lodge. "I also just love to nerd out about literature."

"I agree. That's why I majored in English even though I wasn't sure what good it would do me in life."

"You're doing fine." He pulled perfectly straight into a parking space and shut off the car, then turned to face me. "Also, you look absolutely spectacular. That dress."

I flushed, pleased. "Thanks. You look nice too." He wore a light-knit black sweater with a mock turtleneck collar that accentuated his spectacular jawline and a pair of dark denim jeans that hugged his muscular thighs.

"I should have said something earlier." He reached across to brush something from my cheek. A piece of lint or hair. I wanted to grab his hand and place it next to my heart to show him how he made it beat wildly. Of course I didn't. Way too much. Even I knew that.

"But you took my breath away, and my speech too," Darby said. "It won't be hard to pretend you're my girlfriend."

"Darby?" My voice was uncharacteristically quiet and a little husky.

"Yeah?"

"Is it just pretend? Us, I mean."

His eyes softened. "It's not pretend. To me, at least. What about you?"

"Not for me either."

"But?"

"There's no but," I said. "Only an uncertainty about what's really going on here. It's been a long time since I cared about anything besides my business. You know, I've had to be singularly focused, on every decision about what would get me closer to my dreams. I'm afraid to let myself get wrapped up with you. That's the truth."

"Why? Because it distracts you from work?"

"Not that exactly, although part of me worries I'll lose everything if I let myself fall in love. Mostly, though, I'm afraid it will destroy me when you leave."

He breathed in my words and seemed to pull them from the air with his hand and bring them close to his chest. "Because ultimately, men leave. Isn't that what you think, deep down?"

"That's what I think. And it's not that deep down. Isn't it only a matter of time for women? Even if they get two good decades with a man, he leaves her when she's no longer in full bloom?"

"You've seen that with your parents. I lost my mom when I was young. What does that leave us with, though? A life where we don't love because we're afraid to be left? Is that really living?"

"Probably not, but it's less scary than being all-in with everything."

He lifted my chin with his fingers, forcing me to look into his eyes. "Is it so hard to believe that a man could love you forever? The right man, that is. One who will relish your aging body and graying hair, thinking good Lord, I'm a lucky bastard to grow old with the most exciting woman I've ever met."

"Is that what you think? Of me?" I blushed, hot and embarrassed. Why couldn't I keep my words inside my head instead of letting them all spill out this way?

"Yes, Jamie, I think you're the most exciting and interesting woman I've ever spent time with. Is that so hard to believe?"

"It is." Out of the corner of my eye, a pink coat caught my attention. Arianna.

Darby placed his hand over my knee. "Even so, your feelings of inadequacy have no bearing on what I really feel, what I see. Okay?"

I smiled back at him. My bottom lip trembled from the surge of emotions flooding through me.

"Will it ruin your lipstick if I kiss you?" Darby asked softly, twisting a finger into a long lock of my hair.

"I wouldn't care if it did." I breathed in the scent of him, shaving soap and a subtle spicy cologne. The orange light slanted through the side windows. His eyelashes, fine and stick-straight but dark, seemed to wave at me when he blinked. He'd shaven before he picked me up, I thought, noticing a small nick near his cleft chin. "Does it make it hard to shave?" I gently rubbed the indentation with my thumb.

He covered my hand with his, holding my gaze. "A little, yes. Do you hate my cleft?"

"What, no. Why would I?"

"One time when she was drunk, Arianna told me it made my chin look like a butt." His gaze flickered toward the entrance of the lodge, where pink-coated Arianna and the man who must be

Rob, dressed in a gray blazer and jeans, were walking through the double doors.

"No way." I giggled. "That's ridiculous."

He laughed too, his white teeth gleaming. "Now you see it, don't you? Now my chin is a butt to you."

"No, it's the best chin ever."

He moved my fingers to his mouth and kissed them, one by one, before moving to my lips, taking them softly between his own. The tip of his tongue met mine for the briefest of moments before he backed away. "We should go in."

"Yes, we should."

He traced his thumb under my bottom lip, wiping away the smear of gloss I felt certain was there. "I've smudged you."

Reluctantly, I turned away and pulled down the shade to reapply my lipstick, but there was no mirror. He looked sheepish. "This car is so ancient."

"Never mind that," I said, pulling out my compact and quickly swiping my mouth with my favorite plummy color. "Let's do this."

He jumped out to open my door. The sweetest gesture. I loved it. Rare these days, whether because men were afraid to offend the modern, independent woman or were too preoccupied with themselves, I wasn't sure. All I knew is that it felt nice to have a man behave chivalrously.

We held hands as we crossed the parking lot to the main entrance. The palm of his hand was dry and comforting. *Darby is solid and strong,* I thought to myself.

Built in the second decade of the twentieth century, the outside of the lodge had not changed much in a hundred years. The architecture was that of the American lodges of that time period, with logs, river rock, and wide beams, dramatic as opposed to quaint and elegant like my inn. There was room for both, right? Or was my little inn always going to be second place to this monolith?

The lobby had high ceilings and windows that looked out to the ski mountain and had been remodeled not long ago. They'd done a good job at keeping the vintage feel while updating with modern touches, like gas fireplaces, shiny hardwood floors, and white wainscoting and trim. Still holding hands, we made our way across the lobby, past the enormous river rock fireplace to the formal dining room. Arianna and Rob had already sat at a table by the window when we arrived at the host's lectern. She greeted me with a friendly hello and asked about how business was going. This was a small town. All of us in the tourist industry knew one another.

Darby let go of my hand when we got to the table. Rob Wright stood to greet us, holding out his hand to shake Darby's and then mine. When we were all seated, I looked over at Arianna. She was staring at Darby with what looked like love in her eyes. Was it possible she still had feelings for him? If so, what did that mean? Why would she marry someone else?

I thought of Annabelle. She'd loved two men. Was it possible that Arianna did too? And if she did, where did that leave me? I did not wish to share him with anyone, especially her.

15

DARBY

The first thing I thought when I greeted my former friend and ex-girlfriend? They seemed a little plastic. I half expected them to reveal themselves as wax versions of their previous selves. How had I never noticed how much makeup Arianna wore? All that toner and blending she used to do had seemed normal to me. Compared to Jamie, who seemed fresh and natural, Arianna looked like an evil doll in a horror film. Also, her lips seemed bigger than they once were. Puffed up like one of those fish. What had she stuck in them to make them do that?

"It's so good to see you." Arianna gave me one of her best fake smiles, the one she perfected for selfies, with her chin jutted outward and her mouth not quite up over her teeth. God forbid any gum would show above her teeth. How had she perfected that smile? In front of the mirror? Countless selfies until she landed on the right one?

"You as well." I turned to Rob. His jaw was clenched and his gaze darted around, obviously looking for our server. He wanted a drink. I didn't blame him. It's not every day one comes face-to-face with the friend you betrayed.

My nerves had my thoughts jumping around with no logical sense. I must focus. Present my best self, or at least the one I wanted her to see.

"How are you, Rob?" I asked. "It's been a while."

His gaze was directed a little to my right, over my shoulder, avoiding eye contact. "Yes, it sure has been a minute. I'm good. Business is good. We bought a competitor recently. Got to crush them one way or the other, right?"

"Tell me about your little company," Jamie said.

I hid a smile behind my hand. Jamie knew his company wasn't little. She wanted to take him down a notch.

I might love her.

"You haven't heard of my company?" Rob asked. "Do you live under a rock here in Colorado?" He aimed for a droll tone, I thought, but didn't quite make it. His natural nastiness was evident despite the way he'd attempted to mold into someone charming over the years. At school, he'd always been the guy who controlled through fear. We were always worried about what he would say in front of whoever one of the rest of us wanted to impress. It was always something that would cut us down, make us look ridiculous and him glib and cool.

I might hate him.

"I've heard of it only recently," Jamie said, smiling brightly, as if she hadn't picked up on his disrespect. "I looked you up in preparation for our dinner tonight."

"I'm in the story business," Rob said as if he hadn't heard Jamie. "In the form of video games. Have you ever played *Loader*? Or heard of it? That's my baby. We've expanded into other games, of course. One has to in this market. Young people always want better and faster, right?"

"I don't spend time playing games," Jamie said. "Nor do my friends, apparently, because I've never heard of it. I'm old school. I prefer my stories to come from books."

Arianna laughed, tinkling like a bell. The one she used when she was uncomfortable. She might try to fake it around me, but I knew all her tricks. Everything was done with a purpose in mind. She was indeed an "influencer," obsessed with her image and her carefully cultivated online persona.

She'd been enamored with Rob's world, his money, and access to celebrities. I hadn't stood a chance. Was I like poor Clive Higgins? Simple and humble. Not the man a woman like Arianna would want for a husband. She'd never asked me questions about myself as Jamie had over the last few days. Probing questions. Ones that revealed who I was under my protective layers. Now I could see how ill-suited Arianna and I were. How had I not known it before? How had this woman broken my heart?

"Ari tells me you run the little inn," Rob was saying to Jamie. "She has her heart set on the wedding there, as you know."

"Yes, we're delighted you chose us," Jamie said, still stiff. She didn't like Rob. "And we're scrambling to get it exactly as Arianna wants it for your big day."

"I should have predicted those carpentry skills of yours would come in handy one day, right?" Rob asked me. "Shame they don't pay teachers more. It must be hard to take all these side jobs just to pay your rent, huh?"

He was a jerk. He'd always been that way, too. I hadn't seen that clearly before, either. His aim was always to put the other person off-kilter. Even though his words were not necessarily unkind, I knew the truth. It was a game he played to make himself feel superior.

The server came and asked if we wanted to order drinks.

"Ah, there you are finally," Rob said to the server in an overly friendly tone while simultaneously looking at his watch. "It's slower here in the woods, I guess. We've been sitting here for five minutes. We're from LA and conditioned to the treadmill going full speed ahead. I can't tell you how nice it is to slow down a little."

"Yes, sir, what can I get you?" The server was young and ruddy, probably a passionate skier who had decided living in Emerson Pass was worth whatever type of job he had to take so he could keep skiing.

"We'll have a round of cocktails and then I'll pick out a bottle of wine for dinner." Rob tapped the wine menu and then winked at me. "Leave this for me, please. I'm taking care of tonight so you order whatever you want. What a treat it is to spend time together after all these years. I'll have a Macallan. No ice. "

"Yes, sir. Jamie, what would you like?" Our server obviously knew her. His voice had warmed when he said her name. She was well-liked in her industry. Who wouldn't like her? She was as smart as she was pretty and had such a genuine spirit.

"Martini for me. With a twist, please. And I'll have your top-shelf vodka," Jamie said. "The most expensive, pretentious one you have. That's the only one that will do, I'm afraid. I'm very fancy." She fluttered her lashes.

The server's eyes sparked with humor, but he only nodded and turned toward Arianna. "And you?"

I slid my gaze to Rob. His cheeks had flushed pink. He might be a pretentious jerk, but at least he knew when he was being mocked.

"I'll have the same as my fiancé," Arianna said.

Scotch? That was new. When we were together she'd liked sweet white wine, often with ice cubes.

I ordered an IPA and our poor server, probably thinking it was going to be a long night, made his escape.

"How long have you two been together?" Arianna asked.

We'd rehearsed this one. I let Jamie answer. "Since around this time last year. We have a lot of mutual friends and one day I just looked over at him and thought—you've been blind. He's been here all this time."

"How sweet," Arianna said. "He's a good one. Lucky you."

If I was so good then why hadn't she wanted me?

Arianna turned to me. "What about you? When did you know there was something between you?"

We had this one figured out too. "Oh, I liked her way before that. I was too shy to ask her out."

"Too afraid of rejection, this one," Rob said. "Always been that way. I used to tell him that life was going to pass him by if he never took his chance."

"Once I showed interest, he didn't hesitate," Jamie said quickly. "He was the perfect gentleman, too. Slowly reeling me in until one day I realized I was madly in love with him. No one's quite like him. Such a combination of brains and brawn."

"Reeling you in like a fish," Arianna said, laughing. "So Colorado."

"I know a good thing when I see it," I said. "She's the best thing that's ever happened to me."

Jamie tipped her head to my shoulder. "He's always saying the nicest things. It took me a while to get used to being treated with actual respect and loved for exactly who I am."

"Why aren't you engaged yet?" Arianna's eyes darted from one of us to the other. "Or is it a money thing?"

Ouch. She really knew how to dig at a person right where it hurt.

"Oh, we're engaged." Jamie grinned. "Didn't I mention that part?"

"Where's your ring?" Rob asked. "Or is old Darby still as tight as a USC cheerleader's bottom?"

"Rob, really?" Arianna's mouth pursed the way it did when she was irritated. She wasn't so far gone that she could not see when Rob was behaving like a jerk.

"It's being sized," Jamie said. "He found the most exquisite vintage ring for me. I like pieces that have history, and he found the perfect one."

Was that true? Did she like vintage? I'd have to ask her about that. We hadn't covered that during our preparation.

Our drinks came, and I took a grateful sip from my beer. We then spent a few minutes looking over the menu. Jamie and I both decided on the steak. Arianna said she'd do the fish. "Trying to keep my girlish figure for the wedding."

"Babe, no, not the fish," Rob said. "I'm ordering a cabernet."

"Right." She smiled, but this time the varnish wasn't quite as shiny. "I'll get the steak too."

She hated beef. Strictly fish and chicken for health reasons. I remembered even if she'd forgotten who she used to be.

"Yes, good. I'll get the ribs then," Rob said as he picked up the wine menu and made a great show of looking through the options. "This isn't a bad list. Better than I thought it would be out here."

"People come from all over the world to ski here." Jamie squeezed my knee under the table. "All winter we see the rich and famous walking in town, spending money. This town was built around this mountain, and people come from far and wide to enjoy what the Barnes family started all those years ago. It's quite a fascinating history, actually."

Rob seemed not to hear her, because he didn't look up from the menu. My hands balled into fists. To keep myself steady, I reached over and laid my hand lightly on Jamie's thigh.

He must have decided on what wine he wanted to order because he slammed the leather-bound menu shut and picked up his drink. "So, should we talk about what's really going on here?"

"Babe, not here," Arianna said. "We're having a nice dinner."

"No, old Darby doesn't mind hashing it all out over a drink, do you, buddy?" Rob gestured at me with his glass.

"What are we hashing out exactly?" I asked. "There's not much to say. You were screwing around with my girlfriend behind my back. Which is basically how you roll, isn't it? Didn't you steal the idea for the game from Mikey?"

"Don't be absurd," Rob said. "That was always my idea. He may have written some of the code, but that's my baby."

"And he's been compensated for his contribution," Arianna said. "There's no bad blood there."

"Good for him," I said, enjoying myself. "But that's not really the case here. There's bad blood between us, and we all know it. If you want to talk about it, let's go. What do you have to say for yourself? Either of you?"

Arianna had paled. Her hand trembled when she picked up her glass of scotch. "We didn't mean to hurt you. It just happened. The heart wants what it wants, all that. One day, I just knew I couldn't live without him. I didn't feel that way about you, Darby, and for that I'm sorry."

My stomach hollowed and filled with an ache, that old familiar pain from her betrayal slamming back into my body. She didn't have to say it that way. We all knew she hadn't loved me as she obviously did Rob. Why had she felt the need to do that?

Next to me, Jamie radiated heat. She was mad. This amused me, distracting me from the humiliation for a moment.

"Listen, dude," Rob said. "It's like she said. We fell hard. Did it help that I could give her what you couldn't? She says no. It's just me she wants, not my money. She and I, you know, fit together. Soulmates. And when that happens—when a man meets his destiny, there's nothing either of us could do to stop it."

"Actually, there something," Jamie said. "You could either have walked away or told Darby the truth before you acted on your feelings. At least be honest. Both of you. You behaved badly and now you want to make it seem like Darby did something wrong. It doesn't work that way."

"No one said that," Arianna said. "I know you didn't do

anything wrong, Darby. And she's right. We should have told you the truth instead of sneaking around behind your back."

"How could you do that?" I asked. "Pretend like you still loved me? Let me buy that ring and take you to the beach. Didn't you know I was going to propose?"

"I did." Arianna's knuckles whitened as she clasped her hand around her water glass. "Have you ever started down a path and not known how to get off and go a different direction? I cared about you and believe it or not, dreaded hurting you. I let it go on for too long. I know that. And I'm sorry."

"There you have it." Rob splayed his hands onto the tabletop as if to push it deeper into the floor. "All right then, there it was —the big apology. Now, let's move on. Darbs, I'd love to hear more about your life here in the country."

Darbs. My old nickname. I'd almost forgotten he used to call me that. His mouth smirked every time he said it, as if it were ironic somehow.

"Did you just call him Darbs?" Jamie asked.

"That's what we all called him back in the day. Less feminine than Darby, don't you think?" Rob grinned, reminding me of a child in need of attention who thought the way to get it was by saying smart-mouthed quips.

"I always thought it was because he was so good at darts," Arianna said to Jamie. "He was really good at them."

"Why would we call him Darbs, then, instead of Darts?" Rob shot me a look as if to say, *Can you believe how dumb this chick can be?*

"I thought it was a mixture of the two," Arianna mumbled.

Rob ignored her. "It's pretty here in Colorado—I have to give you that. Now that I'm here, it's a little easier to see you here, Darbs. I never saw you as a rugged type of guy, but it seems like you fit right in."

"Living here doesn't require one to be rugged," Jamie said, loud enough that the table next to us turned to look. "But we do appreciate simple, straightforward, and polite people." The unspoken words were obvious. *And you're clearly not.*

"Don't get me wrong." Rob glanced toward the window. "It's great here. I can see now why all the rich and famous come to ski and look for a moose or whatever. It must be rough to see all the tourists come and go, throwing money around when you're a humble teacher, giving to the community." Rob looked even more pleased with himself for being gracious and kind to poor old Darbs.

"I've done fine," I said. *Pretentious prick.*

"He's a very popular teacher," Jamie said. "With parents and kids. He teaches reading and writing to adults for whom English is a second language."

"What a Boy Scout you are," Rob said. "Master carpenter and saving the old people of Emerson Pass."

"They're not all old," I said under my breath, and then had some of my beer.

"You're so busy," Arianna said. "How do you keep up with it all and still have time for Jamie?"

"I'm not that busy," I said. "The carpentry jobs aren't often, plus my summers are free. Jamie and I are more about quality time than quantity anyway." What did that even mean? This night was wearing thin already.

"This is a close-knit community," Jamie said. "When my inn burned down, the whole town rallied around me and I'd only recently moved here. That might be hard for you to understand, Rob, given what you do."

"What I do?" Rob asked.

"Big corporate money and all that," Jamie said, lifting her chin slightly.

"You're mistaken," Rob said. "My company has a philanthropic element. At least that's what my accountant tells me." He laughed.

"What about your buddy Mikey?" Jamie asked. "You screwed him out of what was rightfully his and everyone knows it."

Rob's face went from smugly pale to outraged red in a second. "What? How would *you* know anything about that?"

"I know how to use a computer," Jamie said. "There were quite a few stories about how he wrote the code and then you ousted him."

"Those stories were exaggerated by the press," Arianna said. "He and Mikey parted ways with no hard feelings, isn't that right, babe?"

"Sure. He made a lot of money for his *actual* contribution," Rob said. "Regardless of what the rumors say. People have been coming for me ever since."

"Ever since when?" I couldn't help but ask.

"Since the IPO," Rob said. "People go insane when there's money involved."

"It's only a rumor that Mikey sued you for firing him and taking credit for all his code?" Jamie asked innocently as the server approached with our first course, a garden salad made with arugula and cherry tomatoes. "Or is that all made up too?"

Rob spoke through gritted teeth. "Like I said, Mikey's been well taken care of for what he did for us, but the man was not the leader we needed to take us public and meet the demands of our stockholders." His mouth twitched upward into a smile. *He looks like a ferret*, I thought.

I took another grateful sip of my IPA. A little tart with a hint of citrus for spice. Kind of like Jamie. If she were a drink, she might be this IPA or a glass of hearty red wine.

Beside me, Jamie nudged me in the ribs. "Don't you agree?"

"I'm sorry, what?" I asked as I stabbed a tomato.

"That you can't believe everything you read." Jamie smiled but her eyes glittered with intensity. "And big money controls the narrative these days, doesn't it?"

"Always has," I said.

"People without it seem to think money's evil," Arianna said lightly. "But we can change the world with our wealth."

"Are you planning on doing that?" Jamie asked. "Saving the world?"

"I have some ideas," Arianna said, tightly. "But right now I'm focusing on the wedding and my business, of course."

"You may or may not like it," Rob said to Jamie. "But the world needs people like me. I'm a visionary and not afraid to make the hard decisions."

"If you say so," Jamie said, as sweet as could be. She could match Rob perfectly that way. Both of them fakes. "Still, I wonder what your ex-partner would say about it all?"

"Funny girl," Rob said without an ounce of humor in his tone.

No matter how much money or how well he dressed, Rob couldn't hide the fact that he was a soulless liar. Men like him won in the short term but someday it would catch up with him. Or maybe not. It didn't really matter much to me or my life. This was the past. Sitting next to me, lighting up the room with her smile and her spirit—was she the future?

No sooner had I thought it than I realized how much I wanted her to be in my life. Maybe forever. Not since Arianna had I been so smitten. This was a good thing. I might have a chance for happiness. The kind that Arianna had with Rob. As much as I disliked him, she was happy, and that was good. I'd truly moved on. I could sit across the table from her and that giant engagement ring and feel nothing but happy for her. That didn't mean I had to like either one of them.

Our main courses arrived. Rob muttered something about the quickness of its arrival after our drinks and asked where the bottle of wine was. The server, who appeared to be shrinking with every interaction he had with Rob, looked desperately over at his bartender, who was in the process of setting a bottle on the counter. "I'll bring it right away."

Arianna looked horrified by the portion and the blood trickling out of her steak. Jamie let out a delighted squeal. "I'm sorry for the cow who had to die for my dinner, but I'm going to enjoy every bite."

The server reappeared with the wine. I watched as his hand shook when he pushed the corkscrew in and tugged it out so fast that several drops of red wine spurted out and landed on my shirt. The poor man looked as if he were going to cry. "I'm so sorry."

"No big deal," I said.

"I can pay for it to be cleaned," the server said.

No, he couldn't. He was living paycheck to paycheck, week to week like most of us. "Dude, I promise, it's not a big deal," I said. "A stain remover will get this out no problem."

"I could send my mom over," the server said.

Jamie laughed. "Could you send her to my house too?"

"No, please, it's not necessary." I gestured toward the empty glasses. "Let's give this a try."

The server poured a small portion into Rob's glass, who then made a big thing of swirling and sniffing before lifting it to his mouth. "Yes, that's fine," Rob said.

I draped my arms around Jamie's shoulders and gave her a quick kiss on her temple. She looked up at me in surprise. "What was that for?"

"For being you."

16

JAMIE

The unexpected squeeze and kiss from Darby had me glowing from the inside out as I gobbled up my steak and a mound of buttery mashed potatoes. Fortunately, the rest of the night went a little smoother. Rob acted less cocky and condescending. Still, I couldn't wait for the night to end and I could leave here with Darby.

We walked to the car hand in hand without talking. The stars had come out while we were inside. Out here by the lodge, they were more visible than in town. At the car, I stood looking up at them for a moment, breathing in the scents of the fall night—dry grass and decaying leaves mixed with pine and fir needles and a hint of a wood-burning fire pit on the other side of the lodge. Voices and laughter from guests enjoying the fire and s'mores punctuated the night.

"Maybe I should have a fire pit," I said as I got into the car. "At the inn."

"I'll build you one, if you'd like." Darby turned on the car but didn't back out yet. "Maybe with river rock or something?"

"That would be lovely."

We chatted about where it would be safe to have one out at

the inn as he pulled out of the lot and onto the road that would lead us back into town.

"You were awesome," he said as we drove into town.

"I was?" I asked, pleased.

"I've been waiting all my life for someone to put him in his place. You knocked him down a few pegs, which he didn't see coming. I've never seen anyone fluster him before."

"Well, good. He deserves to be flustered. He is not a good person."

"He's the worst," he said. "I can't believe I spent so much of my life feeling bad about myself around him. When I saw him tonight I realized that's just part of his thing. He likes to keep people down and off-kilter, and he's a genius at knowing just the right buttons to push."

"I can't believe she's marrying him. Because actually, she's not that bad," I said. "Compared to him, anyway."

"The bar is not too high."

"What was it you saw in her?" I asked. All night, I'd been thinking about that and wondering what it was that had drawn him to her in the first place.

"She's smart and charming. You can see that, right?"

"Yes, I can. But also vapid and not very interesting."

He laughed. "I didn't see her that way at all. The whole time we were together, there was a part of me that wondered when she would leave. Not totally consciously maybe, but I never thought I had what it took to keep her happy for long."

"You were right."

"Yeah, I was."

"I wonder what would have happened if you hadn't felt that way? If you'd been cocky as hell like Rob. Maybe you caused her to leave because you expected it."

He appeared to think about this for a few seconds before answering. "I've never expected much from my life, and I guess we get what we believe we deserve. I don't know."

"Is that why you haven't asked me out until recently?" Lights from a car going the other way illuminated his profile.

"I didn't think you would say yes."

"Well, now you know," I said. "And we can both agree I'm a catch."

"Um, yeah?"

"Meaning, if I'm interested in you, then you must not be all that bad after all." I smiled, flirty and loose from the drinks and my full stomach.

"I guess you're right." He looked over at me for a quick moment. Just then, the car sputtered and lurched. He cursed under his breath and slowed, veering onto the side of the road. The motor coughed and then died. We sat for a moment before he looked over at me. "Well, it looks like this old girl's finally dead. I thought the shop had resurrected her for a few more miles but maybe there's no saving her."

"Do you think so? Maybe it's just the battery? Isn't it almost always the battery?"

"Maybe." He rested his forehead on the steering wheel for a moment. "How am I going to get to work? I can't borrow Breck's truck again. It's too humiliating."

"You can borrow my car," I said. "If you need it."

He turned to face me. "That's really sweet, but last time I checked, you needed your car to get to your own job. I was hoping she'd make it until we got paid for the gazebo job. And now I'm going to have to pay for a tow truck." He rubbed his eyes and scrunched over the steering wheel. "Being broke makes me feel like a total loser."

"You're not a loser." I touched his shoulder. "Don't say that about my friend."

He lifted his head to look over at me. "Can you really look at me and think I have any potential to be a good partner? My father's a criminal. I'm broke. I have no car and student loans galore. I'd never be able to buy you a nice house or one of those big fat rings like Arianna's."

"Your father's a criminal, not you. It's not a crime to be struggling financially."

"No debtors' prisons like there were in the past," he said, with a hint of humor in his tone. "But you know what I mean. Next to a guy like Rob, I don't stand a chance."

"Maybe for Arianna. Not for every woman." I twisted in my seat to get a better look at him. "Not every woman cares about all that."

"Most women do." His face was barely visible in the dark, but I could hear in his husky tone how discouraged he was about life. "Arianna didn't waste any time after she met Rob to make her choice."

"I'd rather be with an interesting man doing something meaningful with his life than married to Rob Wright. He's all wrong, if you ask me. Actually, the guy's a total jerk." I shivered and wrapped my hands around the tops of my bare arms. Without the heater, the cool night air was chilly, and I hadn't brought a jacket. We would have to walk back to town or call a friend to get us. It was already after nine. Our happily coupled friends would probably be in bed watching television and snuggling. Suddenly, a longing filled me. I wanted that with someone. Was it Darby? Could it be him, after all this time? Had he been right in front of me all along? "If it were up to me, I would choose you over him every time. I don't care how fat a diamond he offered. He's pretentious and full of himself and was hellbent on making you look and feel bad tonight."

"He succeeded," Darby said.

"He may have made you feel bad, but he didn't succeed in making you look bad. Not to me. The opposite, in fact." I placed a hand on his thigh. "You seemed smart and funny and really interesting. The kind of man the *right* woman would be grateful to have in their life. Not Arianna." The very thought of Darby with her made me want to claw at a hard object with my finger-nails. "But you have to see it for yourself."

"See what?"

"How great you are. No one can tell you that. You have to believe it in your own heart." I leaned closer. "Now, kiss me before we figure out how we're getting home."

He did as I asked, taking my breath away with the intensity of his mouth on mine. When we pulled away, we were both breathing harder than the moment before. "Thanks for tonight," he said. "You were spectacular. Remind me not to get on your bad side."

"Impossible. You're already in here." I tapped my chest. "Now, who should we text to come get us? I'm cold."

"I'll text the guys and see if anyone would mind coming to get us. I don't think we can get a tow truck this time of night anyway, so we'll have to leave her on the side of the road here."

He pulled out his phone and typed for a moment. "We have a group text. Mostly we give each other grief."

A second later, his phone dinged. "It's Huck. He and Stormi are coming back from dinner with his parents and are going to swing by and get us."

"Great."

"What should we do while we wait?" Darby asked, drawing nearer and stroking my bare arm with his fingers, giving me goosebumps. "Make out like teenagers?"

"I never did that when I was a teenager," I said.

"Really? Why not?"

"I don't know, really. Just wasn't ready. Things were tumul-tuous at home with my dad. His temper made it so we never knew what kind of night we were about to have. It took every-thing to keep it together well enough to get my schoolwork done."

"What was he like?"

I closed my eyes, summoning an image of him from when I

175

was a teenager. He ruled the house with an iron fist with rules like ways to fold towels and hang clothes. If anyone deviated from his instructions, he would grow enraged but never say it out loud. Instead, he would ignore us or say cruel things unrelated to what he was mad about. One night, I came home from an evening studying at my friend Mary's house to find my mom crying at the kitchen island. Stacks of dishes were in the sink. I caught a faint scent of charred meat. An open bottle of wine and a glass were on the countertop in front of her.

I'd rushed to her side. "Mom, what is it?"

She'd looked up at me, her mascara and eyeliner smeared from tears. "I burned the steaks. I left them on Broil and started talking with Max and forgot. You know how charming he can be. Max, you know. Your dad was furious with me. He got so mad he took Max and Stan to a steak house and left me here." She lifted the wine glass to her mouth and drank.

"Did he ridicule you in front of them?" I asked, my stomach churning.

"No, that's not how he is," she said, as if I didn't know. "He pretended like it was fine, all lovey and passive-aggressive." She tossed back a little more wine. Had she had the whole bottle? Not like her. My mother was always perfectly groomed and dressed, never one to draw attention to herself. I hadn't seen her like this before, all smeared and messy and drunk. "And he told the guys I wouldn't be able to join them for dinner because I needed to be here when you got home. They left hours ago. He whispered in my ear on the way out that I should be medicated. Something made for stupid people so they could get their act together."

They do make medicines like that, I thought. My best friend Lottie was on one for her ADD. "Mom, you don't need meds. It's easy to leave a piece of meat under the broiler and have it burn."

She raised bleary eyes to me. "You're a much better cook

than me. You know, I was sitting here thinking about how little I do well. Actually, I couldn't think of one thing."

I sat next to her and drew her into a hug. "Mom, that's not true. He wants you to think that. He wants all of us to think that way. Trey said he barely got out of here alive." I smiled to take the edge off my words, but we both knew the truth. My father had terrorized Trey, just as he did Mom and me. He was subtle but thorough. At the end of the day, we all felt sure we were nothing. Undeserving of the life he'd provided for us.

Now, Darby played with a lock of my hair, drawing me back to the present. "I could hear a whole story without you having to open your mouth just by your expressions." He kissed me, tenderly this time. An emotion stirred inside me, like a tapping on the inside of my chest that made me ache with a combination of longing and gratitude for the sweet man sitting across from me. "I'm right here if you ever want to tell me the dark stories. You can't scare me. Not after growing up with my dad."

"When I was seventeen, I came home to find my mom crying." I told him the story of finding my mother that night. "I heard him come home later and tromp up the stairs. He started in on her—yelled how she'd embarrassed him in front of the other partners. Called her useless for anything but…" I couldn't finish the sentence. Saying it out loud seemed like a betrayal to my mother. *Anything but sloppy sex.*

Darby nodded, murmuring that he understood and that I didn't need to say it. He knew. "Sounds like our dads would be great pals if they'd ever met. Abusive in different ways, but that's what it is nonetheless."

"It took me a while to figure out that not all fathers were this way. Max, for example, was a really good guy." I'd always thought he'd been a little in love with my mom. Had that been part of it, I wondered now? Had my dad picked up on something between them? Had that been the trigger? Or was it really the steaks? Probably the steaks. "Sometimes I worry I'm just like him." I'd never said that to anyone before. "I'm particular about things too. Everything has to be perfect or I get anxious."

"Are you cruel to your staff? Or to boyfriends who aren't quite as tidy as you?"

I chuckled against the dull ache in my throat. "No, I'm not. I have high standards at the inn, but I would never come down on someone for simply making a mistake. It's on me to train them correctly in the first place. Maybe that's how my dad felt? Like he'd done his part and trained us exactly how he wanted things, but then we fell short, which enraged him."

"I know just how that is," Darby said softly. "I wish you didn't, though."

"Do you ever worry you're too broken to be with someone?"

"All the time," he said. "But it's the lie they told us about ourselves that makes us think that. Being with Rob tonight, it all came back to me. The way both he and my dad chipped away at my confidence until there was nothing left of who I really was."

"But they didn't win."

"Seems like they did," Darby said. "Tonight, anyway."

"You're great just the way you are. Better than great."

"Do you always do this? Make people feel better?"

"I'm not sure," I said. "Maybe it depends on who I'm with. You make me feel good. Like I'm more than the sum of my parts."

"Or bank accounts?" Darby asked.

"Yes, right." In the distance, a pair of headlights appeared. "I bet that's them."

I was glad to be rescued, but at the same time knew that what had happened between us had made us closer. "Darby?"

"Yeah?"

"Do you want to stay over tonight?"

He stiffened and turned toward the front window. The headlights, nearly upon us, illuminated his face. A muscle in his jaw twitched. "Is that what you really want?"

"Yes, it's what I want. Do you?"

Slowly, he twisted to look at me. "I don't know that I've ever wanted anything more. At the same time, I don't want to wreck anything."

"We won't." I hoped I was right. Having Darby in my life was starting to feel just right.

———

WE WERE SOON SITTING in the back seat of Huck's car that smelled of new leather and mint gum.

"I think she's a goner," Huck said, referring to Darby's poor car. "I'm afraid to say."

"She's been on borrowed time," Darby said. "I need a truck anyway if I'm going to do construction. I've been borrowing Breck's to haul stuff, but that can't go on forever."

"Let me know and I'll go with you into Louisville to buy something new," Huck said. "I love shopping for vehicles."

"With nothing to trade in, I'm not going to be able to get much," Darby said. "But thanks."

"Do you want to borrow my car until you figure it out?" Stormi asked, turning back to look at us. "I don't really need it since Huck and I drive into work together."

Darby rested his head on the headpiece and shook his head. His hand reached out to find mine. "I have good friends," he said under his breath. "I forget how good sometimes."

"Yeah, we both do."

"You guys want to stop at the grill and get a drink?" Huck asked.

We exchanged a look. "No, we'd like to get home," Darby said. "Big day tomorrow."

Big night, too, I thought.

———

"Good Lord, what was that?" Darby flopped back onto the pillows in my bed. "It was better than I remembered even, and that's saying something."

I was too tired and satiated to move and closed my eyes. "Even better. What is this between us?"

"Extreme chemistry?"

"I guess that's what you'd call it." I rolled over to my side facing away from him, hoping he would curl up next to me.

"Is this okay?" Darby slid into place behind me and draped his arm over my hips.

"Sure. As long as you don't mind?"

"What would I mind?"

"My last boyfriend didn't like to snuggle after sex," I said. "He always rolled to the other side of the bed as if I were too hot or something."

"You are hot." Darby nuzzled my neck.

I giggled. "Not yet. You have to give me a little recovery time."

"How long will that take?" He kissed my shoulder and made circles on my hip with his fingers.

"It's a miracle. I've recovered already."

"A modern medical miracle," he said, pulling me on top of him.

The morning would come soon, I thought, as I wrapped all four of my limbs around him. And I didn't care if I woke tired. Losing some sleep would be worth every moment.

DARBY

I yawned through first period the next morning, and every muscle in my body reminded me of the night before. By lunchtime, I'd decided I would lock my classroom door and take a nap and woke after twenty minutes feeling much better, and even better after another cup of coffee. By the time the last bell rang, I was ready to conquer the second part of my day. The portion that would include Jamie. Thinking of her gave me energy.

After school, I headed out to the inn. Breck had lent me his truck for however long I needed it, for which I was grateful. Once I got the payment for the gazebo project, I could put a decent down payment on something new. Maybe a small SUV? I could picture Jamie and myself in it together as we drove to the park for a run. Then we'd go back to our place and cook dinner and share about our days. I could tell her about my students, and she could relay stories of her customers.

I blinked away the daydream as I pulled into the parking lot of the inn. The sight of Jamie's car made my stomach flutter. *You're a fool for love*, I told myself. *You could get hurt.*

I told myself to shut it and parked in the back, near my

construction site. My muscle aches had subsided and I was ready to get to it. If all went as planned, I'd be done by the end of the week with plenty of time to spare. The wedding was still a couple of weeks away. Jamie would be able to rest easy knowing that all would be just as the bride requested. I wanted her to know she could trust me to do as I promised. In all things, not just the project. The more time we spent together, the more I could see how she watched me for clues for when I would leave or let her down. Not if but when. A distinct difference.

I worked for a good hour, listening to music in my head-phones as I sawed and sanded and nailed. The weather, although sunny, was cold and crisp. A gorgeous fall day that required work gloves and a quilted vest to stay warm. The scent of woodsmoke from the fireplace reminded me why autumn was my favorite time of year, especially in Emerson Pass.

Mostly, I'd kept my insecurities from taking over my brain today. However, as I worked, it worried me that Jamie had not come out to say hello. Was she regretful about the night before? Had we taken it too far and now she was worried about how it would affect the project and our friendship? That one worried me the most. What if she wished she'd never agreed to work with me or spend all this time together?

When I looked up from my work, Jamie was striding across the lawn toward me. I yanked out my earbuds and stuffed them into my pockets. My chest filled with warmth when she smiled at me and waved. Darn, she was gorgeous—all business today with her hair in a bun and dressed in black slacks and a beige turtleneck sweater.

"There's a sexy man in the garden of my inn." Jamie held out a napkin with a gooey-looking cookie wrapped inside. "I thought I better come investigate and see if you needed a cookie."

I pulled her into an embrace. "I'm glad you did. I was starting to think you were avoiding me."

"No, I just got really busy. Lots of check-ins today, which I'm excited about." She wrapped her arms around my neck. "But all I could think about was getting out here to see you."

"Really?" It was as though she could read my mind and knew just what I needed to hear. "I was out here thinking you might have regretted last night. I didn't hear from you all day and you know, my mind kind of spiraled."

"I totally understand." She pressed her mouth to mine. "But that wasn't it. As a matter of fact, I can't stop thinking about last night."

"Full disclosure, I had to take a nap at lunch today. Not that I'm complaining."

She laughed. "I did the same thing in my office. If we meet up tonight, we should try to get a little more sleep."

I doubted I'd be able to keep my hands off her if she allowed me another night in her bed. But I couldn't let the good feelings keep me going. "If we meet up? Would you like to?"

She kissed me again. "I would like to meet up tonight and will even feed you."

My limbs buzzed with joy. She was going to feed me. She wanted to see me. "I'm there."

She pulled me behind a tree to kiss me again, this time a properly messy one. "I'll see you tonight."

Holding hands, I walked her back to the patio. It wasn't until we were at the steps that I saw her. Arianna stood just inside the French doors, watching us. Even with the glare of the window, I could tell she didn't like what she saw.

So much for faking our relationship, I thought. Whatever Arianna had witnessed was real. I was in. Fully in. No one could change my mind about pursuing Jamie, not even Arianna. My broken heart had healed at last. All it took was a few years and the kiss of my favorite innkeeper. If only I'd pursued her earlier.

But no. I wasn't ready then, and maybe she wasn't, either. Now, though, we both seemed willing to see where this could take us. I was grateful.

I lifted a hand to wave at Arianna. She fluttered her fingers at me and plastered a fake smile across her face in tandem.

"Looks like we had an audience." As soon as I said it, I wondered if she'd known Arianna was standing there watching and had come out to give her a show. Or were the kisses real? I inwardly groaned. *Why must I torture myself this way? Take things for what they seem.* It was impossible, though, not to wonder all the time about people's motives and whether they would strike out at any moment.

"Seems that way." Jamie's eyes sparkled, and she squeezed my hand. "No, I didn't know she was there. That's not why I kissed you."

"How did you know I went there?"

"Because I would have too." Jamie turned to face me, giving me another light peck. "We're the same."

"Messed up."

"Messy, for sure. Always looking for the moment when betrayal first becomes evident."

"Yeah, that," I said.

She looked into my eyes. "Maybe this time we won't be left and made to feel like it's our fault." One of her staff came out then and called out to her that they needed a decision on wine for happy hour. "I'll see you later, okay?"

I nodded and watched her prance up the stairs in her black pumps. Those pants clung to all the right places, I thought, as I turned to head back to work. That smile, too. It was as genuine as Arianna's was fake. How had I not known that all along?

I WAS PUTTING the last of my tools in the truck when someone called out to me. Arianna's voice. I turned to see her coming down the steps of the patio. Wrapped in a knit shawl that engulfed her, she seemed cold and way too skinny.

Leaning against the truck, I waited for her. "What's up?" I asked when she was standing in front of me.

"I saw you out here and thought I'd say hello." She hugged herself and shivered. "Got cold all of a sudden, didn't it?"

"Yeah. I hope you have a warm wedding dress."

She ignored that and launched into the reason she was here. "I wanted to say—I'm sorry about last night. I know it was kind of a disaster."

"Seemed fine to me." Liar.

"Jamie doesn't like Rob, that much was obvious."

"Is there a reason she should?" I asked, amused.

"Well, no. It's just I thought it would be good if we could clear the air and all be friends. But after last night, I see that's not going to happen."

"There's too much of a past between us," I said. "My relationship with Rob was really toxic. I see that now. And the one with you was about the same. I used to do that, you know. Surround myself with people who treated me like crap, maybe to prove to myself that my suspicions were correct. I *was* crap. I don't do that anymore."

"I'm sorry if I made you feel bad."

"You wanted me to be someone else. Until you found the one you really wanted. The one who you didn't need to change."

She tilted her head up to the sky, which was that beautiful twilight color of blue with a hint of violet. "I don't know what you thought happened between us that was toxic."

"You cheated on me with my nemesis. How about that?"

"But in the middle, before Rob, did I treat you poorly?"

It was obviously something that bothered her. She wanted absolution so she could walk away, back to her new shiny life, without feeling like a bad person. "You were fine," I said. "Don't worry about it. Marry Rob and have the life you wanted. I'm happy for you."

"Yeah, okay. By the way, Rob was kind of an ass last night. If you could see him like I do, you might understand why. He's jealous of you, and his solution is to try to cut you down."

"Jealous of me? Why?"

"He always has been. The way you are with people, how they flock to you and worship you. He wishes he had that quality. Even if he'd never admit it, I know that's what it is. You remind him of all the things he hates about himself."

Interesting theory. Was she right? Perhaps, but regardless, she obviously knew Rob better than I ever had. "I hope you'll be happy," I said. "Truly. You don't have to feel bad about me anymore."

"I can see you've made a good life here. And Jamie seems good for you. The girl's feisty and wicked loyal. That much was evident last night. She'd defend you to the death. That's the kind of love you need, Darby."

"Isn't that what we all need?"

"Some of us need it more than others, I think." She gazed down at her tan pants tucked into brown riding boots. "That was the thing about us. I couldn't ever be that person for you. You deserve to be with someone who can be."

I nodded and left it at that. "I've got to run. Jamie's expecting me."

"Sure, go. Thanks for all your hard work on this." She gestured toward the gazebo, which now had posts all the way around. I'd put on the roof tomorrow.

Out of nowhere, Arianna thrust herself against me. I stumbled backward as my arms instinctively wrapped around her. She reached up to kiss me, but I moved my face just in time and it landed on my ear.

I put my hands on her upper arms and physically moved her aside. "What are you doing?"

"Saying goodbye?"

"That shouldn't be a question. You said it a long time ago. Go find Rob. There's nothing for you here. I'm madly in love with Jamie. There's a real chance for us to be happy together. Can't you leave it alone? Leave me alone? Haven't you done enough to hurt me?"

I got in the truck and started the engine, expecting her to walk back inside. Instead, she stood watching my truck head out to the road. The slump of her shoulders made me curious. Was she really as happy as she claimed to be?

You know what, I thought. *It's not my problem. Whatever she does is her business. I have my own life.* One that included really good friends and the possibility for real love with an amazing woman. Books and students, too. Life was good. For the first time since the disastrous proposal, I realized how truly rich my life had become, regardless of what was in my bank account.

The only emotion left was one of indifference. She could do whatever she wished to do. I was free. With that came a tremendous burst of energy. I could not wait to see Jamie. I'd splurge and stop for flowers. They were overpriced at the market, but what the heck? Jamie deserved something pretty, something frivolous. We were at the beginning of something wonderful. There was no way I was letting that spoiled, lying woman ruin it. She was a narcissist through and through. I hadn't seen it before. How could I not have? It was so obvious, the way she'd come out there to quash whatever good had come into my life. She didn't want me, but she couldn't just let me be happy. I didn't get it, but I could see it.

Roses or mums? That was the more important question.

18

JAMIE

From the great room of the inn, while my guests mingled over their wine and cheese, I'd watched the interaction between Darby and Arianna. I'd felt like a voyeur and knew I was invading their privacy, but I couldn't look away. *Trust*, I'd thought. *I need to show some trust.* But then Arianna had thrown herself into his arms. From my angle, I hadn't been able to see if they'd kissed on the mouth. *Oh, God, if he kissed her I might die.*

Seething with distrust and insecurity, I moved from the window as Arianna headed across the lawn toward the back entrance. Soon, she would step foot in my sanctuary and my dream come true. Somehow, knowing she and Darby had exchanged words made me wish I could send her back to California, regardless of the extra money she'd brought into my life. She was poison.

But what of Darby? Was he truly over her? What had passed between them? Was there a part of him that still wished for her to be his wife? Had she seen the error in her own judgment when she chose that idiot Rob over Darby? And if so, how would that knowledge change Darby's feelings for me? Was I second best until first place presented itself?

I turned from the window and walked over to a clump of my guests to offer them a refill on their wine, pretending that my insides were not a quiver of nerves.

"Another of the merlot, please?" Mrs. Hennings, who had checked in with her two adult daughters that afternoon, asked me. She was a slim woman in her late fifties and smelled of expensive perfume. They'd come from Washington state and would stay a week. Their annual "girls'" vacation was the highlight of her year, she'd told me when they checked in. This was their first time at my inn. They planned on coming last autumn but unfortunately, the inn was nothing but charred wood by then.

My employee John had left to grab more crackers and another bottle of white. We weren't accustomed to so many guests and had not put out enough. Normally, my nearly full inn would have made me giddy with relief and joy, but I couldn't shake my dark thoughts about Darby. Was he like my dad, ready to leave whenever a shiny object presented itself?

Glad for something to do, I went over to the bar and poured Mrs. Hennings another glass of the Merlot. After delivering it to her, I looked around to see if anyone else needed a refill. The daughters, beautiful young ladies in their early twenties, were curled up together on the couch looking through one of my coffee-table books on historic inns across the world. They were almost finished with their glasses of rosé. I picked that bottle up to give them a refill.

Gerald's piano playing lent a perfect soundtrack to the evening with his achingly beautiful music. Outside, the setting sun's orange glow blanketed the grass and trees. The sprinklers over the grass spurted to life, sending cascading drops of water into the air that sparkled in the silky twilight.

My dozen or so guests took up various locations in the great room. A pair of honeymooners were cuddled in an oversize armchair talking quietly. They had eyes only for each other. As it should be.

A middle-aged couple, celebrating their empty nest, was on the window seat with a puzzle laid out on the coffee table next to them. A group of young women on a bachelorette trip were sitting around one of the round tables, planning out their evening while sipping glasses of white. Another couple, gay men in their forties, were near the piano, clearly enjoying the music.

This was my dream. A reality finally, after all my saving and hard work. Why didn't it feel better? I was still me, I realized. Maybe that was the problem.

Darby would be on his way home. Would he still want to meet later? I itched to pull out my phone and see if he'd texted but kept myself in check. Being present for my guests was my job now. Even if one of them was Arianna Bush, who at the moment had entered the lobby and headed toward the bar.

I met her there, with my bottle of rosé still in hand. "Arianna, may I get you something to drink?" I sounded too formal and slightly suspicious, even to my own ears.

She darted a glance my way, then ran her fingers through her dark hair, which hung straight and shiny down her back. I'd been brave at dinner but now, standing here with her, I wanted to slither away and hide under a rock. How could I ever compete with her? No wonder she was a successful influencer. She glowed.

I hated her.

"I'd love a glass of chardonnay," Arianna said. "But I see you don't have any."

"John will be right back with some," I said. "Would you like a little rosé while you're waiting?"

She made an impatient, almost imperceptible sigh. Had she grown that accustomed to everything coming to her exactly when she wanted it? Was that what wealth provided? Did it make one troubled over the tiniest of inconveniences when everything suddenly appeared whenever they wanted?

I poured her a quarter-full glass of the rosé and tried to think of something to say. "He's making great progress on the gazebo."

"Yes, he is." She drank half of what I'd poured her in one gulp.

"Where's Rob tonight?"

"He went into town where the internet was better. Something for work." A dig? Maybe, but who cared anyway? This was a spoiled, duplicitous woman who thought only of herself. She was dangerous. My sense of sanity wanted to slip away. This was why I didn't become involved with men. They only hurt me in the end. Trey was the only man I could trust to always be there for me. Why had I hoped for anything different? Men leave.

"He'll be back to take me to dinner," Arianna said.

"Good. I hope you'll have a nice evening." I set aside the bottle of rosé. John returned with a tray of cheese and crackers and a bottle of the white tucked under his arm.

"Everything all right, Miss Wattson?" A retired air force pilot, John was in his early sixties with silvery hair and a broad jaw.

"Yes, fine, John. Thank you. Ms. Bush would like a glass of the white, though."

He gave her his best American hero smile before splashing a generous pour into a glass. After she had it in hand, he set out across the room to offer my newlywed couple a refill.

"Thanks again for last night," I said, not meaning a word. "It was a generous thing to do."

"We have the means, so it's no big deal." Arianna's hand shook as she brought the glass to her mouth.

"Is everything okay?" She seemed upset and jumpy. What did

it mean? God, I wanted to just sit her down and make her tell me everything they'd talked about.

"Yes, fine." Her gaze flickered to my face. "Seeing Darby's had more of an effect on me than I thought it would."

My stomach dropped to the floor. This is it. The beginning of the end. Why had I been so stupid? "In what way?" I managed to ask without my voice shaking.

"Are you two really engaged?"

"Um, yeah. Why?" Had he told her the truth?

She looked me straight in the eye. "You don't seem like his type."

"Opposites attract?" Was that what she meant? Or was she implying that she was his type and not me?

"You're not opposites. You're exactly the same. Which I've heard doesn't always mean a good relationship. In the end, couples need to challenge each other. You two seem like a comfortable old pair of shoes. Boredom could set in at any moment." She watched me over her tipped-up glass before placing her glossy lips to the rim. How did she keep that lipstick intact while drinking?

"Things that work," I muttered instead. Like Guy Clark and his Susanna.

"I'm sorry?" Arianna watched me with those big, fabulous, perfectly made-up eyes.

"Nothing."

"I'm going to be honest with you," Arianna said, "and tell you that I don't think Darby loves you. I mean, woman to woman, right? We need to take care of each other."

My throat was so tight I could barely speak. Sweat dampened the palms of my hands. "Why would you say that?"

She leaned toward me, conspiratorially. "You should ask Darby. Hopefully, he'll tell you the truth before he hurts you worse."

"How would you know what he feels?" I asked, quieter than I wished.

"He and I just have one of those relationships. It's special. We understand each other very well."

"If it was so special, then why did you break his heart?"

She hesitated for a moment, and her mouth curled up in a mean-girl smile. The same one I'd seen last night directed at Darby. "Sometimes I wonder that myself. It might have been one of the biggest mistakes of my life."

This was a game to her. It gave her pleasure to mess everything up for anyone she sensed could be happy. She couldn't stand the idea of Darby with someone else even though she didn't want him herself. Insidious, like a virus one didn't know they had. Doing damage, little by little until it was too late to save yourself.

"Does Rob know your feelings about Darby?"

Her eyes flickered, ready for a fight. "Are you threatening me?"

"Threatening you? With what?" I asked, forced innocence in my voice. "That you kissed my fiancé?"

"You saw the kiss, did you?" The same evil cat smile played at her mouth. "I'm so sorry. We should have been more discreet. Of course, I didn't expect anyone to be creepily watching us from the windows."

I crossed my arms over my chest in a gesture of self-preservation. "I'm starting to get you. I see what you're up to."

"Up to? Don't be silly. I consider you a new friend and wanted you to know that Darby may not be telling you the whole story."

"Which is?"

"He's never gotten over me, and this whole thing with you was simply a distraction. Now that he's seen me again, all the old feelings came back. I mean, what did you expect? He told me once that I'm the love of his life. That doesn't go away just because you're sleeping with someone else."

"You don't want him. Why are you messing with him like this?"

"I'm not messing with him. Goodness, you *are* delusional. I'm sorry to have upset you. I shouldn't have said anything. I was trying to help. The same reason I wanted to have the wedding here and the gazebo built."

"To help *me*? How's that exactly?" This woman needed help. She was sick.

"I heard about your troubles with the fire, and I wanted to give you some business."

"What about the sentimental reasons? Your mom and all that?"

"Of course that played into the decision, but it doesn't matter what you think about me. The truth is—I was trying to do a nice thing by having my wedding here instead of the lodge. Everyone knows how much financial trouble you're in here. Once I realized you were a friend of Darby's, I wanted to help even more. I had no idea you were dating until later."

"How did you know I was a friend of Darby's?" Did she mean before she came to the inn and asked about booking her wedding here? "When did you know that exactly?"

"I know about his life here. I keep tabs on him."

"But how? How would you know about me?"

"Fine, I knew about you back in Cliffside Bay. I went looking for Darby that night I broke up with him. I was worried sick about him. I saw the two of you leave that bar and I followed you back to the resort—saw you go up to his room together. Then, recently, I saw photos of you and him online and figured you had followed him out here. Or the other way around. He's like a puppy dog that way. Once he gets even a pat on the head, he loves you forever."

"He's not online." Something about this wasn't adding up. In fact, she wasn't making any sense at all. She'd just told me he didn't love me, and now he was a puppy following me around. "He purposely got off social to avoid you."

"It was a photo of the two of you at that art opening. Rob knows Crystal, or knew her late husband, and wanted to support her by buying a piece of artwork from the gallery. Stormi had an online version of the opening so that people could see the art without having to be there. You two were standing near a painting, obviously together. I was delighted that he'd finally moved on. That was before I knew the full story."

It took me a moment to place what she was referring to. Then it came back to me. The art gallery opening. We'd all been there to support Crystal and Stormi. Darby and I had talked for a few minutes that night in front of a painting we both liked. That had been one of our only interactions that evening, but apparently, it had been captured in a photo. She was right. I had felt an attraction that night. Maybe he had too? As the reality of what she was saying to me sank in, a sick feeling in the pit of my stomach overwhelmed me. This was a dangerous woman in front of me. She was not at all what she'd seemed to be. Not now or two years ago when she'd been dating Rob behind Darby's back. Again, it occurred to me that this was a fun game to her. How many lives could she mess with before it was all finished?

"What do you want?" I asked. "For real. You came to town to see Darby. To rub it in his face that you bagged Rob Wright. But then once you arrived and saw him again you realized that it wasn't enough to let him be? You needed to know if you could still get him back. But why? I don't get that part. You got Rob and broke Darby's heart. Wasn't that enough?"

"You're being really weird right now," Arianna said in her well-honed gaslighting voice. "None of what you said is true. I was trying to be nice and give you some business. It was the least I could do for Darby's new girlfriend. I have so much and you have so little. Gosh, it seemed like the right thing to do. I had no idea he would be the one to build the gazebo. That was a happy coincidence, because it's obvious he really needs the work. Poor baby. One can't live on passion alone. I mean for his work, not you."

"No wonder the men didn't know what you were doing. Or who you actually loved. You talk in circles until the other person starts to believe it's them with the problem. Did you take some kind of gaslighting course at influencer school?"

"Don't be ridiculous." She set down her glass of wine. "Anyhoo, I must run. I'm meeting Rob for dinner." She squeezed my arm. "But sweetie, for your sake, please ask Darby about our exchange this afternoon. You deserve someone who's honest with you. I can't bear to see someone as nice as you get hurt, especially when this business venture of yours is so tenuous." She clucked her tongue. "I really do feel for you."

With that, she turned on one high-heeled designer boot and left the room. I remained, shaking and wondering what the heck had just happened, coming out of my stupor only when John asked me a question. I turned to him and tried to focus on what he was saying. All of this would have to be sorted out later. I had a business to run.

But even as I gave myself these instructions, I couldn't shake the sense of impending doom. I would have to ask Darby about what happened between them. And I would have to be strong enough to hear what I'd feared all along. He loved Arianna. Not me. No matter how good it seemed from my side, he was obviously pining away for someone else. A sick, manipulative nightmare of a woman. If that was who he chose, even though she would stomp on him again, then he wasn't the man for me anyway. The sooner I knew, the better. I was fine. I would be fine. It wasn't as if we were dating for a year or something. Not as we'd pretended to be. When did the line between make-believe and truth blur?

I drove home from the inn about an hour later, alternating between tears one moment and overwhelming rage the next. It was twenty-to-eight by the time I arrived at my apartment. He would be here any moment, and I had nothing to cook. I'd been so distracted I'd forgotten to stop at the store. But it was for the best. I was not cooking for a man about to leave.

19

DARBY

I knew something was wrong the moment I stepped inside her apartment. Despite being an obtuse male, I picked up on the clues right away. For one thing, there were not the usual good smells coming from the kitchen. Secondly, she stiffened when I tried to embrace her. Thirdly, she wouldn't meet my eyes. Fourth, she didn't even notice the flowers, or if she did, was choosing not to comment.

"Hey, everything all right?" I asked.

"I'm fine." She hugged her middle, as if protecting herself. From what? Me? What had happened?

"Did you just get home?" I gestured lamely toward the kitchen and stepped inside the apartment. *Nice, Darby. Ask her why my dinner wasn't made like a total idiot.*

"Not long ago." Jamie shut the door behind her. "After an interesting talk with Arianna."

I froze. What had she done now?

"Telling me all about your kiss. Which don't bother to deny. I saw you."

"That was not a kiss," I said, thinking as quickly as I could. "She tried to kiss me."

"It seemed she succeeded." She moved away from the door. Better than shutting it in my face, I suppose.

"She didn't. Trust me. I made sure she knew it was not a welcome advance." I moved toward her with my hands out in front of me. "Whatever she told you was probably a lie. You know that by now, don't you?"

"The question is, do you know that? I can't decide if she's still duping you or not. After the other night, I thought things were...I thought there was something real between us."

"It was last night," I said as gently as I could. "And from my perspective, there *is* something special between us. Whatever you think you saw with Arianna—it's not what happened." For a moment, I quieted, searching for the right words to convince her of my innocence. "She came out there with an agenda. I don't know why, but she doesn't want me to be happy with someone else. Even though she didn't want me. Doesn't want me."

She collapsed onto the couch. Her hands gripped the edge of the cushions. "Darby, I don't know if I can do this."

My heart stopped. It was coming. Of course it was. How was I stupid enough to think this would work out for me? Add Arianna into the mix, purposely misleading Jamie, and I stood no chance. Anger bubbled up from deep inside me. I hadn't known how much of the hot black tar lived in me until this very moment. Arianna Bush had nearly ruined my life the first time. Now, when things were actually looking up for me, she had arrived to torture me further. "Do what exactly?" My voice sounded flinty and defensive. Already my protective layers were hardening. Soon, no one would be able to get in. I would not make the same mistake. Not again.

"I don't want to be a fool," Jamie said. "Or get hurt when you decide you're still in love with her. Or maybe you've already decided that. I don't know. All I know is this doesn't make me feel safe. And I want that, Darby. I want to be able to trust you with my heart, and right now it doesn't seem like I'll ever be able to."

"There's nothing between us. She's nothing to me, other than a source of intense anger. I'm sorry she got to you. I should have known and called you right away to explain what really happened."

"What did happen?" She lifted her eyes for a second before returning to gaze down at her knees. Such pretty knees, poking through the ripped denim.

"She told me a bunch of crazy stuff about missing me and that you and I weren't a good match. I can't remember half of what she said. I just wanted to get away from her."

"I need a little time to think," Jamie said.

"Okay. Sure." For God's sake, I might cry right here in front of her. "Jamie, I would not hurt you. Not if I could help it." I sat on the edge of the coffee table, feeling sick to my stomach.

"That's just the thing. Even if you don't mean to, you will. I'm not strong enough to fall in love with you and have you leave. Not when I finally have my life back on track."

"This is a matter of trust. If you can't trust me, then we have nothing. You're right about that." I stood, having aged a thousand years since I'd come in here so happy and excited to see her. "You're wrong about me. For the record. I'm the most loyal guy in the world. How do you think I got involved with Arianna in the first place? I was too stupid to see her for what she really is, and she's succeeded in ruining my life one more time."

I still had the stupid flowers in my hands. I placed them on the table. "I'm sorry you won't give this a chance. I really am."

I walked toward the door, hoping she would call me back. She didn't. So I walked out of there and down the hallway to my apartment. Eyes stinging, I unlocked my door and went inside, only to collapse on the floor. Leaning against the closed door, I let my head fall to my knees. *Just feel it*, I thought. *Feel the disappointment and hurt. Don't run from the pain.* I'd taken a chance, and it had proven to be a mistake. But I couldn't let it wreck me forever, living in a shell as Jamie had chosen. Arianna had taken away a lot from me. I would not let her take anything further.

———

I WASN'T hungry but knew I should eat something if I was going to have another beer. I'd already sucked down one, staring at the wall and wondering how I'd fallen so fast and hard for the girl down the hall. Talk about the girl next door.

With a bag of pretzels in one hand and a new bottle of beer in the other, I wandered over to my futon and sat. I took a swig of beer, then turned on the television. Maybe there would be a new PBS show to watch. Anything to take my mind off Jamie.

My phone had buzzed several times and my heart had leaped with hope. But it was not Jamie. One text was from Arianna, asking if we could talk.

I might have gotten you in a little trouble with your girlfriend.

You did. Big trouble.

I deleted the message. Then I blocked her. I should have done that a long time ago. Funny that this was the first time she'd texted me since we broke up. It took me having someone else that had awakened this sudden affection.

She was mentally ill. That's all there was to it.

The next text came in from Huck.

You okay?

Yeah. Jamie dumped me. Thinks I'm still hung up on the wicked witch of the west.

Nothing came back for a few minutes, other than those three dots indicating that someone was writing back. Finally, another one popped into the feed.

I'm sorry. That wasn't what I meant, though. You haven't seen the news? About your dad?

What now? I thought. Had he appealed or something? Before

I could text back, the phone buzzed again. This time with a live call from Huck.

"Hey," I said.

"Listen, you might want to sit for this."

"I'm already sitting."

"Okay, well, the thing is—I just saw it come over the AP wire. They found your dad this morning in his cell. He took his life, man. I'm sorry."

It was as if someone had kicked me hard in the stomach with a steel-toed boot. I started to shake. *Not that, Dad. Not that.*

I took in big gulps of air as I stared down at the beer bottle between my knees. The end of his life. Just like that. How had he done it? Did I want to know? Was all this happening while I was at school or later when I was trapped by Arianna in the garden? What did it matter? He was dead. He'd chosen to leave me long before this. We were no longer family. Not if love is what made one. Yet he was my father. The only living relative I had left. No longer.

Could I blame him? Facing prison after what he'd done?

A sob rose up out of my chest. No, I could not let it get to me. He was nothing to me any longer. But a voice whispered to me. *He was your dad. He gave you life and a home, fed you and kept you warm.*

But what kind home had he raised me in? One of fear and anxiety. Where love was transactional. Every moment an uncertainty of what would come next.

Why, then, was I crying like a baby?

———

HALF AN HOUR LATER, I'd finished crying into my beer and was now working on another one. I hadn't been able to keep myself from pulling out my laptop to do a search. It wasn't hard to find. The headlines said it all.

Fallen cop found dead in cell.

Disgraced cop dead from hanging.

The details described a suicide watch. They must not have watched him very carefully, since he'd done it with a sheet.

I thought about the last time I'd seen him. My high school graduation night, I'd come home from the ceremony to change for a party. He hadn't been there. A shift had kept him from attending. I'd told myself I didn't care. His work was more important than seeing me walk across the stage. He was uncomfortable with formal ceremonies. All the excuses I could think of didn't keep me from knowing, deep down, the truth. He was not interested in seeing me do much of anything, even graduate.

I was surprised to see him in the kitchen. He had a whiskey bottle open on the table alongside a bag of pork rinds. Disgusting. He stood with his back against the counter and raised his glass when I came in. "To the graduate."

"What are you doing home? I thought you worked tonight?"

"I was sent home."

"Why?" My mouth fell open. Sent home? What did that mean?

"Some bullshit thing about excessive force, son." He rubbed a hand over his closely cropped hair. Lately, I'd noticed the crevices on the sides of his mouth had deepened and his hair was starting to turn more and more silver. When he was like this, drunk and sour, he seemed older than his forty-five years. "They want us to act like little girls. Like pansies. And treat criminals like they should be at a resort instead of jail where they belong. The world's all upside down, kid." He stared blankly at the wall behind me. "Sometimes it seems like I don't fit anywhere anymore."

I gritted my teeth. What should I say that wouldn't make him mad? In this kind of mood, he was feeling sorry for himself and appeared cowed and docile, but I knew that he could change in a split second. Anger was still his favorite gear.

"What? Got nothing to say? You too good for me now? You're always siding with the rest of them, aren't you?"

"The rest of them?" Who was that exactly? I could decide all on my own that I hated him and feared him and wished he was different and loved him too. That was the thing. No matter what he did, he was still my father.

No sooner than I'd had that thought than he threw his glass against the wall about a foot from my head. Then he lunged at me, putting his hands at my collar and shoving me against the wall hard enough to knock the wind out of me.

"You think you're better than me, don't you?"

"No, sir. I do not." I could barely speak. The palm of his hand pressed into my neck. My Adam's apple throbbed against the force. He put his whole body into it, as they'd taught us at football practices. Commit to it, they'd said. My father knew how to hunker right into it.

His eyes had the glazed, enraged look they got when he was just about to start hitting my face. I'd wanted to go to the party, but I wouldn't be able to if my face was all banged up and bloody. I braced myself as the first punch came, knocking my head against the wall with the force of his fist to my chin. The second blow was to my nose.

Out of the corner of my eye, I noticed a movement outside the windows. Rob. He was here to pick me up for the party in his new car. Why had I agreed? Now he would see the truth.

My father jumped away from me. I wiped under my nose. Blood was everywhere.

Rob, outside the window of the kitchen door, seemed frozen in shock. I'd never told anyone what my father did to me. Not even Rob.

Without another word, my dad picked up his whiskey bottle and left the room.

That night, after Rob helped me get cleaned up at his house and lent me a new shirt, I told him how bad it was and that it had gotten worse. He'd offered his house for the summer. His parents were hardly ever there. We could have a summer of parties before we left for college.

Now, as I sat here, remembering that night, it occurred to me that Rob's behavior that night had been one of the reasons I overlooked so much of his poor behavior. He'd been supportive and considerate. I'd cried at the beach party and he'd been kind to me.

I didn't move in with him that summer, but I did leave my father's house the next day. I left him a note, saying I would not be back. I'd earned a scholarship for college. I didn't need him for anything. And that day had felt like the first day I'd ever felt freedom. I never had to see him again. He could no longer hurt me.

But he did hurt me. Memories last longer than bruises. All these years, I'd been running from those memories, trying to build a new life for myself based on love and good work. *You've done that*, I told myself. *You made your own way.*

If only Jamie could find her way out of her past, her memories, and see that I was right here in front of her offering her everything I could possibly give her. My heart.

But she didn't want me. Or she was too afraid. Either way, I was alone on the night of my father's death. Trying to make sense of my life and what to do next, just as I'd always done.

2 0

JAMIE

I couldn't believe what I was seeing on television. Darby's father had died in prison. Before I could fully absorb what had happened, my phone rang. *Stormi.* She would be calling to see if I'd seen the news yet. Concerned, obviously. I didn't pick up, though. I couldn't trust myself to talk and not completely lose it.

Instead, I sent her a quick text to tell her I couldn't talk but would call her later. *And yes, I saw the news.*

What should I do? I asked myself this as I paced around my apartment. As hurt and angry as I was about what I'd seen earlier between Darby and Arianna, I was also concerned about him. Would he be comforted by her? Maybe she was at his apartment right now, offering solace and support with her body.

My stomach churned at the thought of them together.

I went to the window and opened it a few inches to let some of the cool autumn air into the room. Breathing deeply of the pine-scented evening, I closed my eyes and leaned my forehead against the window frame.

A sudden knock on my door startled me. Hustling to the

door, I yanked it open with unnecessary force. Rob Wright stood in the hallway, dressed all in black jeans and a turtleneck. He wanted to look like Steve Jobs, I guessed.

"What do you want?" I didn't need to pretend to be nice or to act as if I liked him. He'd shown me who he was at dinner. How betrayed I felt by Darby at the moment made no difference in my opinion of Rob.

"I saw the news."

"And?" I raised both eyebrows.

"I called Darby, but he's not answering his phone. I'm concerned."

"Okay." I glared at him. Apparently, he wasn't getting the hint, because he didn't move.

"Can I come in? I'd really like a chance to talk to you. Clear up a few things."

"Fine." I stepped back to let him inside, then shut the door behind us.

"I thought he'd be with you," Rob said.

"We had a fight. You might want to ask your fiancée why."

Rob rubbed his eyes. He looked terrible, unshaven and red-eyed. "Yeah, about that—she's a complicated woman."

"Complicated? Is that what we're calling it?"

He paled and sank down onto my couch. "She has some issues."

"And what are those exactly? That she's a total narcissist and a liar?"

He sighed and looked around the room as if he wanted a drink. I didn't offer him anything.

"What are you doing with her?" I asked. "Other than you seem to love besting Darby. Is that what this is for you? A way to win?"

He ran a hand through his already disheveled hair. "It might have been at first. Darby and I used to compete in a lot of ways, including girls. They always loved him and thought I was a total nerd. I went to college and reinvented myself, you know? So I could be the one the girls noticed. When Arianna showed up in his life, I was floored by her. Absolutely besotted."

"Besotted?" What a weird word to use. A pretentious word, just like him.

"Obsessed. Was it because I wanted to steal her from Darby? Maybe. But I fell for her. Hard. I've never been as consumed with a woman in my life. I had to have her."

"Even though you had to betray your best friend to do it?"

"Even then." He splayed his hands over his kneecaps. "I'm not proud of it. In fact, I acted like a complete ass last night because I'm deeply ashamed. Especially when I saw how well he was doing. With you and his work. He found a home here, and God knows he needed one after his father."

"I saw them kissing." It came out like a confessional.

"You saw her attempting to kiss him," Rob said. "There's a difference."

"How do you know that?" A twinge of hope rose in me.

"I have people who keep an eye out for her," he said. "More security than anything."

"But also your spies." This guy was as psycho as his girl-friend. They deserved each other.

"I guess you could call it that. If you were feeling unkind."

"Don't talk to me about kindness." I narrowed my eyes, trying to understand this man before me. He paid people to watch Arianna. But why?

"It's not that I don't trust her," Rob said.

"But you don't?"

"I don't, no. She's troubled, I get that. She has this unquench-able need for love and attention. When she saw how in love Darby is with you, she couldn't help herself. She had to prove to herself that she could still get him."

"Have you confronted her about this?"

"Yeah, we had a really big fight just now. But she did admit to me that she can't stand the thought of him with anyone else, even though she chose me. I don't expect you to understand. I don't myself. All I know is that I love her and accept her as she is. I've got my own issues, as you probably witnessed."

"Control. Distrust. Pretentiousness. Cruelty even—when it comes to Darby anyway. Should I continue?"

He grimaced. "No, I think that's enough. It's stupid, the way I feel so competitive with Darby. If you'd known us back in the day it might be easier for you to understand. He was the golden boy. Great athlete and student. Teachers loved him. Girls worshipped him. Guys dug him. He had all the friends and the bright future and all of it. I was a geeky little wannabe hanging on to him for dear life. Still, as much time as we spent together, he never told me what was going on at home."

"What do you mean?" I sharpened. What was he about to say?

"He never told me about his dad. About how bad it was. I didn't know until graduation when I saw what was happening myself." He shuddered, as if the memory still scared him. For a slight second, I saw him as he must have been then, skinny and nervous and socially awkward. How had he and Darby become friends in the first place?

It didn't appear that he was going to elaborate, so I prompted him. "What do you mean—what was happening?"

"You don't know?" He seemed surprised.

"I know a little, but I'd like to hear it from you. Darby downplays it."

"Yeah, that's what he did back then too." Rob ran the palms of his hands against his thighs. "It was the night of our high school graduation. My parents had gotten me a car as a gift and I offered to pick Darby up for the party. When I got there, I waited for him to come out but after a few minutes, I decided he must not have heard me drive up. I went up to their back door off the kitchen. That's when I saw it with my own eyes. His dad was whaling on him—beating the crap out of him. Blood was coming out of Darby's nose, but his dad didn't stop." He closed his eyes. "I can see it like it was yesterday. Mr. Hanes just kept hitting him. Darby put his arms up to defend his face but it seemed half-hearted, as if he knew it was no use to try to protect himself. Like he'd been there many times before." He opened his eyes and looked straight at me, but his gaze was toward the past. "Darby just stood there, taking it. It was a regular occurrence. That much was obvious. All the bruises over the years suddenly made sense. He always made excuses about football practice or a baseball or he tripped in the middle of the night. I never thought anything of it except that sporty guys were often bruised or scraped. I don't know why it never occurred to me. Except that I never imagined a cop would be bad. Isn't that stupid? I mean, I'm a smart guy, but I'm also simple. To me, all cops were good. They were not child abusers."

"Yeah, right." I'd thought that as a child too. But as in all professions, there were good and bad people. Mostly good. I hoped, anyway. "Darby's told me he didn't want anyone to know when he was a kid. Not even you."

He nodded. "That night, we talked, and I told him to get out of there and never look back."

"That's what he did." I gave him a long, hard look. "I don't understand how the same person who told him to get away and helped him do so would then steal his girlfriend later."

"Because love is messy," Rob said. "I love Arianna. I'd do anything for her. I had to have her. It felt like life and death. As much as you might think so, I didn't purposely hurt Darby. Was I jealous of him growing up? Yeah. Do I see everything as a competition? Yes. But Arianna, she was different. It wasn't about winning. I love her."

"Even knowing what you know about her?"

"Even then." He stood, seeming a little unsteady on his feet. "Will you check on Darbs? I know him. He's hurting right now.

This will put him back years on the progress he's made to separate from that bastard. He'll talk to you. You're probably the only one who could provide comfort to him. And as far as whatever you think you saw between Arianna and Darby—it wasn't what it looked like. She told me Darby said he's madly in love with you and can see now that what happened between them was for the best."

"He said that?"

"Why should that surprise you?" Rob stared at me with those intense eyes.

"Because your fiancée told me that something had happened between them today. She went out of her way to make sure I knew and acted like she was helping me by telling me the truth. What are you doing with her?"

He fiddled with the silver bracelet on his wrist. "Like I said, I can't live without her. I have a feeling Darby feels the same way about you. The way he was last night—the way he looked at you —he never looked at Arianna that way. Even before he knew about us."

I walked him to the door. Before he left, I put my hand on his arm. "Be careful, Rob. Don't let her wreck your life."

"I will." He smiled and for the first time since I'd met him, I softened toward him. Just a little, mind you. He was still the jerk who stole Darby's girl and spent way too much energy making him feel bad about himself. All because of his own insecurities. How often we let them rule our decisions instead of love, I thought, as I escorted him out of my apartment.

I KNOCKED on Darby's door a few minutes after Rob left. Suddenly, I couldn't wait another moment to see him. He'd told Arianna he loved me. Was that part of the act? Was it true?

"Who is it?" Darby asked from behind the closed door.

"It's Jamie."

The door opened, and he looked at me with puffy red eyes. "What do you want?" Guarded and hurt. Alone.

"I heard about your dad."

"Yeah." Wooden and without emotion. So unlike his usual warmth. It took me aback and made me want to run away. But no, I needed to at least tell him I was sorry.

"I'm sorry I overreacted about Arianna. If you'd heard her, though, you might have gotten scared too."

He stared down at the floor. "Is that it?"

"No. Darby, can I come in? We should talk."

He backed up and I slipped past him. There were three empty beer bottles on the coffee table. The windows were open, making the room uncomfortably cold.

"I'm sorry, Darby. I got scared."

He plopped onto the couch and picked up one of the bottles and dipped it backward into his mouth and then set it back on the table. "Empty."

"Shall I get you another one?" I sat down next to him on the couch.

"I shouldn't. I have to work tomorrow." He still had barely looked at me.

I turned to face him and put my hand on his knee. "She's a psycho. You should hear what she said to me." I described as best I could her strange circular conversation, including her confession to knowing I was his girlfriend. "Or, she assumed we were because of the photograph. She didn't say it but I think she came here to stir up trouble for you. All in all, she wanted to put doubt in my mind about the two of us."

"But why would she do that?" Darby asked. "Why bother? She got what she wanted. Why can't she just leave me alone?"

"You know her better than me," I said. "What do you think?"

"She's a narcissist who craves drama in her life. In this case, she had to create some because there wasn't any."

"You can be sad. I'm going to be right here." I teared up, anxious and uncertain of what to do next.

"I thought it was over between us. I'd let myself fall for you. I'd broken all the rules I'd made for myself, but I thought it was okay because you seemed to feel the same way. There's such an ease between us that's natural and good. And then here come Rob and Arianna to make me miserable one more time."

"For what it's worth, Rob does care about you." I explained what Rob had said about feeling jealous of him. "He said you had it all—friends, girls, sports, and grades." I ticked them off on my fingers. "And he was a nobody. A geek."

"He *was* really geeky, but I liked him because he was smart. It wasn't until later, when we were in high school, that he started undermining me. He's not well, either."

"They deserve each other," I said. "As long as they stay away from us, I couldn't care less."

"Us? I like the sound of that."

"I do too." I placed my hand over his. "Can you forgive me?"

He nodded as his face crumpled into tears. "I needed you. Only you. Huck called to tell me. He'd seen it come through his feed at work. I don't know what to do with this. He left me with one final blow, didn't he? This…this is…unimaginable. I don't care about the man, so why is this hitting me so hard?"

I put my arms around him and tucked his head against my chest. "Because it's your dad and this has been really awful."

"When I think about him all alone in that cell—it's too much. I can't figure out what to think or do. How am I supposed to process this when I haven't seen him in so long?" He paused for a moment, taking in a shuddering breath. "That last night I saw him, I thought he was going to kill me. If Rob hadn't come just then, he might have. Rob can be a jerk and you're right, he goes out of his way to make me feel bad about myself, but he saved me that night. He and his mother helped me come up with a plan to get away from my dad. I will never forget that."

"I know. He told me the whole story tonight," I said. "He said he hadn't known until then."

"I did a great job hiding the bruises. Do you know I even perfected using concealer to cover my purple spots?"

"Oh, baby, I'm so sorry."

"I am too. I'm just so sad," Darby said. "I don't want to be sad. He doesn't deserve it."

He sobbed, shoulders shaking. I let him cry it out and when he was done jumped up to get him a wad of tissues.

"I'm here now," I said. "If you want me, that is."

He lifted his tear-soaked eyes to mine. "I want you. Very much. I thought she'd ruined this wonderful thing in my life. I'm in love with you for real. No faking."

"I think I'm in love with you too," I said. "Although it's a little early to know for sure."

"Give me a chance to prove to you how right I am about us?" Darby asked.

"Yes. Yes, I will."

I climbed onto his lap and kissed him and was about to go in for more when his stomach growled. Laughing, I got up to scare something up for dinner.

21

DARBY

A week went by without mishap. I finished the gazebo and was quite pleased with how it turned out, even if it was for my ex-best friend and girlfriend. Rob had reached out several times but I hadn't called him back. Maybe someday I would contact him, but for now, I didn't need the toxicity in my life.

We were surprised when Arianna left a note for Jamie at the inn the day after the gazebo was finished.

Dear Jamie,

I've decided it's not good for my mental health or that of my relationship with Rob to have the wedding here. I'm sorry about the gazebo. But hopefully this check will make up for it.

Best,

Arianna

"Can you believe it? After all the trouble we went through?" Jamie asked, cheeks pink. "She actually paid in full. I wasn't sure she would pay at all."

"It's kind of her usual mode of operation but we lucked out," I said. "Thank God she's moving on from us. I feel sorry for the next people she ensnares, though."

"Me too."

We happily took our share of the money. I was able to buy a new vehicle, a truck this time, to make my construction projects easier. Jamie paid off all of her credit card debt and still had enough left over to put aside for a rainy day.

Then, around Thanksgiving, another surprise came. This time from my dead father. One day my phone rang with a number from California. I almost didn't answer, figuring it was a sales call. I'm glad I did. The call was from my father's estate attorney. My father had sold his house before his prosecution to pay for attorney bills. However, even after everyone was paid, there was a sum of two hundred thousand dollars, which he'd left to me.

To say I was stunned would be an understatement. There was no letter to go with the money. No explanation or apology. But the old man had left me money.

"In a million years, I wouldn't have predicted it," I said to Jamie that night.

"This is amazing. I'm glad for you. Maybe you can buy a house now."

I grinned. "My thoughts exactly. I have someplace I want to show you."

The next afternoon, I drove her out to the Barnes property. A cottage not far from the main house had been empty for years. Mr. Barnes said it would need to be gutted and completely redone. But would I be interested? He asked for much less than he could make on the open market. Since I could do a lot of the work myself, I jumped at the opportunity.

Now, I pulled down the driveway toward the cottage. Mr. Barnes had said we could take care of the sale when I had the money in my account and had given me the keys to the place.

Snow had begun to fall as we'd headed out of downtown and was sticking. We would have snow for Thanksgiving.

"Where are we?" Jamie asked as she got out of the car.

"This is my new cottage. Well, a very old cottage that needs a ton of work."

"Darby, really?"

"Yes, and I want you to see it and help me pick out the finishes and everything else." I took her by the hand and almost dragged her onto the porch.

Once we were inside, I explained about my deal with Mr. Barnes as she looked around the empty cottage. "This is where Flynn and Shannon lived with their family," I said.

"He's the one who opened the mountain for skiing, right?"

"That's right." I took her down the narrow hallway, showing her the two bedrooms and then the kitchen, which had not been updated since the seventies. Remnants of the pink flowered wallpaper remained, but the avocado-green appliances had been hauled away. "Out back, they had the prettiest garden, according to Mr. Barnes. Flynn liked to build things, just like me." I explained to her about how I would take out the wall between the living room and kitchen to make a great room. "And upstairs there's another bedroom and a small space that would be perfect for my office." I showed her some of the details, like the hardwood floors that I planned on keeping and refinishing. There were arched entryways, and the fireplace was made from river rock.

"Can you do all this yourself?"

"I'll need a little help from my friends," I said. "But Huck and Breck have already volunteered. Isn't that the best?"

"They are, yes." Jamie smiled. "I'll be happy to help you pick out interiors, but we'll get my brother to help too. He'll do it for my boyfriend."

"Come on. Let's go outside. I want to show you the garden before it gets covered with snow."

We went down the hallway and out through the kitchen door. The garden was contained behind a sagging wooden fence. A fire pit and the brick patio remained.

"Strangely enough, this has all held up really well for a hundred years," I said. "We can landscape this out here and maybe even put in an outdoor kitchen."

Jamie's eyes lit up, obviously pleased for me. Her gaze traveled to a picnic basket I'd brought out earlier that day. "What's that for?"

"I thought we'd have a picnic." I gestured toward the fire pit, where I'd made a tepee of kindling over some newspaper. I'd brought two camping chairs out as well. "We can sit out here if you'd like?"

"This is very romantic." She put her arms around me and kissed me before taking a seat.

After lighting the fire, I brought over the picnic basket and took out a bottle of bubbly and the sandwiches I'd picked up from Brandi's bakery. Amazingly enough, despite the falling snow, the fire burned hot. I tossed a few logs on and then set the basket by her feet. "Oh, that's strange. There's something else in here." I opened both flaps to show her the small blue box tucked into one of the wine glasses. "What do you think that is?"

Her eyes widened. "Um, I don't know."

I took the box out and knelt at her feet. With the sky dropping fat, dry flakes that caught in her hair, I proposed with the diamond I'd bought her with some of the money my dad had left me.

"Will you marry me and come live with me in this cottage and raise a family and grow old together?"

"Darby, really?"

"Yes, really."

Her eyes glistened. She nodded, clearly unable to speak. "Yes," she managed to croak out.

"Thank God. I was worried maybe I was jinxed when it came to proposals."

Her laugh rang out in the quiet yard. "You had the wrong girl before."

"And now I have the right one. Give me your hand, please." She did so, and I slipped the princess-cut solitaire on her finger.

"It's beautiful," she said. "But it's so nice. Should you have spent the money?"

I reminded her about the money my dad had left, along with Arianna and Rob's guilt money. "There was enough to get the one I wanted for you. I figure it's something good from the money of a man who hurt me my entire life. The only nice thing he ever did for me. This is a fresh start."

"For me too," Jamie said, still admiring her new diamond. It looked even better on her delicate hand than it had in the box. The diamond sparkled as brightly as her eyes.

We had our picnic and talked about the future and what kind of wedding we would have. "Small and at the inn," I said. "Maybe in the gazebo."

We had a good laugh about that.

The snow ceased, leaving us in silvery light. Warmed by the fire, we snuggled close together and dreamed the dreams of lovers. I hadn't thought it possible to be this content, with our whole lives ahead of us. Together. That was the best part of all.

22

JAMIE

After Thanksgiving, Maisy and I decorated our great room at the inn with garland and mistletoe. Darby had cut down a giant noble fir, and we asked our friends to come out for an afternoon of cookies and cider to help us decorate. We wanted everything to be perfect for the season.

I'd thought of Annabelle and Bromley as I placed an angel at the top of the giant tree. How strange and unexpected life could be at times. Annabelle could not have foreseen the twists her life would take. She had only faith and a deep commitment to honoring her vows, even when that bond had been tested by her attraction for another. Did doing the right thing bring eventual joy? I liked to think so. At least in her place, it had. She'd been a good wife to Clive until his dying day and had given herself the chance to grieve. What waited on the other side of that sadness was a union better than she could have imagined.

We'd learned through Mr. Barnes's research that Bromley had indeed come to Emerson Pass as Annabelle's new husband. Mr. Barnes had stopped by one day shortly after Thanksgiving with a letter he'd found in one of his archives that told us the end of the story. "This explains the rest of it," he'd said to me as he handed me the letter.

Dearest Quinn,

I am sorry it's taken me such a long time to write a proper letter. I'm glad to know you received the letter I sent telling you of my safe arrival in Florida. Thank you for writing back with news of home. I've been busy and preoccupied since then but have retired to my room early so that I might write to you. I'm sitting at the desk in my room at the Huntings'.

Bromley was waiting for me at the station, looking dapper and more handsome than I remembered. Fine lines around his mouth and eyes in addition to several silver strands in his mop of blond hair hinted at the eight years since our last meeting. I am sure he sees the same in me. But it was the same between us, except now we were free to allow ourselves to fall in love. The years had not been kind to his heart, he said to me that first night as we dined on oysters and drank cold white wine as the surf ebbed and flowed. He'd left part of his heart in Florida. All these years, he'd remained unattached. "No one was you," he said.

When he learned of Clive's death, he'd thought and thought about whether to write to me. A few months later, he finally made up his mind. He didn't think I would write back to him and most certainly didn't think I'd agree to come to Florida. I told him I didn't think I would either.

What can I tell you about him? He's a good man. An honorable one. A man who understands my artistic disposition and my ambition. But, dear sister, there's something hard to describe about what it is exactly between two people. What is this thing that makes it hard to breathe if the other is not near? This desire to be with them, to hang on their every word? I've decided, after all this time and through the curves in the road of my life, that love is mysterious and almost unexplainable to anyone other than the one who loves. He is the man for me. How long will I have him? I can't know. I thought Clive would outlive me. With his sturdy, strong body, I thought he would live forever. But it was not to be. Instead, one part of my life ended and another began. I suppose that's all we can hope for. To be able to adapt to the changes that come in this unpredictable life and have faith that after grief, love can come to us again.

Clive's life might have been shorter than I'd have liked, but the years he spent on this earth were joyful ones. We had such a lot of good days, small moments that gave us both joy. And now I believe he's somewhere giving me his blessing.

I never told you this, but years after I came home from Florida, I told Clive about Bromley. I'd told him how I'd felt a deep pulling toward him but that I'd not acted upon it. Clive understood and had instantly forgiven me. "What's to forgive, since you walked away anyway, dearest?" Clive said. "I cannot expect that in a long life of loving each other that there won't be times we're tempted. What matters is the choice we make. You chose to come back to me."

"Have you ever been tempted?" I asked.

"Not in the way you were. But I admired your sister a great deal before she chose Alexander."

I'd smacked him then and wiped away tears. "My sister. That's much worse."

We'd laughed together, and then he'd kissed me and taken me to bed. With the confession, I'd let go of Bromley and the white sand and blue sea. It turns out that was better than burying a box. I'll have to tell you about that some other time.

Now I have returned to the sea and my lovely Bromley. The days are long here. We spend them exploring the beach and riding horses in the surf. I've learned how to play tennis, if you can imagine. Bromley's family has embraced me and offered me a room in the house for as long as I wish to stay. Last night, as we sat on the patio enjoying our dinner, he proposed to me. I wanted to say yes immediately but there was something I had to ask first. Would he be willing to spend at least half the year in Emerson Pass?

He'd agreed, saying we could spend all our days there if I wished. However, Florida is part of me now too. In fact, it's inspired a whole new line of wedding dresses made for warmer climates. No one wants a bride to melt as she walks down the aisle with her father.

We've decided to elope to save the trouble of a wedding, since we're both older and married before. We shall do so and have a party when we return as man and wife.

I cannot wait for you to meet him. I know you will love him eventually, even if you still hold Clive near your heart. It is indeed possible to love two men at once. How it all sorts out in heaven, I cannot say.

Thank you, my dearest, for all you did for me when I was young. The sacrifices you made were always clear to me, even back then. I can still remember the day Mother and I sent you off on that train. We wept, scared we might never see you again after sending you to the wild country of Colorado. How wrong we were to weep. We were scared only of the unknown. If we'd known that your true love waited there for you and how much those precious children who had lost their mother needed you, we would have dried our tears and gotten on with things. I shall never forget your generosity or bravery. I hope someday to look back on my own life and say that I was brave. Flawed, yes. But courageous just the same.

I shall close now. Bromley is waiting for me on the beach so that we might stroll along the edge of the water and smell the briny air and speak of the future. The one we will make together. God willing.

I'll be home with my new groom by Christmas. Please set a new place at the family table.

Much love,

Annabelle

She'd had her happy ending, twice it would seem. It had me thinking about the death of those we love and the avalanche of grief they leave behind. For his part, Darby had been able to move through his shock and grief from his father's death. "Ultimately, I have to let go," he'd said to me one night. "But it's particularly hard when the people we're supposed to love let us down so terribly by the way they lived. When they go, it's hard to know how we're supposed to feel."

I'd nodded and held him close—that night and many afterward. Until one day, he woke with a new resolve to move forward. His father had not been a good person. He'd accepted it and decided that no longer would he let the past dictate the future. Yet sometimes, I caught a moment of grief that passed over him when he thought I wasn't watching. I hoped they would not come forever, but perhaps they would. Regardless, I was impressed that he allowed himself to mourn what had been and what would never be.

It was the same for me too, I suppose. Darby's love for me, and mine for him, had changed the hardness I'd carried around for so long. Strangely enough, the more committed I felt to him, the freer I became. He had become my family and me his.

My brother Trey had agreed to come out and help design the interiors of Darby's new cottage. He'd come with my sister-in-law, Autumn, and my two adorable baby nieces for Thanksgiving and a two-week stay afterward. They'd surprised me by bringing our mother as well. Although business had increased with the snowfall, I had enough rooms for them at the inn. My mother had insisted on paying. To my delight, she told me that her divorce with Dad was final and that she'd come out very well. She would not need to work for the rest of her life. However, she'd decided she wanted to work and had taken an administrative position at my brother's firm. "I'm the mother hen of the office," she'd said. "And I love it."

My brother created our design plan for no cost, asking only if we would babysit so he and his bride could enjoy some time alone. Darby, loving children, had readily agreed. Somehow in those short weeks together, my mother and Autumn had fallen for Darby almost as hard as I. My brother, although more reserved in his affection, admitted to me how much he liked him. "You're like Autumn and me. Together you make the other stronger and better. He's helped heal you and vice versa, am I right?"

"You're right." For some reason, that made me cry.

Instead of the wedding of Arianna and Rob that we'd antici-pated, we had had Huck and Stormi's to help plan and attend. Desiring a small, intimate wedding of just close family and friends, the happy couple had asked if they could get married at the inn. I'd excitedly agreed. "A Christmas wedding," I'd said to Darby. "Totally exciting."

"Kind of Dickensian," Darby had said.

Which made me laugh.

Both Tiffany and I were bridesmaids, with Breck and Darby acting as our groomsmen. The weather cooperated very well on the day of the wedding. Several days before, we'd gotten a foot of powdery snow. But the day of the wedding, the sun shone brightly, glinting off the icicles that hung from the rafters of my inn and the gazebo.

As if we channeled the lovebirds of old, we were a merry, joyful group that gathered the day of their wedding. I watched my friends enjoy food and dancing with the scent of our Christmas tree in the air and shook my head in disbelief. This was my life. Soon, I would marry Darby and move into the cottage. All of my dreams had come true.

"May I have this dance, Miss Wattson?" It was Darby, looking more handsome than a man should in his black tuxedo.

"My dance card has only one spot left." I rose to my feet and into his arms. "And it has your name on it."

"I shall throw away any such dance cards from now on. I am the only name you need." Darby kissed me before twirling me around the floor.

"You are the only one," I said. "Now and for all the Christ-mases to come."

I hoped we'd get fifty or so Christmases together, but one cannot know for sure. Only the current moment was certain. What a moment it was.

A NOTE FROM TESS...I'M so happy you followed the stories of my Emerson Pass friends all the way here. Sadly, this is the last book in the contemporary series but there's still more to come in the historical books. THE REBEL comes out January 22, 2023. You can pre-order HERE!

Have you signed up for my newsletter yet? You'll get a free ebook just for doing so! Visit my website to sign up at www.Tesswrites.com

MORE EMERSON PASS!

The Historical Series

The School Mistress
The Spinster
The Scholar
The Problem Child
The Seven Days of Christmas (a novella)
The Musician
The Wordsmith
The Rebel

Sign up for Tess's newsletter and never miss a release or sale!
www.tesswrites.com. You'll get a free ebook!

ABOUT THE AUTHOR

Tess Thompson is the USA Today Bestselling and award-winning author of contemporary and historical Romantic Women's Fiction with over 40 published titles. When asked to describe her books, she could never figure out what to say that would perfectly sum them up until she landed on...Hometowns and Heartstrings.

She's married to her prince, Best Husband Ever, and is the mother of their blended family of four kids and five cats. Best Husband Ever is seventeen months younger, which qualifies Tess as a Cougar, a title she wears proudly. Her Bonus Sons are young adults with pretty hair and big brains like their dad. Daughters, better known as Princess One and Two, are teenagers who make their mama proud because they're kind. They're also smart, but a mother shouldn't brag.

Tess loves lazy afternoons watching football, hanging out on the back patio with Best Husband Ever, reading in bed, binge-watching television series, red wine, strong coffee and walks on crisp autumn days. She laughs a little too loudly, never knows what to make for dinner, looks ridiculous kickboxing in an attempt to combat her muffin top, and always complains about the rain even though she *chose* to live in Seattle.

She's proud to have grown up in a small town like the ones in her novels. After graduating from the University of Southern

California Drama School, she had hopes of becoming an actress but was called instead to writing fiction. She's grateful to spend most days in her office matchmaking her characters while her favorite cat Mittens (shhh...don't tell the others) sleeps on the desk.

She adores hearing from readers, so don't hesitate to say hello or sign up for her newsletter: http://tesswrites.com/. You'll receive an ebook copy of her novella, The Santa Trial, for your efforts.

Made in United States
North Haven, CT
29 June 2023

38398184R00137